J. F Clark

The Society in Search of Truth

Or, stock gambling in San Francisco. A novel

J. F Clark

The Society in Search of Truth
Or, stock gambling in San Francisco. A novel

ISBN/EAN: 9783337048570

Printed in Europe, USA, Canada, Australia, Japan

Cover: Foto ©Andreas Hilbeck / pixelio.de

More available books at **www.hansebooks.com**

THE

SOCIETY IN SEARCH OF TRUTH;

OR,

Stock Gambling in San Francisco.

A NOVEL.

BY J. F. CLARK.

Formerly a Member of the Pacific Stock Exchange.

DEDICATED TO
ALL THE LOVERS OF TRUTH IN THE GREAT AMERICAN NATION,

PUBLISHED BY THE AUTHOR,
ROOMS 57 AND 58, No. 120 SUTTER ST., SAN FRANCISCO.

OAKLAND, CAL.:
PACIFIC PRESS, PRINTERS, STEREOTYPERS AND BINDERS.
1878.

DEDICATORY.

To the Lovers of Truth:

Ladies and Gentlemen (for the followers of that sublime virtue are of both sexes): I dedicate this effort of my pen to you because you, and you alone, appreciate the fact that all honor, all virtue, and all true nobility are born of Truth, which is the Sun of Moral Life, whose beams illuminate and beautify the Social World and tinge it with the hues of Heavenly light, or having set, leaves it enveloped in the gloom of blackest night.

THE AUTHOR.

PREFACE.

The most difficult part of an author's labors is the preface to his work; because in it he has to speak of himself and his objects, and is conscious of a certain amount of egotism and self-assertion, without which he would fail to be either forcible or lucid.

With this conviction firmly impressed on my mind I proceed to inform my reader that I have chosen the form of a novel in which to illustrate the evils of a system that is fraught with corruption and injustice, not only in California but in other parts of the United States, as well as in foreign countries.

I have made San Francisco the arena of the exploits and experiences of my various characters because I have had better opportunities in that city than in any I have visited, during the wanderings of many years, of observing the frauds and trickeries the ramifications of which I have endeavored to portray. It is but just to state that the same characteristics are to be found wherever stock gambling exists.

Joint-stock corporations are a necessity of the age. By the aggregation of capital many benefits have been conferred on mankind which could not otherwise have been realized. It is the manipulations of stocks by designing capitalists that are productive of such disastrous results. The shamelessly unjust handling of the properties of corporations by the controlling powers demands the exercise of legislative functions. The properties of corporations held in trust by the directors are too frequently used as a means for their own enrichment, without regard to the rights or interests of outside stockholders. Stocks are assessed and dividends declared irrespective of the wants or condition of the corporations solely to lower or raise market prices. By these iniquitous means the mining business is being brought into disrepute.

In California mining is one of the greatest of industries. San Francisco owes its present position mainly to mining, which is an honorable calling. For years the efforts of some of its leading capitalists have been directed to the propagation of the false theory that "the market" and not mining is the legitimate means by which wealth is to be accumulated. By a series of "deals" a very few have become wealthy, gathering in the earnings of the masses and living in luxurious ease on ill-gotten gains in the midst of widespread poverty. Pursuing this same phantom, "the market," which they have been educated to believe exists only in connection with mines of the Comstock lode, numberless wealthy men and women have been reduced to poverty.

On the other hand there are in California a great number of people who are engaged in legitimate mining; who are content to let the market alone; who are sole owners or stockholders of private corporations, the stocks of which are not manipulated on the market; who are benefitting the State and enriching themselves.

With regard to my characters, they are drawn from observations of actual life. There is not an individual or a living thing, from my reader's favorite hero down to Rose Pye's pony, "Poor dear old Taffy," whose counterpart I have not at some time seen and known. Neither is there an incident or circumstance recorded for which I cannot find a parallel in my own experience or observation. I have endeavored to make THE SOCIETY IN SEARCH OF TRUTH a record of living facts, which I have embodied in a form I trust will prove acceptable to all who love the truth.

THE AUTHOR.

NOTE.—The rights of translation and of dramatization reserved.

CONTENTS.

viii   CONTENTS.

THE SOCIETY IN SEARCH OF TRUTH.

CHAPTER I.

THE ORIGIN OF THE SOCIETY.

"Gentlemen, I propose that we resolve ourselves into a society, its object to be, to search for Truth."

"It is a good suggestion, Judge," answered General Sterne, "but where and how do you expect to find Truth? Do you propose to discover it by the aid of your gold-rimmed spectacles, or to avail yourself of the Lick Telescope (when it is built), or will you put the lies of the day under a microscope and pick out the golden grains of Truth; that is if you can find any?"

"General," said Commodore Pye, "you are too cynical. There are two sides to every question, you always choose to see the shady one; every institution and every human being is compounded of good and evil; you elect to see their imperfections and ignore their virtues; by this means you rob yourself of one-half of the pleasures of existence. The true philosopher looks on the sunny side of life."

"Gentlemen," said Judge Bland, "I do not jest— I am in sober earnest. I propose to you the formation of a society, its object to be to search for Truth. Truth is worth looking for. It may be hard to find, what of that; gold is hard to find, yet men search for it; diamonds are bard to find, yet

hard

men seek for them.   Truth may be hard to find, but it is well worth seeking.   We have the time, we have the dollars—like Othello we are minus occupation, therefore let us unite and seek the Truth.   By pursuing this course we may win for ourselves immortal fame.   There have been discoverers before us.   Did not Gallileo discover the motion of the earth; did not Harvey discover the circulation of the blood; did not Columbus discover America; their names have been handed down to posterity, but what of their fame, ours will infinitely surpass theirs if we discover Truth."

"That is so," said the General, "and we shall deserve all the fame we get.   Do you know that I entertain the belief that it is this same Truth the Wandering Jew has been looking after these eighteen hundred years, and that General Grant has been roaming over Europe in search of it ever since he left the presidential chair.   Deceit and lies so closely surrounded him whilst he filled it, that he wanted a change.   Whew!   If he finds it, the Truth is not the thing to win a third term election with."

"One might suppose," said the Commodore, "that the General does not believe in the existence of Truth, but is convinced that Truth is dead, and is prepared to maintain that he assisted at its obsequies, and is therefore in a position to treat us with ridicule, as though we were ghost-hunters, when we speak of seeking Truth."

"Judge Bland and Commodore Pye," said the General, speaking slowly, and with great sententiousness, "I have no desire to ridicule you. Ridicule is a vulgar weapon. The argumentum absurdum is not my forte. I do not love the world, it is a sham; man is an all but universal fraud; life is for the most part an acted lie. Look at our politicians, do not lies and frauds put them in office; and do not their trickeries and frauds open our eyes to their true character? Look at the press! are not its columns divided between the exposure of the crimes and lies of others, and inventions of its own. Look at the courts of law (I will not say of justice)! Does not money get away with justice all the time? Look at the pulpit! does it not pander to rich supporters and condemn all poor sinners? Do not preachers always see a divine call when a new charge offers a higher salary? You want to establish a society to search for Truth. You remind me of Diogenes who went out in broad daylight with a lighted candle to look for an honest man. Your prospect is more Utopean than Bennett's expectation of hoisting the Stars and Stripes on the North Pole. Nevertheless, gentlemen, I will commit one more folly; I will join your society. I will aid you in the search—but I warn you that our efforts will be fruitless, though I admit they may be laudable. I will second the Judge's motion, and move—

" 1. That the society shall be called the ' Society in Search of Truth.'

" 2. That it shall consist of the three persons now present, with power to add to their number.

" 3. That Judge Bland shall be its President.

" 4. That General Sterne shall be its Vice-President.

" 5. That Commodore Pye shall be its Secretary."

The motions were carried without discussion.

" In addition to which," said the Commodore, " I beg to propose that the meetings of the Society be held weekly on Tuesday evenings at 8 o'clock, and that the President is hereby requested to deliver an inaugural address at the first meeting."

Agreed to.

" Gentlemen," said the Judge, rising from his chair with much dignity, and assuming a smile, the blandness of which was ineffable, " I accept the honor and trust, and thank you.   This is the proud-est moment of my existence.   I feel my bosom swell with mighty exultation. My heart embraces our work. We shall win golden honors and glorious fame. The world will thank us and posterity will revere our memory.   And when the ephemeral proceed-ings of other socities are lost on the dim vista of the past, ours shall live enshrined in the hearts of the people, and blazoned on the scroll of never dy-ing fame."

" Bravo !" said the Commodore.

" Humph !" said the General.

CHAPTER II.

I INTRODUCE THE SOCIETY TO MY READERS.

It would be difficult to find three men, and all gentlemen, more dissimilar than the three members of the " Society in Search of Truth."   So unlike

were they, that to the unreflecting there appeared
an incongruity, in the tripartite friendship, which,
despite sundry small, trifling misunderstandings,
had now endured through several years. The fact
was that each saw in the other two some sterling
qualities which he was conscious of lacking himself. A wise dispensation of the Omnipotent Creator has provided that man, with all his vanity and
egotism, shall have a keen perception of his own
weaknesses and failings which is clearly shown in
his friendships and his loves, and acts as an equal-
izing force in the economy of human life. Thus
we see the stern and morose yoke himself with the
buoyant and cheerful; the sad and the silent with
the gay and talkative; the bold and vivacious with
the quiet and dignified; the noisy and excitable
with the sedate and grave; tall men have ordinarily a penchant for little women, and small women
are brave enough to dare the acceptance of big men,
whilst undersized masculines are often seen to take
to their guardian care or place themselves under
the protection of giantesses. Thus is the equilib-
rium of development preserved. Were it otherwise
ordered, the human race would soon be divided into
Brobdignageans and Lilliputians. And with regard to mental qualities the same remark has equal
force. In love and friendship, the acids and alka-
lies of mental organisms blending neutralize each
other and give effervesence and sparkle to life. In
the case of man and his wife, or man and his friend,
if both are inveterate talkers, they will necessarily
bore each other, or if both are habitually silent,

they will inevitably weary of each other. The happiest unions are generally those of opposites. In homes and in social circles, there should be listeners as well as talkers. A good talker likes a good listener quite as well as a good listener likes a good talker. Humanity delights in contrasts and in change. Variety gives esprit to life. We like to go forth into the sunshine, and again we like to seek the shade.

Judge Bland was a bachelor arrived at that doubtful age when the glass is often consulted by single men who are anxious to know what new marks receding time has recorded on their hair and features. Possessed in his youth of an ample fortune, he had nevertheless studied law, and had attained considerable success and some fame as a jurisprudent. He was born and reared in Massachusetts, and had received a liberal education. A lover of art and fond of travel, when by the unexpected death of a cousin he fell heir to a second fortune, he abandoned his profession, spent several years in visiting different countries, and finally found himhimself in San Francisco, studying, he said, the ways and manners of the most cosmopolitan city in the world, and devouring a mixed multitude of literary productions forwarded to him by his own order, once a month from New York. An enthusiast on many subjects, somewhat pedantic in his speech, an ardent admirer of beauty, always gallant to the fair sex, a welcome guest in all drawing-rooms, his heart had been often assailed, but for some unexplained reason he had never married.

Commodore Pye was an Englishman by birth, and possessed a fine property in England; married in his twenty-second year, he was a widower ere he had completed his twenty-third. His wife he had almost idolized. She left him a parting legacy, a baby daughter, whose hold on life seemed so precarious that it was long despaired of. But as the months rolled by the fragile blossom gathered strength, and when at the expiration of a year she had developed into a healthy child, he left his estate in the hands of his steward, conveyed his little daughter to the south of France, and committed her to the care of an elder sister, long widowed, and then took to the sea. He had visited all parts of the world. Naturally fond of adventure, when the civil war broke out he at once repaired to America, he warmly espoused the Federal cause, and entered the navy in charge of a gunboat; and so ably conducted the various commands entrusted to him, that he was rapidly promoted, step following step, until he had achieved the highest dignity he could attain in his profession. He had been duly naturalized, having determined to remain in America. At the conclusion of the war he retired from nautical life and had made San Francisco his headquarters—from which he made occasional trips to India, China, and Japan, but had never returned to Europe. If the thought of filling the place of his lost wife had ever crossed his mind, no one was the wiser. He yet remained a widower. He was a man whose great characteristic was common sense. Regular, almost methodical, in his habits, plain and

outspoken when occasion demanded it, yet naturally
inclined to reserve, courteous and affable at all
times, yet rather inclined to listen. than to talk;
punctillious in matters of honor, a whole-souled
man and a staunch friend; a great statistician, particularly in matters relating to finance, population,
and agriculture, so much so that his friends prefer-
red to use his knowledge on those subjects rather
than refer to any cyclopedia.   Such were the characteristics for some or all of which he was highly
esteemed by his few chosen friends.

General Sterne was a Virginian, proud of a long
line of descent, which he could trace back for many
centuries, and of an unsullied name.   He was tall
and slight, of a somewhat swarthy complexion,
had dark, almost black eyes, and strongly marked
eye-brows, wore a full beard and moustache; he was
a decidedly handsome man.   To those who did
not know him, there was an undefinable something
in his bearing which seemed to say approach not too
near.   Those who understood him knew that he
had a kind heart, and that his hand was often
opened for the assistance and relief of the less fortunate than himself.   Left an orphan in his boy-
hood in charge of his father's brother, who had an
only daughter some two years younger than the
General, it was the earnest desire of her father that
the cousins should love and marry.   Fortune seemed
to favor his wishes, the General formed a sincere attachment for his cousin, and in due course proposed
and was accepted by her.   Time rolled on and the
marriage day was fixed for the fifteenth day of Sep-

tember following. This was in June, 1859. Meantime, the General resolved to take a trip to the north, taking with him some valuable jewels—heirlooms in his family, which he desired to have reset for his beautiful bride. His object attained he returned home, to find that his promised wife had eloped with a neighboring planter, a man of inferior position and doubtful character. Deeply wounded and greatly disgusted—a changed man, his youthful freshness gone, a look of sad sternness settled on him—his faith in woman completely destroyed, he at once disposed of his estates, and wandered in Europe and Asia for several years, where he avoided society, especially that of woman, and tried to persuade himself that he hated the human species. When, however, the civil war commenced he immediately returned to America, and taking service in the Confederate Army entered upon his new duties with so much ardor, and cool daring, that he speedily rose from captain of a company to be a general of the army. The war ended, he again left the South and visited Europe, Africa, and the Australias, and finally landed in San Francisco— where he had now resided several years. I have made my recitals as brief and concise as possible. I would not have troubled my readers with them, were it not necessary that they should know something of the history of our characters, in order that they may have a just appreciation of the peculiar characteristics of the three original members of the " Society in Search of Truth."

B

CHAPTER III.

JUDGE BLAND DELIVERS THE INAUGURAL ADDRESS.

On the Tuesday evening succeeding the events recorded in the first chapter, the Society assembled in its appointed place of meeting, the Judge's private parlor in the Palace Hotel. The Judge, who was somewhat fastidious in his tastes, had provided such additional furniture as the importance of the occasion and the gravity of his position seemed to him to demand. They consisted of a chair of massive proportions and elegant workmanship, the back of which was very tall, and was surmounted by three figures. In the center was a carved statue of Truth; the draperies drawn aside from her left breast disclosed a pane of glass, through which her heart was visible. Towards it the wand she held in her hand was pointed. On the right was Justice holding her scales, and on the left one of Solomon's life guardsmen holding up an infant by one leg with his left hand, whilst his right hand grasped a huge sword, which he held above the infant, waiting the order of the wise King to make the segregation he had decreed. This was the President's chair. A long table standing in front of it was ingeniously filled with a reading desk, which could be raised to any height or sunk into the table at pleasure of the President, by pressing a spring. Upon the table there were ample supplies of gold pens and elegantly tinted paper, and three silver inkstands, each of which was adorned with the dove of Noah, holding in her mouth the olive branch of peace. At the other end of the table was the Vice-President's chair, though smaller than that of the President. It was of similar workmanship, and had also three well-executed figures, Faith, Hope and Charity, on the top rail. The Secretary's chair, which stood on the right of the Vice-President's, though of the same character, had no special ornament.

"Gentleman," said the Judge, "I trust the arrangements I have made for your comfort and convenience, meet with your approval."

"They are admirable," said the Commodore.

"Precisely so," said the General, at the same time casting a dark look at the three female figures surrounding his chair, next flashing it for a moment at the Judge, and then returning to Faith, Hope and Charity. It was evident he was debating a point in his mind. It might have been that this adornment of his chair appeared an innuendo of the Judge aimed at him, or probably he did not like the proximity of the three females. Anyway he took his seat and drew forth his cigar case, and lighted a cigar (he only occasionally smoked). Perhaps he hoped the graces would resent the odor of tobacco smoke and move off. If so, he was doomed to disappointment.

The Commodore having also taken his seat, the President, holding his gold-rimmed glasses in his right hand, rose to his feet and said:

"Gentlemen and members of the Society in Search of Truth: Never in an existence of some (ahem), say forty years, have I experienced such pleasurable emotions as those which now well up from the center of my being, and permeate every pulse and every nerve and every fiber, and fill every portion of my corporeal frame, from the greatest part to the remotest atom, with pure and unalloyed delight. We have met to-night to inaugurate a great and glorious work, which will result in universal benefactions to our country, and secure for us everlasting niches in the immortal temple of fame. .

' Magna est veritas et prevalebit.'

The Truth, gentlemen, is a ray of God's sunlight sent down from heaven. Clouds may obscure, but cannot destroy it. It is an emanation of the Omnipotent. It may be hidden, but cannot be obliterated. It is like its author, indestructible. It is a spark of immortality which may be covered, but cannot be extinguished. We are drawn to the violet by its fragrance. Hidden in deep bosses of green leaves, which bury it from our sight, we could never find it if we did not part the leaves.

" We must seek for the Truth as we would for violets. We must part the rank leaves that overshadow her. We must rend away the vile overgrowth of lies which hide her from our vision. We must break through the barriers which a wicked world has reared around her, and we shall find her clad in all her pristine beauty, fair as the lily, pure as the snowdrop, fragrant as the violet, and lovely as the seraphim who wait upon the majesty of heaven."

The Commodore, moved by the eloquence of the Judge, nodded his head approvingly, and said " Aye, aye, sir."

The General glanced uneasily over his shoulder at the three figures on the back of his chair, and smoked on in silence. He was thinking he would have liked Truth better in any other form than that of a woman—

The Judge resumed :

"In seeking after Truth, we shall do well to remember what Tacitus says :—

'Truth is established by investigation and delay.'

"We must recall that line of Ammian :—

'Truth is simple, requiring neither study nor art.'

We should also bear in mind that Casaubòn says—

'The study of Truth is perpetually joined with the love of Virtue, for there is no virtue which is not derived from Truth.'

"We should not forget those lines of Bacon :—

'It is heaven upon earth to have a man's mind move in charity, and rest in Providence, and turn upon the poles of Truth.'

"We may be encouraged by Colton, who says :—

'The adorer of Truth is above all present things.'

"And allow our interest to be stimulated by Byron's observation, that—

'Truth is always strange,
Stranger than fiction.'

"I will not tire you with further recitation of the opinions of writers with whom you are familiar, but invite the Society to adopt as its motto the words of Shakespear :—

'I will find
Where Truth is hid, though it were hid indeed
Within the center.'

Again the Judge paused, awaiting to observe the

effect of his oratory upon the Society. And here I may inform my readers, that through a long course of desultory reading, the Judge had always kept a literary diary, in which he recorded the opinions of the works he read, and into which he also copied what he deemed to be choice passages. These he had classified and arranged in alphabetical order, so that on occasions like the present, it was as easy for him to give a hundred quotations as half a dozen, and by this means he had in some cases succeeded in conveying the impression that he was possessed of astonishing erudition.

As the Judge surveyed his audience, the Commodore said emphatically, " Hear ! hear !

The General, still conscious of the obnoxious female presence, smoked in silence.

" I must now," continued the Judge, " outline the *modus operandi*, which I shall commend to the ' Society in Search of Truth.' In conducting our business, I deem it advisable that we should appoint committees to examine the various institutions and organizations we propose to investigate.

" Our field is a large one. We have abundant material. Politics and religion, the theatres and social life, the stock boards, and our railroad systems, the judiciary and the customs, woman and teetotalism, the mint and the public press, politicians and lecturers, the Workingmen's party and communism, the Republican and Democratic parties, the social evil, woman's rights and domestic happiness, protection and free trade, labor and capital, national honor and the corruption of office, the vexed question of the presidential election, in which Hayes triumphed over Tilden, the Beecher and Tilton scandal, the Tammany ring, the Desert Land Act, municipal corporations, the water companies, the gas companies, saving banks, specie resumption, the rights of the North and the South, the Irish Catholic difficulty, religious supremacy, the centralization of government, the Chinese question, astronomy and the public schools, social science and necromancy, spiritualism, the Indian agencies, infidelity and the authenticity of the Scriptures, life and death, the influence of art, the sciences, the patent office, the past and future of our country. These are all subjects for our careful consideration. Some few others I will suggest at our next meeting."

The Commodore, who had regarded the Judge with amazement for some minutes, wondering what would next follow, now arose from his chair in an apparently exhausted condition, and rang the bell. When he was again seated, the General, first glancing at the female figures which seemed to haunt him, rose to his feet, and drawing himself to his full height, said :—

" Mr. President, do you expect this society to live forever ? Do you claim for us immortality of the body as well as the soul ? It would be necessary for us to live a thousand years, to separate the Truth from the filth which surrounds it, were we to undertake all you have suggested. There is one subject alone, sir, that you have named, which would absorb all our lives, and when they were ended, we should be no nearer a solution than we are to-day. It is beyond our comprehension, sir. We cannot grasp it, or if we could, we could not fathom it. That subject is woman. I suggest, sir, that that subject be struck from the list. I shall not discuss it—"

At this stage a waiter entered and asked, " Did you ring, gentlemen ? "

" Yes," said the Commodore, " bring us a magnum of your best champagne. Quick, and three glasses."

The General continued :

We have started on a fool's errand. We shall be fortunate if we do not receive a fool's reward. We have resolved to look for Truth. We are like the man who looked for a needle in a haystack. Our folly equals that of Don Quixote, when he charged a windmill. The President has suggested subjects enough to bring to our remembrance ten thousand lies, through all of which, could we live long enough, we might wade knee-deep, and never find one grain of Truth. But as we have resolved on the search, I shall not beat a retreat."

Here the waiter returned with a two-quart bottle of champagne and glasses. The Society refreshed itself. The Commodore dashing off two bumpers, seemed to revive, and said :

" Gentlemen, I suggest that we take one subject at a time, and that we first resolve ourselves into a committee to investigate stock operations, the General, the Vice-President, to open the question."

Carried.

CHAPTER IV.

JUDGE BLAND MEDITATES AND SOLILOQUIZES.

To say that Judge Bland was not chagrined at the abrupt termination to which his inaugural address was brought, would be to deviate from the truth. He had not delivered more than half the subject-matter he had prepared when the remarks of General Sterne brought him to a stand-still. He had suggested enough work for the society to find employment for twenty such societies for a lifetime. He had yet more to suggest. And then, he had not reached the grand peroration, which he had prepared with great art and elaborate skill, and which he honestly believed would rival the choicest oration of Cicero, of Burke, or of Clay. To make it perfect he had culled the choicest figures of speech from his favorite authors, and now as he sat alone, his guests having retired, he placed an extra chair in front of the presidential seat in order that he might have a full view of the statue of Truth, and continued for more than an hour to read and re-read his manuscript, pausing every few minutes to rest his eyes on the emblematic figure before him. What a loss to the "Society in Search of Truth!" "What a loss to the world," he said to himself, was that unfortunate interruption—this masterpiece of genius, this sublime effort of immortal mind, is lost to the world forever. Had not the General made it impossible for me to proceed, those glorious thoughts of mine would have been transcribed on the records of the Society, and in due course would have gone forth to the world, but now they are destined to go down to oblivion; they will be buried forever. Oh, Glorious Truth," said he, fixing his gaze on the statue, "how do the ways of man bury thee from our sight. But I will dig thee up, though thou wert buried in the reeking, steaming earth, down deeper than the Savage mine."

I have already informed my readers that the Judge was an enthusiast. He had pondered the formation of the "Society in Search of Truth" until the undertaking had become a mania with him.

I have long entertained the belief that every member of the human family has a mad spot somewhere in his mental organization, which is shown by the triumph of imagination, passion, or appetite over reason. To illustrate my meaning: The strongest instinct of animated beings is the preservation of individual life, an instinct supported by reason, hence I maintain that whoever attempts his own life is at least momentarily mad. His act is a violation of the Creator's universal law, it is the triumph of a passion or a feeling over reason. Its immediate cause may be a cowardly fear or dread of shame. It may be loss or disapppointment. In any case it is a defiance of the immutable decree, and is therefore madness. The perfectly sane man or woman, if such can be found, allows reason to govern every desire, imagination, passion, appetite, and vanity. When inclination gets the mastery of reason, it is always a species of madness. It may be of a dangerous character, tending to the destruction of life, as in the case of the excessive drinker, or smoker, the libertine, or the glutton; or it may be in the comparatively harmless form of the pursuant of some chimerical project or ideal excellence which, absorbing the mind, warps and turns reason from its true course. Of such a character was the Judge's mania. He had contemplated his ideal Truth until he thought he saw her triumphant everywhere, and hoped and believed that the Society would show the world that it was a much better world than it had any idea of, which, to say the least, was a noble aspiration, if a slightly mad one, on the part of the Judge. How far his dream was to be realized the future records of the Society will show.

The General was his antithesis. Though some years younger than the Judge, he had seen quite as much of the world, but he had viewed it through a distorted medium. For nearly twenty years he had lived in hotels or under a tent, and during the whole of that period had shunned the walks of social life and had never entered a domestic circle. He believed the world to be false and hollow. He hated the conventionalities of life. He never allowed himself to be introduced to a lady if he could avoid it; he was always sarcastic, sometimes satirical, and not unfrequently severe; hence he was never popular; he disguised a naturally generous heart under a cloak of cold austerity. He had formed a sincere friendship for the Judge. It is true they seldom entirely agreed, but their deep-seated mutual esteem warded off any approach to actual quarrel. He had entered into the Society to please his friends, and meant to do his duty. The Commodore, with his plain, straightforward common sense, was a decided contrast to them both. He might have been the balance pole upon which they, as scales, were suspended. There was an equableness about him which to know was to admire. He regularly attended church on Sunday mornings, and not unfrequently the theatre in the evening. He was a whole student some part of every day, and half a Bohemian every night. Moderate in his appetites and desires, he always seemed to hold himself in hand. In the society of ladies, in the Bohemian Club, on the street or in the office of his agents, at home or abroad, he was always the same self-poised, unchangeable man. He had joined the Society projected by the Judge from two motives. He really enjoyed the company of the Judge and the General, and he hoped to enrich his already valuable collection of statistics from the facts which in course of its proceedings would be brought forward and investigated.

The morning succeeding the night of the first meeting of the Society the Commodore's servant brought to his room a letter and a small package. They both bore the French stamp and post-marks. The Commodore finished the paragraph he was reading in his morning paper; he then broke the seal of the letter and read :—

"MY DEAR PAPA: We are coming to visit you. Dear aunt has requested me to write and tell you that she hopes to be in California in about two months' time, and intends to bring Geraldine with us. You don't know Geraldine, of course; you have never seen her. She is my dearest friend. I always call her my sister, but she is not one bit like me. She is one year older than I am; she is dark and I am fair; that is, she has black eyes and raven hair; my eyes are blue and my hair light-colored. She has lived with us ever since her father, Lord Stanley, died, five years ago. Aunt thought it would be pleasant for me, and so it has—but there—is it not funny for me to be describing myself to my own dear p apa—whom I cannot remember to have seen, and I nearly nineteen years old. I hope you will be glad we are coming. We do not like leaving dear sunny France, but aunt thinks we ought to see the world, and that I ought to know my dear papa.

"From your loving daughter,   Rose.

P. S.—I send you a miniature likeness of myself, so that you may know what I am like now.

The Commodore very deliberately opened the package. Taking the painting to the window. he stood for some minutes gazing earnestly at it. He next walked to his secretaire and opening a secret drawer, drew forth a case. It was of ivory, mounted with gold and magnificently carved. He touched a spring and disclosed another picture. Returning to the window he held them side by side as if comparing them. For nineteen years no eyes save those of the Commodore had ever looked upon that second picture. At length a deep-drawn sigh escaped him. "And so like," he said, "how can I bear it; the eyes, the mouth, that golden hair, and that fair, open forehead; 'tis Rose herself repeated. How can I meet her child—so like her. Am I cowered? Where is my boasted stoicism? Must I hold up my heart before the world and let the idle babblers read the story of my sorrow? Spirit, be brave; strong-will control my heart, and hide from human eyes the grief no time can heal." And even as he spoke he wiped the moisture from his eyes, and sinking into a chair he buried his head between his hands. Was this the impurturable man of the world? that strong-willed unmoved man, the Commodore? It was he.

CHAPTER V.

GENERAL STERNE INVESTIGATES THE STOCK BUSINESS.

General Sterne, having undertaken to investigate the stock business, was not the man to do it by halves. The same indomitable energy and strength of purpose which had led him to calmly face the fore front of the battle in many engagements, where some generals we know of would have kept at a very safe distance, and which had earned for him the sobriquet of "Cast-iron Sterne," now prompted him to visit the bull rings, in which the bears from time to time assail with more or less effect their constant foes the bulls. He therefore gladly paid the five dollars demanded as admission fee by the San Francisco Stock Board, the price the geniuses of that institution charge the gudgeons for the privilege of seeing their twenty-dollar gold pieces made into tens, and their tens into fives, and their fives into thin air. Now the General was well known as a man of mark, and a heavy capitalist—but he had never been known to deal in stocks, when, however, he had been seen several days within the unhallowed precincts, some of the more enterprising of the brokers detailed cappers to track him up and run him in. They had no doubt of his intention to invest in stocks, and well knew that if they could draw in one ten thousand of his coin, it would be comparatively easy to find a way to ease him of a few score thousand more. Little did they dream of the motive which had drawn the General within those walls, which had witnessed the demolition of so many fair fortunes. Had they known it they would have shunned him as they would have shunned a grizzly bear on the war-path. My reader must understand that the " Society in Search of Truth" was a secret society, and that it was agreed that no member or visitor was to be admitted to its counsels without first taking an oath to preserve silence upon the subject of its existence. This course was deemed absolutely necessary. It was presumed that the information desired by the Society would be difficult to obtain if the purposes for which it was required were generally known. Even the newspaper reporters, who have intruded themselves in so many places where they are un-welcome guests, for many months did not know of the Society's meetings. Had they known of them they would inevitably have been a source of annoy-ance to the members, for they have impudence enough to push open the gates of heaven, could they find them ajar, and to walk in unasked; though they will know that they would be sum-marily expelled the instant their presence was de-tected.

The General knew that to accomplish his purpose

it was necessary for him to unbend—to relax the sternness of his bearing and appear like other men. It went against the grain, but the iron will of the soldier triumphed over inclination and habit. Some who observed the change attributed it to a just appreciation of the greatness of the Stock Board and the incomparable talent of its members, whilst the enterprising brokers before alluded to began to flatter themselves that the high-toned Southerner was going to be an easier prey than they had anticipated. Meantime the General, with a watchful eye, was regarding all their movements. Accustomed to the din of battle, his ear speedily accommodated itself to the roaring of the beasts (I mean the bulls and bears,) around him, and his eagle glance soon took in every movement and change that was made in the marshaling of their respective forces. At the same time, though he never could have been induced to trust any material portion of his fortune to any one of them, he only resolved to risk a trifle, in a test operation, as a means of enabling him to observe what he could not otherwise learn. When, therefore, Will Wily who was a taut for a well-known firm of brokers approached him and told him he had a " point," he gravely listened with much assumed interest until he named the stock. It was Lady Washington which Wily said was a dead sure thing for a rise. " Sir," said the General, his dark brows contracting and his eyes assuming the old warrior-like blaze, " I do not want the Lady at any price. Is there nothing else ?" Wily somewhat discomfited, ruminated for a moment and replied: "Yes, I know another stock, it is closely pooled. Grayson has put up the coin, and it will have a big deal directly." "What is it?" asked the General. "Julia," whispered the tout. The General at this announcement said abruptly, "Good morning, sir," and left the hall muttering to himself as he went, "The fool—to offer me anything with the name of a woman."

But though annoyed and disgusted, the General was not the man to quit the field without achieving the purpose for which he entered it. To do or die, was his motto, it was graven on the hilt of his sword, and it was graven on the inflexible will of the man. He speedily returned to the charge, and to the astonishment of all who knew him, was seen conversing with all kinds of men, on the prospects of this mine, and the deal in that, the chances of a spring rise, the movements of the Bonanza firm, the probability of Sharon and the Bank of California making a deal in South End stocks and other leading topics in stock circles of the day. In all these conversations the outside observer saw, or thought he saw, another gudgeon about to take the bait—the men with whom he conversed saw a man of known great wealth, were flattered by the graceful courtesy with which he listened to their assertions, and failed to notice that his observations were all intended to draw them out, and that he committed himself to no expression of opinion to them. It was a peculiarity of the General, who was void of fear, in fact, did not know what it was, that he never showed his opinions except to his

c

very few chosen friends. I have said he had resolved to buy some stock. Glancing over the list his eye rested on Savage—he liked the name, he had often envied the savages, who, knowing nothing of civilization, followed their instincts and lived a life of freedom, undisturbed by the shams of conventional life. His object was not to make money, he had enough, more than he required, and had no greed of gain. His object was to try a hazard, but it must be recommended to him. He was a member of the Society in Search of Truth. He did not expect to find it; he expected to find the reverse of Truth everywhere. He therefore wished to have and to act upon positive assurances, and was willing to lose all he intended to venture. The opportunity soon presented itself. He was speaking to a broker of the great depth and heat of the Savage mine. when a well-known whipper-in touched his sleeve and requested a moment's private conversation. This the General cheerfully granted.

" You were mentioning the Savage mine, General; if you want to do anything in Savage, I have all the points and know all the inside tracks." As the capper spoke he assumed a look of mysterious wisdom.

" Indeed," replied the General, " I should be glad to know something about it—I was thinking of buying some of the stock—what do you think of it for a speculation ?"

" It is a dead sure thing, General; there is a deal on, in it now. A big development is being made. It is sixteen and a half to-day, it will be twenty-five before to-morrow night."

" Is that so ?" said the General, feigning an interest and pleasure he was far from experiencing, " do you think there is any ore in the mine ? If I remember rightly, within the past three years there have been declarations of developments in all the mines on the Comstock line. In some of them once, in others two or three times, not one of which has proved of any value."

"That is so," replied the tout, " but this is another affair, General, entirely. I will show you a dispatch which I received to-day,"—glancing around to see if he was observed—he handed a telegram to the General, who read as follows :—

"Got it sure—improving all the time—big bonanza—certain —buy all you can."

" Thank you," said the General, " I think I will buy some."

The tout now suggested to the General that there was a great difference in stock-brokers ; " Some," said he, " are careless, and some are, well—not quite on the square. Now my brokers are Trackem & Cinchem. They are a smart firm and as square as a die. I should like to introduce you."

The General expressed his willingness and soon found himself in an expensively fitted office, which was as showy as French polish and gilding could make it.

He was introduced to Mr. Cinchem.

Mr. Cinchem had often seen the General ; he was most happy to make his acquaintance.

"Do you think, Mr. Cinchem, that the Savage is a good mine?" inquired the General.

"There is no doubt of it, sir; none whatever. It is near the Bonanzas, and now the Sutro Tunnel is cooling the air, we shall soon see what it will do," answered Mr. Cinchem.

"Do you think it is likely to rise in price?" queried the General.

"Well, you see, General, that is a subject on which we never offer an opinion, and" (assuming an air of great candor) Mr. Cinchem added, "the market and the mine are two different things—the mine no doubt is good. We never express opinions about the future price of stocks; on that subject we never give advice, sir; never."

CHAPTER VI.

HOW IT IS DONE.

It is only justice to Mr. Cinchem to say that his statement regarding the custom in his office was true. The firm assumed a virtue at all times in abstaining from offering any opinion as to the price stocks were likely to realize at any future period. Mr. Cinchem would remark: "You understand, sir, the market is by no means regulated by the actual values of the mines. There are wheels within wheels, sir, and when the mine is looking its best, the stock may decline. That is the result of manipulation, sir." The fact was that the firm of Trackem & Cinchem were but in the position of the cat, whose paw was used by the monkey to pull the chestnuts out of the fire. They were employed by the controlling powers of certain mines, to do a certain amount of work, for which they were liberally rewarded. They were used to draw into the net all the fish they could catch, be they great or little; they had no scruples of conscience, and they asked no questions of their employers. It was to them a matter of supreme indifference whether they gathered in the superfluous coin of the bloated aristocrat, or the savings of a lifetime of the workingman. They were told to bull a certain stock and sell it, or to bear it and buy, and they did it to the best of their ability. In doing it they did not scruple to act upon the inside knowledge necessarily committed to them, not openly, but through the agency of lesser brokers, who were glad to receive patronage of the great firm, and thus their treachery was hidden from their employers. At the same time they claimed to be an eminently respectful firm, doing a plain commission business only, and as a matter of policy, adopted the practice of assuring their clients, that they knew nothing whatever of the manipulations of the market. "It is a fair gamble, you know, sir;" they would observe to an anxious inquirer, "they go up and they go down; buy them when they are low and sell them when they are high, any man can make money by watching the market. If I were out of business, sir, I could make a fortune in 'em in no time." At such times he forgot the hundreds of accounts closed on his ledgers, closed only because the victims had no more coin to put up—to use a Californiaism,

" their mud was exhausted."   At the same time, if
they had instructions to bull a stock, they never
hesitated to say the mine was undoubtedly good—
" every indication of a bonanza;" or if their instructions were to bear the stock, then the prospects were very doubtful—the water in the mine
was excessive and new pumps would be required,
necessitating heavy assessments," or 'the depth
now attained would immediately involve the necessity of erecting new hoisting works." But we are not
to suppose because the firm of Trackem & Cinchem
would give no opinion as to the price stocks would
command in any number of days, that they did
not influence the public mind in that respect. Whilst
they were far too respectable to do such work themselves, they did not hesitate to employ a number of
broken-down and unprincipled stock operators, who
for a small pittance propagated the theories which
furthered their interests, who intimidated would-be
buyers when stocks were low and hunted them up
and incited them to purchase when they were inflated.   Into the hands of one of these cappers the
General had voluntarily fallen.

" Will you please buy me one hundred shares of
Savage, Mr. Cinchem ?" said the General.

" Certainly !"

The form was produced and the blanks filled
out ; General Sterne attached his autograph.

" What deposit do you wish ?" he inquired.

Mr. Cinchem hesitated a moment and then said:
" Oh, none from you, General ; the stock will be here
to-morrow at 12 o'clock.'

The General wished the broker good morning and retired ; the tout remained.

"I have brought you a —— good client, Cinchem —he is worth at least half a million."

" Yes, but what has induced him to go into stocks —I never heard of his dealing before, did you ?"

" No," said the tout, " and he wouldn't be dealing now if I hadn't hunted him up and run him in. I worked him up good, I can tell you. You'll make a big haul out of him, Cinchem. You'll have to divvy and come down handsome, by the bye, just pungle down five dollars ; I'm stumped."

Mr. Cinchem felt in his pockets and finally found and paid the money.

Will Wily, for it was he, pocketed the coin and immediately proceeded to Frank's saloon to liquidate it. Wily was naturally smart. A few years earlier his name stood high in San Francisco. He was now a broken and reckless man. When Trackem & Cinchem first started in business, Wily was one of their best clients. He was possessed of a considerable amount of real estate and a good bank account. Trackem was the first to make his acquaintance, which he assiduously cultivated. Wily had an unfortunate propensity for boon company and wine. This Trackem steadily encouraged. Wily thought him the best fellow in the world and shortly made the firm his brokers and bankers. Trackem having played his part now handed him over to Cinchem, who did his work so expeditiously that in six month the funds and properties of Wily had all changed hands. The firm was rich, and

Wily was, to use another Californiaism, "a busted community." From that time to the present he had been a hanger-on of the firm, and was sorely grieved if they did not give him enough change to enable him to get exceedingly full every night. With some variations in the detail of circumstance, there are hundreds of others who have had Wily's experience in San Francisco. Their money entirely lost in stock-gambling, they seem utterly demoralized, and hang about the entrance to the stock-boards as if they expected to see their coin handed back to them from within the doors which engulphed it.

As the city clock struck twelve the succeeding day, the General, who was always prompt and punctual, walked into the office of Trackem & Cinchem and demanded his bill. It was handed to him, with the stock; it ran as follows:—

General Sterne in account with Trackem & Cinchem.

To 100 shares of Savage @ $17¾ $1,775 00
" Commission...... .... 9 00

$1,784 00

The General wrote a cheque for the amount and inquired, "What is Savage selling for to-day ?"

" Well, General," said Mr. Cinchem, "this is an off day you see, things are down, and Savage with the rest. The average price to-day was, let me see— referring to the list—thirteen dollars and a half. Better market to-morrow, I hope. That dollar assessment on Savage to-day has affected it more than other stocks. Is there any other business we can do for you ?"

The General had consulted the papers before coming to the office of Trackem & Cinchem. He had small interest in stocks being up or down—he did not look to see what he had made or lost—he was searching for Truth—and the highest quotation he could find for Savage was sixteen and five-eighths, his hundred shares were rendered to him at seventeen and three-quarters. Hence when Mr. Cinchem asked for further commands he hesitated a moment and finally answered : "Yes, I think you may sell that hundred shares for me to-day. I will leave them with you and call to-morrow."

"Very well, General, if you think it best," said Mr. Cinchem.

The General bowed his affirmative and departed.

Punctual as before the General returned the next day and received his account and a check. The following is a copy of the bill:

General Sterne in account with Trackem & Cinchem.

By 50 shares of Savage @ $12¾ $637	50
" 50 " " " @ $12½ 625	00
	$1,262 50
To commission............................. 6	65
	$1,255 85

As before, the General had consulted the stock lists and could find no quotation of Savage under thirteen and a quarter. When therefore Mr. Cinchem politely inquired if the General had any further commands for him, and later if he would join him in a glass of wine, the General declined both propositions with stately courtesy and left the office

quite satisfied : First that Wily was a trapper for
the highly respectable firm ; secondly, that he had
been robbed both in the buying and selling of the
stock, and thirdly, that he was much nearer right
in his estimate of humanity than the Judge was,
and that he should be able to demonstrate the fact
at the next meeting of the "Society in Search of
Truth."

CHAPTER VII.

JUDGE BLAND INTERVIEWS A BANKER.

If General Sterne was indefatigable in his pursuit of information, the Judge and Commodore were
far from idle. The Commodore might be seen at
any hour engaged in some newspaper office, hunting
up a mass of figures bearing upon the subject of
stock operations, and carefully transcribing them
on the pages of a memorandum book, the fac simile
of hundreds of others, which he had already filled
with statistics, and which he carried with him in
all his travels, having had a trunk specially prepared for their comfortable accommodation. If the
well-balanced mind of the Commodore had that
weak spot which I have shown in a former chapter
is in some form existent in every mental organization, it certainly was a mania for figures. If he had
been asked to demonstrate the authenticity of the
Scriptures, or the immortality of the soul, in both
of which he firmly believed, he would have immediately proceeded to work out the problem by means
of arithmetical or algebraical calculation ; or had

he been asked to deliver his opinion on the Beecher-Tilton scandal, he would have proceeded in this wise: "There are such a number of preachers in the United States, the number of preachers convicted of unchastity is so many, the proportion of detected to undetected criminals I have estimated from a careful examination of all authorities, to be so and so. The existence of strong animal passion in men who have vigorous physical organizations is found in such a proportion of the whole, the number of opportunities offered to man to indulge his evil propensities amounts on the average to so many; the proportion deterred from the committal of wrong by the lack of opportunity or the fear of detection, is so many. Now, sir, I have given you the figures, you must make your own deductions. Mr. Beecher being a minister of the gospel, I shall for my own part give him the benefit of the doubt."

Meantime, the Judge resolved to interview the great head centre of the stock business of the Pacific slope, Mr. Highwater, of the banking-house of Highwater & Obrian. Now the Judge had met Mr. Highwater on various occasions, and the banker had always been very affable to him. It was a well-known fact that he always was affable to men of large means, for though he was reputed to be the richest man in San Francisco, he was known to be as greedy of wealth as the poorest father of a large family could possibly be, and was never loth to devise a means to excite interest in the stocks he controlled, to induce his rich neighbors to invest in them, which virtually meant the transfer of their

funds to his coffers. To accomplish this end he
employed numberless agents, to whom he gave from
time to time opportunities to make very considerable sums of money whilst accomplishing his purposes, but he almost invariably contrived to gather
in their gains when he had used them as much as
he desired. And whilst he plotted to become possessed of the fortunes of the well-to-do, he by no
means lost sight of the working classes, whose earnings he had been so successful in gathering in, that
it was estimated that there was not one in ten of
the entire adult population, of whose means he had
not received from a small portion to the whole; and
yet, like the horse-leeches' daughter and the gaping
grave, his insatiable desire for gain still cried out,
" Give ! give !"   By these means he had succeeded in
gathering the bulk of the coin formerly in circulation into his own vaults, and changing the condition of San Francisco from that of an active, thriv-
ing, growing city, to one of stagnation, with widely
extended poverty and distress.

It would be too absurd to suppose that any bond
of sympathy could exist between Mr. Highwater
and a man like Judge Bland, who, by education and
habit, was every inch a gentleman, whose breeding
and manners were so unquestionable that he was
often spoken of as the Chesterfield of American
society. He was altogether too antithical to the
banker, and so thoroughly indifferent to the further
accumulation of wealth, that Mr. Highwater, whose
soul was too narrow to grasp the excellencies of the
Judge, whilst he was always affable to him, at the

same time really disliked him. He had no doubt he was despised by the Judge, which to do the Judge justice, was not a fact. He therefore had a great desire to lower the Judge's dignity, which in the banker's estimation, could best be accomplished by taking to himself the Judge's ample fortune.

When therefore the Judge called upon him, he was delighted to see him, and when he began to make inquiries concerning the Comstock lode, became cordial in the extreme.

"The Comstock lode," said the banker, " is as far from worked out as ever—work has only just commenced on it, sir."

" But, Mr. Highwater," remarked the Judge, "it is said that the bonanzas are all but exhausted, and that there is no other development on the whole line of the lode that is known to be payable."

" Lies—all of it, sir," affirmed the banker. " Lies put forward by people who want to injure us, and to blackmail us. The bonanzas are liable to open out at lower levels bigger than ever, and with regard to the other mines—well there are several large ore bodies already discovered which will be opened up and worked as soon—well, as soon as we are ready. The Comstock has profitable work in it for hundreds of years to come, sir."

" Do you not think," asked the Judge, " that this prospect, held forth to the people for several years, has been very injurious to San Francisco, and that large numbers of people have been ruined by placing faith in it ?"

" Some may have been," said Mr. Highwater, "but

they were gamblers, anyway, and if they had not
lost their money there, would have lost it at the
faro table.   They do not deserve our sympathy,
Judge.   I have not lost my money."

"But do you not think this stock business en-
courages gambling, and that the Comstock lode is
a positive disadvantage to the people ?" queried the
Judge.

"No, sir ;" replied Mr. Highwater, "the people of
San Francisco will gamble.   It is well for them to
have it to gamble in.   Some of them make large
fortunes out of the stocks, as well as the mines.
Why, Judge, that Comstock lode has built San
Francisco, and if a few people suffer, why—well—
it does not matter.   It has not done me any harm.
I don't see why it should injure any one, besides
there will be any quantity more ore coming out
directly."

"Thank you, Mr. Highwater, for the information," said the Judge.   " I wanted to know the true
state of the case.   Good morning."

"Good morning," and the banker bowed the
Judge out.

" I wonder if the old fool will invest," soliloquized
the banker.   "I must give a hint to one or two of
the boys to go for him.   I would like to see him
cinched.   I must think more of it and see if I can't
take him down a peg or two."   He remembered a
few of those he had taken down from affluence to
poverty.   Some of them were his friends, both men
and women, others he had hated as he hated the
Judge, simply because they had a nobility of soul

he could not comprehend, but which, at the same time, chafed and annoyed him when they came in contact with him. Yes, he would have the Judge roped in, and he chuckled at the thought.

But for once the banker was destined to be disappointed. The Judge was well satisfied with his ample income. He neither sought nor desired to augment it. So he pursued his literary pleasures and his harmless hobbies, and was superior to all the blandishments the most skillful of the banker's cappers could bring to bear upon him.

Very different to the banker's feelings were those of the Judge. He left the office with a feeling of regard for the busy man of mines and banks who had so obligingly responded to his inquiries, to ponder on what he had heard and to prepare himself to speak effectively and throw a brighter coloring over the subject of stock operations than that which he clearly foresaw would be given by his esteemed friend, the General, at the meeting to be held the following evening of the "Society in Search of Truth."

CHAPTER VIII.

GENERAL STERNE ON THE WAR-PATH.

If there was one feature of the strongly marked character of General Sterne that was more purely individual than any other, it was the love of justice and fair play. Under his cold and austere exterior there was a heart, which, hidden away from the vulgar gaze of the world in which he moved, and un-

suspected by it, was capable of the warmest
emotions and the most generous sympathies. This
fact, from time to time, would show itself despite
the vigorous efforts he made to repress and obliter-
ate it. Nothing so much excited his ire as the oppression of the weaker by the stronger. Anything
in the form of wrong or injustice done to those who
were incapable of defending themselves would inevitably bring down his wrath. At the same time,
in smaller matters in which he was the injured individual, he not unfrequently appeared oblivious of
the fact. When in the army he preserved a disci-
pline unknown in other regiments than his own.
He held every subordinate officer directly responsi-
ble to himself for the performance of the very letter of duty, and no influence could move or change
him from his rigid determination to have those
duties performed, and nothing would more surely
bring forth his sore displeasure than the neglect on
the part of any officer to make the most comfortable provision possible for his men. In civil life many
a bully, in the midst of his triumph over a weaker
man, had felt the weight of his iron hand, and many
a troubled debtor had been rescued from the hands
of would-be devouring creditors, and re-established
in possession of his own. Such acts as demanded
the use of his money he always performed through
his attorney; he never alluded to them, and strictly
forbade their mention by any of the parties concerned.

When the General left the office of Trackem &
Cinchem, no one could have known by his bearing

that he was in the slightest degree annoyed. He was, however, seriously vexed, not at the loss of the few hundred dollars, out of which he believed himself to have been swindled; that he was prepared for, and would have neither been surprised nor particularly annoyed if he had lost the entire money he had paid to them. But he was annoyed to have so easily found out, to his full satisfaction, that people who unlike himself could not afford to lose their money, were being pauperized by a wholesale system of robbery, and by a method of gambling, which, in his judgment, was quite as reprehensible as playing at a faro game, and with less chances in the favor of the player, inasmuch as the cards in the stock gamble are dealt in the dark, and the dealers only have the privilege of seeing them. In point of fact, the inside players make up the pack and deal the cards and know them all, the outsider does not know one, but plays entirely on the chances of a card turning up which is rarely dealt to him.

The General returned to his rooms, he opened a drawer and took from it a pocket-book. Unclasping the book, he drew from it a number of slips of paper, and laid them in a row on the table. They were all notes on demand, from various persons to whom he had lent money at different times. Most of them were for moneys lent to purchase (or to keep good margins on) stocks. Selecting these from the rest, he replaced the balance in the pocket-book, returned the pocket-book to the drawer and went out. Leaving the Palace Hotel, he proceeded down Montgomery street some distance, and then passed

D

up a stairway and entered an office. It was the office of his attorney. " Mr. Equity," said the General, " I have brought you these notes ; you know all about them. I want you to proceed with their collection without delay. I will leave them with you. Please give me a memorandum of them. You will find they amount to thirty-nine thousand five hundred dollars. I want you to issue to-day a notice to each of the drawers to take up his note immediately."

"Are you leaving San Francisco, General ?"

"No, Mr. Equity, on the contrary ; I have just entered upon engagements which will prolong my stay."

The attorney was puzzled. Peremptory proceedings on the part of the General were not unusual, but he had never known him to hasten a debtor. And now, this wholesale order, with its urgency and unexpectedness nonplussed the attorney.

" Is there anything wrong, General ?" he asked.

" I am afraid there is a great deal wrong, Mr. Equity; a very great deal. I am afraid I have been unwittingly aiding and assisting in the ruin of all the men whose names are attached to these papers."

" I do not understand you, General," said the attorney."

The General appeared deeply absorbed in thought for a few moments ; then, looking at the lawyer, he answered :—

" You know, Mr. Equity, when I lent the various sums enumerated here, pointing to the notes, I did it with the intention of benefitting the borrowers."

"I am aware of it, sir," said the attorney.

"You are also aware," continued the General, "that all these sums were advanced by me to be used by the individuals to whom they were loaned in stock operations. The total amount is considerable. I do not care to lose it. But, apart from that, I will inform you that during the past few days I have been investigating the proceedings of the brokers and manipulators of the stock business, and, I regret to say, that I have arrived at the conclusion, that, whilst seeking to benefit the drawers of those notes I have been consummating their ruin."

The General would not speak even to his attorney of the fraud he believed to have been perpetrated on him by Trackem & Cinchem. He continued :—

"My observations have convinced me that I have helped them into a net, the meshes of which will entangle them and destroy them. I will not encourage the system by which they are being reduced to poverty. I therefore wish you to be prompt and decisive in the collection of those amounts."

"I will notify the parties at once, General," said the lawyer, "and report to you."

"Do so," replied the General, "and please remember, Mr. Equity, that in this decision I am not to be moved, and that in future you will not entertain any appeals for such purposes on my account. You will not require me in this business ?"

"No, sir; certainly not," answered Mr. Equity.

The General now left to continue his investigations, and ponder the knowledge he had attained, and then he proposed to return to his rooms and arrange the material he had collected, and prepare himself for the task of submitting the result of his observations to the Society in the evening.

Meanwhile Mr. Equity was in a quandary. After the General retired, he sat down on a chair, apparently wrapped in the profoundest thought. In a few minutes he rose and locked the door of his office. He then returned to the table and took up the notes the General had left, and turned them over with great care. He finally selected two—one was for five thousand, the other for seven thousand five hundred dollars. These he laid by themselves, and again relapsed into reverie.

When the General first came to San Francisco, he had transferred to that city a considerable portion of his fortune. He had made sundry trials of attorneys, which had proved unsatisfactory. He finally made the acquaintance of Mr. Equity, who was a young attorney with a family, whom he found it difficult to support. The General recognized in him an amount of intelligence and ability which, combined with his lack of success, excited his interest and sympathy. He therefore decided to give him the charge of his legal business. This proved to be the turning point in the fortunes of the struggling attorney. The fact of the General employing him, led others to believe that he must be an able man, and his business and income steadily increased—so much so, that by prudence and economy he might speedily have accumulated a competency. But unfortunately, his vanity and love of display had led him to increase his expenditures in as great proportion as his gains increased. Hence he was, so far as ready money was concerned, no better off than when the General first found him in poverty.

Some weeks earlier than the time of which I am now speaking, he had received, from what he believed to be reliable sources, a "point" in a certain mining stock. He was ambitious. He was anxious to be rich. Ready money he had none. But then the General had plenty. But how to obtain it? He knew the General did not gamble in stocks, and he dare not risk asking him for money for any such purpose. But he was anxious to avail himself of what he was led to believe was a golden opportunity. Compass it he would, in some way. Now the General had entrusted to him the authority to entertain and submit to himself propositions for loans. He had directed him to ascertain that the parties were deserving, and to particularly favor such as were in danger from the oppression of creditors. Availing himself of this authority, and fully convinced that he could realize a very large sum in a short time, he had presented to the General two notes, each bearing a fictitious name, the one for five thousand, the other for seven thousand five hundred dollars. With regard to each, he had coined such a story as he knew would excite the General's sympathy. He had received the money; had put it all up on a fifty per cent. margin, and in a few weeks had lost it all in stock gambling. And now those notes were handed to him for collection, and the General held his receipt for them all. All these facts passed through his mind as he sat still meditating on the misfortune which, through his own folly and credulity, had overtaken him. What should he do? He dare not confess his duplicity to the General; that would be to sacrifice his favor forever. The generous, but sternly just man, would never forgive him. Should he collect as many of the remaining notes as he could, and then leave by the China or Panama steamer? Should he take the revolver that lay in his drawer and blow out his stupid brains? Should he poison or drown himself? What should he do?

We must leave him for the present, whilst he resolves the doubt.

CHAPTER IX.

JUDGE BLAND RECEIVES A DISPATCH.

The Judge was in a felicitous state of purturbation. He had received a telegram. He held it in his hand and read it and read it again. So many times did he peruse it, that one might have imagined it was one of those eloquent flights of his own imagination, of which he had committed a number to writing, which he loved to look upon, and for which he exhibited all the affection a tender mother could possibly feel for the first fruit of connubial love. He finally laid the dispatch on the table and walked up and down the room. He next went to the fireplace and standing in front of it contemplated a painting that was suspended above it. It was a life-size portrait of a young man apparently about twenty-five years of age, dressed in the uniform of the United States army. The height of the individual represented was above the average, the form well knit. The *tout ensemble* conveyed the idea of elegance and refinement. The expression of the countenance of strong will, blended with genial-heartedness. A broad forehead indicated a comprehensive intellect. The clear grey eyes, firm and restful and charged with intelligence, looked from under a pair of eyebrows which, nearly meeting in the center, showed persistence to be a strong feature of his character. A finely-formed nose surmounted the mouth, that tell-tale member, which was clearly visible through a light curling moustache, and disclosed no trace of vice. The chin was covered by a brown, wavy beard. The whole face and figure conveyed the idea of graceful ease, of conscious nobility, and of high resolve. The Judge returned to the table, and again took up the dispatch and again read:

SACRAMENTO.

To Judge Bland,
       Palace Hotel, San Francisco :
   Wished to surprise you, uncle—shall be with you to-night— Please engage rooms for me, near your own.

MILTON BUCHANAN BLAND.

The Judge could not keep still. If there was one person in the world for whom he would have given up all the rest it was this only son of his only sister, who thirty years before had married a wealthy distant relative of her own name. The Judge always spoke of Milton as "my boy." He loved him with more than a father's love, not merely from the fact that he was his nearest living relative, but because in addition to that, he recognized in him so much sterling worth, so much superior ability and noble purpose, that he would often observe: "If God had let me make 'my boy' myself, I would not have made him one whit different from what he is." From this picture my reader must not suppose that Captain Bland was so completely good as to be immaculate. On the contrary, he was much like other young men. When at Harvard, and subsequently at West Point, he had entered into all the sports and gaities of his fellow-students, with a zest and determinedness in which he had been exceeded by none of them. He had had his flirtations and his follies, but with them all he never forgot that he was a gentleman. His veneration and esteem for his mother, whom he dearly loved, had ever exerted a salutary influence over him, and preserved and kept him from the grosser follies in which many of his fellow-students delighted. With their pursuits he never interfered, and when invited by them to join in what he believed to be unlawful indulgencies, he had declined in such a pleasant and graceful manner that he had never offended them, and was always esteemed one of the best of fellows. Having completed his studies he entered the army as a lieutenant and was now a captain in the —— Regiment. In the army as at college, the same characteristics marked his life; the same faithful discharge of his own duty, and the same obliviousness of the proceedings of others when they did not interfere with him. By those means he had achieved a high status in his regiment, and in the very best circles of society he received an amount of respect and attention rarely accorded to so young a man. When Milton joined his regiment there was a corporal in the company whose time of service had nearly expired. His name was Tim Maloney. Tim was a good soldier. In the discharge of his duties he had incurred the ill-will of several of the men. When he received his discharge he prepared to leave for the West, where he proposed to take up land and become a settler. The evening before his departure he was way-laid by three men of the company who stripped him, bound him to a tree, and were about to give him fifty lashes, when Milton came upon the scene and dispersed them and liberated him. I mention this circumstance because Tim Maloney, as will hereafter appear, had an opportunity to more than repay the good offices of his lieutenant. Having obtained several months' leave of absence, his widowed mother having died the preceding year, Milton determined to spend his furlough with his uncle, who, with all his idiosyncracies and eccentricities, he honored as a true-hearted and noble-minded man, who always called him "my boy," and for whom, both his parents being dead, he entertained a more than ordinary filial affection.

The Judge could not rest. He must be on the move. He sought his hat and cane, and leaving the hotel went in search of the General. He found him as he anticipated, in the midst of the expectant throng, who (like the lame, the sick, and the impotent who waited for the angel to come down and touch the water of the pool of Siloam, each unfortunate hoping to be the first to step in and be healed) continually do congregate in the region of the stock boards on Pine and Leidesdorff streets. There was the General, still persistent in his search after Truth—hopeless of finding it—but resolute to know all he could learn.

"General," said the Judge, "I wanted to see you. I have an item of news to communicate. I have just received a dispatch from Sacramento telling me that a near relative of mine will arrive here this evening, whom I wish to introduce to you, and also to request your consent to his introduction and perhaps an initiation into the Society."

"Is it a lady or a gentleman?" inquired the General, the solid brows contracting.

"Oh, a gentleman," calmly replied the Judge, "it is 'my boy' whose portrait you have often seen over the mantle-piece in my sitting-room. He is a splendid boy. You will be delighted with him, General."

"Ah," said the General, his brows resuming their normal condition, "When will he arrive?"

"This evening, by the overland train. I heard from him this morning. He thought he would give me a pleasant surprise. And he has."

"I shall be happy to see him, privately, and also in the Society's meetings," said the General. "You will introduce him this evening?"

"Yes."

The Judge now hastened in quest of the Commodore, and found him in the Mercantile Library, pen in hand, surrounded by a number of statistical records, from which he was adding to his already voluminous data, all that he could find relating to the production of ore, and the cost of working the Comstock lode. The Judge waited restlessly whilst the Commodore completed the writing of the extract he was making. He then said :—

" Commodore, can I speak with you ?"

" Certainly," said the Commodore. " I am just through."

He gathered together his memoranda, and restored the volumes to their places on the shelves (he was very methodical), and then, turning to the Judge, intimated that he was ready. They descended the stairway together, and, at the Judge's suggestion, adjourned to the Palace Hotel. Arrived in his parlor, the Judge rang the bell, and when the waiter appeared, ordered a bottle of Eclipse. He then took from his pocket the dispatch and carefully scrutinized it. He next walked to the portrait and looked at it long and earnestly.

The waiter returned, and inquired, " Shall I open the wine, gentlemen ?"

" Yes," said the Judge, and commenced to walk backwards and forwards, always pausing a moment when he passed the portrait.

Meantime the Commodore was inly wondering what could be the matter with the Judge, for no word had he spoken to him since he entered the room. Had he lost his wits ? He had always thought the Judge a man of strong mind, though eccentric. Was he ill? No; or he would not have ordered wine, which he always avoided when out of sorts. Had he met with some misfortune? No. He seemed supremely happy. What was it, then?

The waiter having uncorked the wine, and filled two glasses, retired.

Whereupon the Judge approached the table, and taking his glass in his hand, said: "Commodore Pye, you are one of the oldest and most esteemed of my San Francisco friends. I have asked you to join me here, in order that we may drink a health together." Raising the glass in his right hand towards the picture, he said: "Commodore Pye, the health and happiness of 'my boy.' God, bless him."

"Judge Bland," said the Commodore, also rising from his chair, "the health and happiness of your boy, may God bless him." And his thoughts flew away to sunny France, and to that living picture of his lost Rose, who was so soon to join him, a fact of which he had not even spoken to his intimate friends, the Judge and General (the Commodore was always reticent on purely family matters). He was relieved to find that the business on hand was nothing more serious than the drinking of a health, though still silently wondering why the Judge was displaying this unusual demonstration of feeling.

His curiosity was soon satisfied. The Judge proceeded to show him the dispatch, and then to trace to him the history of "his boy," from his childhood up, and dilate on the many excellencies of his character, all of which the Commodore had heard several times before. It was a subject on which the Judge never tired of speaking. And the Commodore sat and listened, and thought sometimes of Captain Bland, but quite as frequently of that bright copy of his lost darling.

The Judge now arose, saying: " I must go to Brooklyn, to meet ' my boy,'" and though it was a full hour too soon, he hastened off to the boat as if he had not a moment to spare.

The Commodore, meantime, retired to his rooms to arrange the facts he had collected, and put them in such form as would be fit for presentation in the evening to the " Society in Search of Truth."

CHAPTER X.

THE SOCIETY RE-ASSEMBLES.

Notwithstanding the excitement experienced by the Judge, on receipt of the telegram announcing "his boy's" approach, he did not fail to make suitable provision for Captain Bland's lodgment, or to provide a special seat for his occupation in the meetings of the Society. He purchased another chair exactly like the Commodore's. Here a difficulty presented itself. The Judge could not bear the idea of his own chair and the General's being ornamented, whilst his boy's was quite plain. But then if he adorned it, so must he also the Commodore's. He therefore found time to inspect the various establishments which dealt in statues, and finally selected Minerva, with a scroll in her hand, which he had placed on the right of the Commodore's chair. Ceres, her hand resting on a sheaf of corn, he caused to be fixed on the left. Faith he caused to be removed from the General's chair and placed in the center, substituting for her Niobe in tears. Why he this change made I cannot explain. He also purchased two handsome figures, one of Venus the other of Adonis, the former he had placed on the left and the latter on the right of the chair designed to be occupied by Captain Bland. In the center, supported by a tiny gilt column, was a figure of Cupid flying with bent bow in hand, the arrow pointed at the heart of the lady. This was an enigmatical illustration of the Judge's belief that the most beautiful woman must necessarily succumb to the united graces and virtues of "the boy." It does not seem to have occurred to him that the shaft of the fickle god might first enter the heart of the Captain.

The hour for the meeting arrived. The General and the Commodore, who had been together comparing notes of their observations and impressions of the subject for the evening's discussion, entered simultaneously.

"Gentlemen," said the Judge, "I have much pleasure in introducing to you 'my boy.' Captain Milton Buchanan Bland, Commodore Pye; General Sterne, Captain Milton Buchanan Bland."

Mutual recognitions and congratulations having been exchanged, the Judge said :—

"With your consent, gentlemen, I have invited

' my boy ' to become a member of the ' Society in Search of Truth,' and he has accepted the honor, and thanks you. Mr. Secretary, will you kindly administer the oath, and then enroll his name."

The initiatory ceremonies being satisfactorily completed, Captain Bland having been declared a member of the Society, and having expressed his thanks in a few remarks which showed that the Judge had made him conversant with its objects and intentions, he took his seat.

It was about this time the General observed the change in the adornment of his chair. He cast a searching glance at the Judge, which the latter did not perceive, but made no remark.

The Judge now rose and spoke as follows:—

"Gentlemen, and members of the Society in Search of Truth :—The subject of our investigation to-night is 'Mining and Stock Operations.' The calling of the miner is an ancient and an honorable one. It dates back to the very earliest times, and next to those of the gardener, which was the business of our first parent, Adam; the farmer, which was the employment of Cain, who was a tiller of the soil; the shepherd, which was the occupation of Abel, is the most ancient kind of labor of which we have any record. We are told, gentlemen, that Tubal-Cain, who was the son of Zillah, was an instructor of artificers in brass and iron. There must have been miners in those days, or there would have been no brass or iron. Therefore the miners' business is older than that of the blacksmith or foundryman. The study of mining is an interesting one.   To search out and find the method by which Vulcan, the god of subterranean fires, rends the earth's crust, and pumps up into the fissures the metals we find so useful in the arts, and also in the common uses of life, is well worthy of our investigation.   The importance of mining, as an industry, cannot be over-estimated.   It gives employment to hundreds of thousands of men, who, thus profitably engaged, are consumers of the products of the farmers' labor and the manufacturers' skill.   Without the miner, who digs from the bowels of the earth the iron and the coal, there could be no railroads, or steamships, which add so much to our comfort and convenience.   Without the miner there could be no copper or tin, wherewith to make vessels in which are prepared so many of the dishes which satisfy the gastronomic wants of man; without the miner, there would be no gold or silver for the manufacture of coin, or of objects of grace and beauty, such as these (here he gracefully waved his hand toward the inkstands, the number of which he had now increased to four).   Without the miner there would be no diamonds, or emeralds or rubies, wherewith to deck the female beauty and the loveliness we love."

Here the Commodore, whose thoughts flew off to his lovely daughter, said: "That is so, Judge."

The General, through his closed teeth uttered a sound which resembled "bosh !"

The Captain, whose heart had never yet experienced the full force of the grand passion, but who was an ardent though always respectful admirer of beauty, gave a pleasant smile indicative of interest. He did not catch the General's ejaculation.

Neither did the Judge, who now continued :

"But, gentlemen, I must not trespass on your time by dwelling on this subject, nor must I anticipate the remarks of General Sterne, who is elected to open the question of ' Stock and Mining Operations.' In the course of our discussions, I shall have the pleasure of conveying to you some impressions I have received from a conversation with that distinguished banker, Mr. Highwater, but I must not forget those lines of Herbert :—

> ' If thou be master gunner, spend not all
>   That thou canst speak at once ; but husband it
> And give men turns of speech; do not forstall
>   By lavishness thine own and others wit.'

"I trust that we shall bring to bear on this important subject, all attainable knowledge. Superficially is always dangerous, and its observations are almost invariably delusive. As Pope remarks :—

> ' A little learning is a dangerous thing ;
>   Drink deep or taste not the Pierien spring ;
> For shallow draughts intoxicate the brain,
>   But drinking deeply sobers us again.'

"Gentlemen, I have much pleasure in calling on our distinguished, esteemed, and able Vice-President, General Sterne, to open the discussion on ' Stock and Mining Operations.' "

The Judge resumed his seat, the Society according him grateful demonstrations of applause.

Rising to his feet, the General pushed back from him his chair, with the two remaining graces and the weeping goddess, and then turning, faced his audience, his head erect, his face expressing and his bearing confirming a conscious power and a stern resolve. He gravely bowed to the Society and said :—

"Mr. President and Gentlemen :—

"I have listened with pleasure to the remarks which have been uttered from the Chair this evening. It would have afforded me great gratification if I could have laid before you as the result of my observations, a pleasing picture of the manner in which stock operations are conducted in San Francisco—for it is to that part of our subject and not to mining, that I have for the present directed my attentive research. If in the pursuance of the object to which I have given my unremitting care, I could have discovered such redeeming features as would have justified me in bringing a gratifying report before you, I should have rendered it to the Society with cheerful gladness. But, gentlemen, I regret to say that the preponderance of evidence so far as I have progressed, is not of a pleasing character. I do not design to affirm that there are no honestly conducted stock operations ; I do not propose to assert that amongst the controllers of mines and the brokers, who are their employees, there are not some honorable men, whose acts are just and whose words are Truth ; but at the same time, the oath I have taken to this Society, whose proceedings are ultimately to go forth to the world, and the duty I owe to myself as a man, demand that I should tell you, that the Truth, if Truth there be, in these operations, is so hidden from sight, that to find it seems impossible. If I may borrow a figure of speech used by the President in his inaugural address, in which he told us that 'we were drawn to the violet by its fragrance, and that, hidden in dark bosses of green leaves we should never find it did we not part the leaves,' I will say that I have found no fragrance so far; I have found the bosses of dark leaves; they were frauds, trickeries and lies; I have parted a great many of them but so far I have found no violets."

At this Captain Bland looked up at the General, astonishment, not to say distress, depicted on his features.

The Judge murmured to himself, "Is it so; was Colton right when he wrote, 'Truth can hardly be expected to adapt herself to the crooked policy and wily sinuosities of worldly affairs; for Truth, like light, travels only in straight lines.' He is right; but why will not men follow Truth?"

The Commodore turned over the memoranda in front of him, but did not speak.

The General continued: "Had I opened Pandora's box, I could not have discovered more evils. I have found, gentlemen, that the method of stock operations, as at present conducted, is calculated to increase the wealth of the few, and to ruin the masses; that great numbers are already ruined by it; and that by false reports of rich discoveries the public are induced to invest in worthless stock certificates, at high prices. I have ascertained that there are a number of so-called mines on the Comstock lode which never had payable ore, and have no prospect of ever getting it, which are now being foisted upon the public, at the rate of from half a million to millions of dollars for the so-called mine. I have discovered that it is the practice of the controllers of these properties, aided by certain banks, from time to time to inflate the prices of the Comstock mines; to have what they term a ' deal,' and then to sell out to the public all the stock they can, after which they heavily assess the stock, and when the stockholders are weary of the tax, the controllers buy in the stocks at comparatively very low prices, and prepare to have another ' deal,' that is, they raise another excitement, and repeat the former operation. I have found that their object is to make stock gambling take the place of mining. I have ascertained that nearly every mine on the Comstock line, has been declared to have a development once, and some of them three or four times, within the past four years, and that not one of those supposed developments has been of any value to the outside stockholders. I have discovered that in some instances the controllers of mines have never paid an assessment, but have collected heavy sums from the outside stockholders, and converted them in part to their own uses. I have observed that in some cases, the controllers of mines are contractors for the supplies and work done for the mines, thus Highwater, Obrian & Co., directors, let to Highwater, Obrian & Co., contractors, the contracts to supply timber, and to do the milling of the Company's ores, at their own prices; and they, the directors, grant to themselves, the contractors, the free gift of all the tailings; and the gratings of the stamper boxes are never made too fine to let the tailings go through. I have found that the controllers of mines employ a number of men to induce individuals to let go their money in exchange for worthless stocks, and that some brokers' returns to their customers are greatly at variance with the authorized quotations of the days on which their orders are executed; and also, that it is a most difficult thing for a stockholder to obtain any reliable information, much more a sight of the property in which he is interested. I have also found, to my amazement that the law takes scarcely any cognizance of these things, and when in the last session of the Legislature, a bill was introduced to regulate some of the evils I have enumerated, a combination of mining men subscribed large sums of money wherewith to give obliquity of vision to the legislators, and so the bill lapsed. Gentlemen, I have honestly sought the Truth, and hoped to have been able to bring before you a different report, but I have arrived at the conclusion that I must have looked in the wrong locality. It appears to me that if Truth ever resided in the neighborhood of the Stock Boards, it has removed into some other part of the city."

The General resumed his seat.

Captain Bland murmured to himself, " Can these things be, and men, like slaves, submit?"

The Commodore glanced at his papers, but made no remark.

The President, looking at the General with great earnestness, seemed to be realizing the fact that the researches of the Society, if this was a fair example, would bring him more pain than pleasure. He hated the turmoil of the world; he loved easy re-finement, and the pursuits of literature and knowl-edge. After a short pause, he spoke :—

"General Sterne, in the name of the Society, I thank you. I must admit my own regret, that the result of your observations and inquiries is a series of disclosures which are painful to hear. But, sir, you have done your duty. If it be our misfortune to have to look upon the deformities which the world seeks to hide under a mask of Truth, we must submit to the inevitable. I will now declare the farther discussion of the subject adjourned to our next meeting, but will repeat to you before we part, some lines of Butler's, that recurred to my memory whilst you were speaking, which should apply to some of those unjust proceedings you have informed us of :—

> " Men venture necks to gain a fortune—
> The soldier does it every day
> (Eight in the week) for sixpence pay.
> Your pettifoggers damn their souls,
> To share with knaves in cheating fools."

"My boy," said the Judge to Captain Bland (when the Commodore and General had gone), "this 'Society in Search of Truth' is a much more se-rious business than I expected."

"Never mind, uncle," replied the Captain, "'Let us have the Truth, though the heavens fall.'"

CHAPTER XI.

THE JUDGE'S DREAM AND WILY'S TROUBLE.

Long after his guests had left, and Milton, who remained for some time responding to the many inquiries of his kind-hearted uncle, had retired to his rooms, the Judge sat in his chair, wrapped in meditation, first recalling many incidents of his past life and then of the shorter history of his nephew. Finally his thoughts reverted to the Society. Its operations were already assuming a form he had not anticipated, and did not desire. An enthusiastic worshipper of the beautiful, governed in all his actions by high principle, wrapped up in the pursuit of literary pleasures, a student of poetry, and trying to see good in all mankind, it was perfectly natural for him to idealize all the virtues. So was he seeking to idealize Truth, and in desiring to establish the Society, his object was to cull the beauties out of every day life, rather than to lay bare the deformities of its vices—which it always pained his generous soul to look upon. But lo, at the very beginning of its meetings, the startling fact revealed itself that if the Society would make the discovery he desired, it must wade (as the General had observed at the first meeting) knee deep in filth to find it. This pained the Judge. He always maintained that man finds enough of evil without looking for it. For this reason he never read such newspapers as sought to fill their columns with sensational and scandalous incidents. But the very first meeting for discussion had disclosed much he would far rather not have heard. "How unfortunate," he soliloquized, "some other subject was not chosen. Could we not change it?" No; he knew the General and Commodore would both insist on the completion of what was already begun. Was there no way to escape it? None; for he was the originator and the President of the Society. He must go on. He finally sought his room and went to bed—to dream. He thought he saw a number of men enter his sitting-room, and that he demanded their business. They made no reply, but walked to his chair, the presidential chair, and loosened therefrom the statue of Truth, and bore it away, he following, up Montgomery street to Pine, down which they turned, and entered the Stock Board, where they planted Truth on the caller's desk. It seemed to him to be early morning; there were no people in the streets.

Their work completed, the men filed out of the hall; he still following, the massive doors closing behind them by the aid of unseen hands. Arrived on the pavement the intruders separated, scattering in different directions. He waited on the steps of the building. Presently carts began to rattle through the streets; the milkmen, newspaper men, butchers, and vegetable vendors were at their early morning work. Soon stragglers began to move along the pavements. Again a little while, and the busy throng of every day was there. Now appeared the janitor, who opened the doors of the Exchange, and stood transfixed, his morning's work undone, gazing at the statue of Truth. The other employees enter one by one, and each in turn becomes immovable. Brokers and multitudes of dealers arrive; they take their seats, all gazing at Truth, and silent as the tomb. Half-past ten has come, a quarter to eleven. The throng increases but no man speaks. Eleven o'clock! The caller mounts his rostrum; he looks at Truth and stands beside her like a statue. The hall is full. Each eye is riveted on Truth; each tongue is dumb; each limb is motionless, as waiting a revelation. It comes at last—a man rises from a broker's chair as if by a more than human effort. It is Trackem. He walks to the desk. He mounts the steps. He seizes the caller's baton. He raises it high above his head—a fearful blow—a mighty crash—and Truth, broken in a thousand pieces, lies scattered on the floor. Then every tongue was loosed, and a shout went up which shook the hall to its very foundations. Anon the President seizes his baton. He strikes the gong. He cries "Ophir!" The brokers rush to the center. The whirl and strife grows fast and furious. The fragments of Truth are ground to impalpable dust, to be swept out by the janitors at the noon recess, and her very existence lost to memory before to-morrow's sun. Excess of excitement waked the Judge; he struck a light looked at his watch and was astonished to find that the events of what had seemed to him to be hours, could but have occupied a few minutes, seeing it was only a quarter of an hour since he had looked at his watch before. Why is there ever this discrepancy between our sleeping and our waking thoughts? Does the soul in our slumbers leave

the body and go on journeys on its own account?
If dreams foreshadow its future, what will it not
accomplish when freed from the trammels of flesh
and time? The Judge relieved to find that Truth
was safe upon his chair, composed himself to rest,
and slept the calm and peaceful sleep of perfect
health and quiet conscience.

Meantime, General Sterne, bidding adieu to the
Commodore at the Palace, had proceeded up Market
street toward the Baldwin Hotel, where he resided.
He had advanced but a short distance when he
perceived a number of people congregated on the
sidewalk, in advance of him. As he drew nearer
he thought he heard a voice with which he was
familiar. Pressing through the crowd, he perceived
that it was Will Wily, who was, as usual at that
time of night, so far inebriated that he might have
been called drunk. Just as the General gained the
centre of the ring, he saw that Wiley was engaged
with a much taller and more athletic man than himself, who at that instant struck him a savage blow,
which felled him to the earth. In a moment, so
suddenly that the bystanders could not understand
how it was done, the General straightened his right
arm, his knuckles came in collision with the lower
left jawbone of Wily's antagonist, and he rolled
over and remained very still, whilst the General,
folding his arms across his chest, and turning slowly
round, faced, in turn, the whole crowd. There was
in his manner an intimation of his thoughts, so
plainly to be read that every one of the crowd
understood him to mean :—

"I have defended a weaker man against a stronger. I am here. If you have cause of complaint against me, state it. If you want revenge, take it; I am ready."

No one moved or spoke. He now turned his attention to the prostrate men, first to Wily, who, he believed, was stunned, but not seriously injured, and then to his antagonist, who was recovering from the stunning effects of the General's well aimed blow, and was sitting on the pavement, endeavoring to collect his thoughts, and comprehend what had happened. When the General turned and faced him, his eyes resting a moment on the General, aided his memory to recall the cause of his prostration. His first thought, as the General approached him, was to spring to his feet; his second, as he glanced at the stern, resolute features, was to make a deprecatory motion with his hands, which he did. It was quite unnecessary; the General had never been known to strike a fallen foe. Looking down on the man, he said :—

"Rise, sir. You have injured this unfortunate fellow. You must assist me in escorting him to the Baldwin Hotel." There was authority and firmness in the command, which seemed to force compliance. The man sullenly rose from the sidewalk, and assisting Wily, who was now conscious, to his feet, aided the General in leading him to the hotel. Arrived there, the General turned to the man and said, "You can go, sir," and, as may be supposed, he gladly went.

The General having engaged a room for Wily,

and ascertained that his injuries were not of a serious character, nevertheless secured the services of an attendant, and gave him instructions to remain in Wily's room through the night, and to take every needful care of him ; to come to his own room and call him at any hour of the night, if necessary, and on no account to allow Wily to leave the hotel in the morning, until he had seen him.

The attendant assisted Wiley to cleanse himself from the dirt which he had gathered from the gutter, and then put him to bed, where he slept the heavy sleep of alcoholic intoxication until the morning.

The General, after leaving Wily, sought his own rooms. They were magnificently appointed. To the furniture they contained when he engaged them he had added a brilliant-toned, though small, upright piano, and a parlor organ, which, though no larger than the piano, was perfect of its kind, and contained all the latest mechanical improvements contrived to give variety to harmonious sound. There was also a fine book case, inlaid with California woods, which was filled with choice works of literature; English, French and German, as well as American. Niches and brackets on the walls, filling the space not occupied by paintings, were adorned with souvenirs of art, in the form of busts and statues. Here and in his library the same peculiarities were observable. In the latter there was no novel, no poem, nor any other work that treated of women. Amongst all his paintings and statuary there was no female form. The observer of this peculiar idiosyncracy, might, with reason, wonder why the General did not embrace the Moslem faith, which allows no soul to woman. And yet, withal, the General was passionately fond of music, which is the poetry of sound, in which the great masters have made their passages question and answer each other, now with the gentle pathos of tender love, and again with the energy and fire of rancorous hate.

The General's favorite music was the oratories. Entering the room, he seated himself before the piano and played that charming little air from Mendelsohn's St. Paul, "But the Lord is mindful of his own." Moving across to the organ he next flooded the room with the harmonies of Handel's grand chorus, "All we, like sheep, have gone astray," and then, closing the instrument, he lighted a cigar, and sat down to think over the incidents of the day, which had crowded one upon another in such rapid succession, that until now he seemed to have had no time for thought. It was at such times the General really appreciated the soothing influences of the narcotic weed.

CHAPTER XII.

WILY IS GENERAL STERNE'S PRISONER.

It may appear strange that General Sterne should have exhibited so much interest in Will Wily, seeing that he had fully convinced himself that Wily was but a tout for Trackem & Cinchem, and that he had waylaid him with the view of decoying him into their office, for the express purpose of affording them an opportunity to perpetrate a legal fraud on him.   The discovery of these facts, which would have utterly disgusted most men, only excited General Sterne's interest.   He had made diligent inquiry concerning Wily's past history, and was satisfied that there were sterling qualities hidden under the vices that now obscured them.   He had been convinced that Wily had been more sinned against than he was now sinning. He therefore resolved that he would do all in his power to resurrect the better man and gain him back to an honorable course of life.   How he could best accomplish this end he had not determined; nor could he see very clearly how he could obtain a sufficiently strong hold on Wily to make him subservient for the time being to his own will.   As we have seen, fortune favored his designs and threw Wily into his hands, and now, this morning, after the circumstances related in our last chapter, he was his prisoner waiting his will.   The General had returned from breakfast to his room, where he intended to remain, until the attendant he had engaged should usher in Wily.   He had taken from his book-case a volume of miscellaneous poems and had just read those lines of Gray's :—

> " The tricking gamester insolently rides,
>   With loves and graces on his chariot sides ;
>   In saucy state the griping broker sits,
>   And laughs at honesty and trudging wits."

He was mentally applying them to the firm of Trackem & Cinchem when a knock was heard at his door.

" Come in," said the General.

The attendant entered, introduced Mr. Wily, and retired.

" Be seated, Mr. Wily," said the General, " I wished to see you. I found you in an unpleasant predicament last night. Will you tell me how it occurred and what had happened ? "

Wily hesitated. Struck down himself before he saw the General, he knew nothing of the blow by which the General had avenged him ; he had a dim recollection of being assisted to the hotel by the General and by the man who struck him, but how or when the General arrived on the scene of action he did not know, nor could he account for the fact of his foe aiding the General in getting him to the hotel. At length he answered : " Well you see, General, it was all a mistake. That man hit me when he meant to hit some one else. It was a joke, anyway."

The General was not to be put off in this way. Fixing his eyes on Wily he said : " Why do you seek to deceive me again ? You did it once when you gave me that point on Savage. Now listen to me, sir ; you are tout for Trackem & Cinchem ; you do their bidding ; you receive from them a daily pittance ; you were rich when they were poor ; they are rich and you are in poverty—they now own all the properties that once were yours, and you take the paltry sums they dole out to you. You do their dirty work, out of which they make their hundreds and sometimes thousands, and in return give you a few paltry dollars, the greater portion of which you every night spend in drink.

Now, sir; you see I know all about you.   Answer my questions and I will aid you if I can.   How did that last night's trouble originate ?"

As he finished speaking the General appeared to Wily to dilate and expand before his eyes, and to be invested with an authority which he endeavored to combat, but felt he was powerless to resist.

Still he hesitated, asking himself : "How did he gain this knowledge of me and my affairs," and then, reflecting, "he knows already almost as much as I can tell him, and why not let him know the whole Truth ? "

He answered : " I will tell you the plain Truth, General.   A few days ago I decoyed him into Trackem & Cinchem's office to buy some stock. When he met me last night he said they had robbed him, and accused me of stealing his money in conjunction with them.   High words followed, and at last he knocked me down."

" But were his charges true or false ?" asked the General.

" True in part," replied Wily, "I certainly took him to Trackem & Cinchem ; he no doubt lost his money, but I did not get it.   If the stock had gone up he would have made money."

" But are not the stocks you are instructed to bull and find buyers for such as are greatly inflated, and about to decline ? " inquired the General.

" I must confess it generally goes that way."

" Now, Mr. Wily," said the General, " I want you to give me the history of your dealings with Trackem & Cinchem.   I do not mean since you lost your money, but before that time. I want you to clearly understand that I do not ask these questions from idle curiosity. I am desirous of benefiting you. In order to ascertain the best way to accomplish that object, it is necessary for me to know all the facts of the case. I have already intimated to you my conviction that you were unjustly dealt with ; I wish to hear your own statement. When you have made it I will instruct you in the course you are to pursue. Now, sir, proceed."

Wily felt himself at a loss to understand the power this man exercised over him. He commanded him to lay open to him the secrets of his life ; he did not know why he should comply. He did not wish to do it, but he glanced at the penetrating eyes the General had fastened on him, and felt himself compelled to yield compliance, and supply the information he wanted.

" Begin at the beginning,'' said the General.

Wily, feeling that there was no help for it, resolved to recount his story. He had never told it; he did not like to think of it, much less speak of it. He now, however, proceeded :—

" When I first made the acquaintance of Trackem I was ranching in ————, Alameda county. I had a comfortable homestead. I was making a handsome living, and saving money, and had purchased several pieces of real estate in San Francisco. I suppose I was worth somewhere in the neighborhood of a hundred thousand dollars. I used to come to San Francisco once or twice a week, and

F

Trackem knowing my places of call, used generally
to hunt me up. The firm were in a small way of
business then. He would often ask me to lunch
with him ; a bottle or two of wine usually followed.
We would talk about all sorts of things, but always
wound up with stocks, when he would tell me that
Ralston had made so much on such a stock during
the preceding week; or Sharon or Keene so much,
as the case might be. This was four years ago. I
always had plenty of money in the bank at that
time. By some means Trackem got to know it ;
how, I cannot tell ; I never told him. He would
then advise me to take a hand, just to try my luck.
For a long time I resisted. I had never owned a
stock ; I was comfortably fixed, and was contented.
But one unfortunate day we had taken an extra
bottle of wine, and I consented to try one venture.
I wrote him a cheque for five thousand dollars, and
acting on his advice, instructed him to buy Ophir
stock with the money. In one week I had sold my
shares and doubled my money. I think that sent
me mad. I neglected my ranch, and spent all my
time in the city. I thought I saw before me a
prospect of making millions without the drudgery
of the work on my farm. Trackem had by this
time made me acquainted with Cinchem. The
greater part of each day I passed either in their
office or in the Stock Board. I bought when they
told me, and sold when they advised it. I made
hundreds and lost thousands, but I still went on,
piece by piece ; my San Francisco real estate went
to the firm; I still went on. At last my ranch

went, and I was a bursted man. That is all, General. I do not think they acted squarely; I know they didn't. If I have never blamed them it is because I think they always acted on my instructions. It is true, they told me what to do first, and I told them to do it afterwards. Since I have been running for them I have seen it all, and know I was a cursed fool for not seeing it before."

" You know that I lost some five hundred dollars through your advice—how did that come about ?" said the General, "and what did Trackem & Cinchem say about me ? "

" Told me to hunt you up and keap you in hand." said Wily, "but about that five hundred dollars, General, I'm real sorry. I would give it back to you if I had it."

" Never mind that, Wily," said the General, "but now tell about that recommendation you gave me to buy Savage ; did Trackem & Cinchem instruct you to do it ?"

" Certainly they did, sir ; " replied Wily, "they knew that deal was over, and that the assessment was coming on. They took your coin, but I guess they never bought the stock at all. They tendered you some customer's stock that they were carrying on margin, used your money and handed you back as the balance, as little as they dared."

The General now reflected for some minutes. At length he turned to Wily and asked, "How is it you indulge in such excess in drink ; from all I can learn, you used to be a sober and respected man ?"

" Trouble, General, and a wish to drown the

thought of my cursed folly, have made me reckless of everything," said Wily.

"Do you think you could overcome this propensity, and be your old self again, if you knew you would be established in a comfortable position ?"

"I know I could, General."

"Very well," said the General, "prove that you can conquer this habit, and I will assist you to recover your own, and re-establish you."

"I will do it, General."

Again the General seemed wrapped in thought, Wily eyeing him the while in anxious suspense. At length the General said : " Very well, Wily, I will trust you from this time out; you will cease to tout for Trackem & Cinchem, but you will frequent their office as usual, and you must be sure to let them know that I intend to invest from one to a hundred thousand dollars in stocks almost immediately; at the same time you may assure them of a portion of my business, and Wily, do not neglect to report yourself to me every night, immediately after dinner, say seven o'clock, and remember, that in order to secure the success of my plans, it is necessary for you to be silent on the subject of my promise. You can go now, but return at seven. Good morning."

"Good morning, General. I will be as mum as the grave."

As wily left the room he felt himself to be a changed man.

What is the secret of that influence which one strong mind exercises over another mind ? What is that subtile power which, going forth from one strong spirit, gives new life, and strength, and hope, to some other spirit; or emanating from a nature powerful for evil, overshadows some weaker one and wraps it in clouds and darkness, and some-times in despair.

CHAPTER XIII.

COMMODORE PYE HAS A SURPRISE.

Purely characteristic of their individual modes of thought and action had been the method adopted by each of the three original members, in preparing for the discussion on stock and mining operations, which was undertaken by the Society at its last meeting. The Commodore had searched the mining records, the official reports of mining corporations, and the governmental statistics of the various States and Territories of the Pacific slope, and had compiled a mass of figures. The Judge had examined his library, and culled from various authors, in both poetry and prose, many beautiful thoughts on mining, and the miners' skill; and had consulted the one man in San Francisco who was most interested in mining operations, and elicited his opinions, or such as it suited him to utter. The Judge's sole object was to invest the subject with poetic thought. The General, on the other hand, had dived down into the life and action of the business. He had steadily pursued a course of observation and inquiry in the very center of the vortex of stock gambling. Hence he brought up a report which, as we have seen, was full of truths of a character it

pained the Judge to listen to, and of a description
unanticipated by the Commodore. The Judge realizing the position had adjourned the discussion to
the next meeting.

After leaving the General, the Commodore repaired to his own rooms, where a surprise awaited
him. Two letters were lying on his table, which
for some reason had failed to reach him in the morning. He recognized the handwritings. One was
from his sister, the other from his daughter. He
opened his sister's letter and read :—

"My dear George —

"Our darling Rose wrote you at my request a week ago, informing you of our intention to visit San Francisco. Having resolved on the journey, we hastened the necessary preparations,
which are now so far advanced that we propose to start one week
from to-day. We shall probably stay a day or two in Paris, then
proceed to London, and leave there for Liverpool in time to catch
the "Celtic," which sails on the 18th instant. We shall probably
be in San Francisco in ten or twelve days after this reaches you. I
hope and believe you will be charmed with Rose ; she is as good
and as beautiful as I should wish her to be. You need be under
no apprehensions as to our comfort, or our baggage being well
cared for. I have in the capacity of courier, your old footman,
James Wily, whom you brought to me with Rose. Some years
ago I made him my butler. He is a most valuable and trustworthy
servant. I also bring my maid, Annette.

"Hoping to find you in good health,
    "I remain, dear brother,
        "Your affectionate sister,
            "Maud Clare."

Having pondered the contents of his sister's letter a few moments, the Commodore refolded it and
restored it to the envelope, and took up the one

which bore his daughter's handwriting. For some minutes he held it in his hand before he broke the seal. What a flood of memories poured through his mind as he looked upon the handwriting. He saw before him his lost wife, as he first found her in the quiet parsonage, the home of her father, in all the freshness of her virgin beauty. He saw her in her bridal robes, as she stood beside him on that proud day when he led her to the altar; he saw her in her dignity and grace presiding over the hospitalities of the old paternal mansion, which he had made her home. He saw her on the narrow bier, still beautiful, clad in the " loveliness of death."

What a mystery of mysteries is memory. It is a house of many chambers. We open one, and the light streaming through it fills our souls with tender thought; we open another, and our hearts are oppressed with fearful, anxious care; we open yet a third, and the sunlight of heaven illumines and fill; our existence with radiant joy; once more we essay to open a door, and thick, black clouds of darkness and despair gather around our souls, and wrap them as in the pall of starless night.

The Commodore at last broke the seal of the second letter. It was but a few lines, and ran as follows :—

" MY DEAREST PAPA :—

" We leave earlier than we expected. I am so glad. I want to see you so much, and I want you to love me dearly. Geraldine sends her love to you. Good-bye for a little while. From

" Your loving daughter,

" Dearest Papa.   ROSE."

The Commodore now took out the two portraits

and sat gazing at them until remembering that he had no time for reverie, but must be making preparation for the reception of his family, he carefully replaced them, and sought his couch, determining to rise early in the morning, and search the city for the very best accommodation that could be found. True to his resolve, he rose and breakfasted early, and spent the entire morning inspecting suites of rooms in private houses, and visiting the various hotels. He finally decided on two magnificent suites in the Baldwin Hotel. He next proceeded to purchase such items as he thought necessary to add to the comfort and luxury of the already handsomely appointed apartments. His first thought was a piano. He selected the most brilliant-toned instrument he could find, which he chose, not for its outside appearance, but for its internal merit. He next turned his attention to pictures and statuary, and collected a number of choice and beautiful works of art, all of which were of a pleasing character. He carefully avoided tragic subjects. These were all arranged in the places he desired them to occupy, under his own personal supervision. Vases, books and bric-a-brac followed, the whole occupying the Commodore's attention for several days, during which, though he met his friends every day, he made no mention of his coming guests.

The time of the expected arrival was fast approaching. The Commodore had become reconciled to the idea of receiving his daughter. Expectancy and anticipation had culminated in longing for her presence. There was, however, one subject on which he was still troubled, which was their first meeting. If the Commodore had a vanity in his plain common sense nature, he was vain of his stoicism. When facing the dangers of the sea, or in the midst of fierce naval encounters, he moved about amongst his men with as much coolness as if shipwreck, grapeshot and bombshells were things unknown or unheard of. Never to be in a hurry, never to lose his self-control, were parts of his creed. But now he felt himself in danger of marring the record of his American life. By what?—the meeting of a simple girl ? But then, that girl was the life copy of a life's idol, whom he had lived for whilst she lived, and whose memory, though she was gone, he still cherished.

There is nothing under heaven that is absolutely perfect. The weak spot in the strong nature had revealed itself. The man who had never shrunk from facing danger to his own life, now dared not meet his child beneath the public gaze. He would have liked to have gone at least to Sacramento. He thought he might be expected there. He wished to go. But then—No. He would telegraph to them at Sacramento. He would tell them that a carriage would be in waiting for them at the ferry. Go himself, he could not.

CHAPTER XIV.

GENERAL STERNE AND CAPTAIN BLAND TAKE A WALK.

After Wily had departed the General sat in his room for some time. He believed Wily's promise to him would be kept. A keen observer of human nature, he had seen a hidden strength under Wily's weakness, and had rightly judged that recklessness, and the desire to render himself oblivious to past and present, had quite as much to do with his intemperance as love of drink. Hence he had resolved that he would endeavor to accomplish two objects at the same time—to rehabilitate Wily, and to make the overthrow of Trackem & Cinchem the means by which it should be done. To attain his object he knew it would be necessary for him to hazard a very considerable sum of money. This he was prepared to do. He might lose it. If so he could endure it; it would not ruin him. He had sketched in his own mind the outline of a plan. He felt sure it would win. But now he would go out and spend an hour or two among the bulls and the bears, and make more observations, and gain more knowledge of " the ways that are dark and the tricks that are vain," in their (to him) uncongenial society. By this course he would be gaining fresh knowledge which he could impart to the Society in Search of Truth, and acquiring a more perfect mastery of the method he proposed to adopt to avenge Wily on Trackem & Cinchem.

The General divided an hour an a half between Pine and Leidesdorff streets (the latter is called by some, Thieves' alley), and the Stock Boards, and adjourned to the Palace, where he had agreed to lunch with the Judge and Captain Bland.

After a pleasant half hour's social chat over the lunch table, the Judge being privately engaged for the afternoon, the General invited the Captain to sake a stroll with him.

It was always interesting to walk with the General, his observations on such occasions, though almost invariably sarcastic, were racy and full of point. When they had crossed Market to Montgomery street, he touched Captain Bland on the arm, and they both turned and faced the Palace Hotel. "There it is, the biggest hotel in the world," he said. "Do you know how the architect designed it? He first drew a square in the middle of a sheet of paper; that was to represent the court in the center; he next made a larger square around it, that was the outer wall; he then drew one bay window, after which he piled up seven or eight hundred more, in rows six high; and thus completed the design of the biggest, if not the ugliest hotel that has ever been built. That architect ought to succeed in life, he is evidently a man of one idea."

As they walked on he added: "That hotel was one of the last of the great undertakings of Ralston, who was the most wonderful man the Pacific coast has ever known. For many years he was the King Regnant, the Prince Bountiful, and the chief speculator of the slope. But he is dead. He performed many generous acts. There," said he, as they passed the Lick House, "is the hotel built by the great philanthropist James Lick, who gave his fortune to charity when he was sick, took it back when he recovered, restored it when his pains returned, and died before he had time to alter his mind again. He too is dead; let him rest."

Crossing Pine street, he pointed to the handsome building of the San Francisco Exchange, and said: " Behold the great mausoleum, the sepulchre of San Francisco's fortunes."

"What building is it?" inquired Captain Bland.

"The San Francisco Stock Board. The center of the operations we were speaking of last night," answered the General, and then facing the Nevada Block, he said: "See where the spider weaves its web, and, like a vampire, sucks the life's blood of the coast."

Arrived opposite the Safe Deposit Company's building, the General observed, "How redundant is its ornamentation. What fools men are. They build palaces to perpetuate the greatness of their name and fame, and leave them as long enduring monuments of their follies or their crimes. There Duncan, like the fabled frog, would swell himself as big as the ox, and swelling like the frog, he burst. They now crossed California street, and the General said :—

" I want to call on my attorney. He is an excellent young man; will you step up with me, Captain?" As he spoke he commenced to mount the stairway and Captain Bland followed. They entered the attorney's office together. The Captain saw before him a finely-built young man, of little more than his own age, but looking much older. He was tall and well proportioned, with fair hair and complexion, indicating a sanguine temperament. His features were marked with lines of care.

" Ah, Mr. Equity, how are you?" inquired General Sterne, " you are not looking well to-day."

" I am not quite the thing, General," responded the attorney, trying to look bright; " I have been working too hard, I think ; I have had several cases which have required close study to bring them out right."

" That won't do," said the General, " health and mental vigor are as much a lawyer's capital as legal knowledge. You must not impair them or you will injure not only yourself but your business. Allow me to introduce to you a friend of mine, who has just arrived from the East—Captain Bland, Mr. Equity."

" I am happy to make your acquaintance, sir," said the attorney.

" I am pleased to meet you," responded Captain Bland; " I am glad to know any friend of General Sterne's."

The attorney meantime scrutinized the Captain with searching care, and inwardly remarked, " Frank, candid and honorable."

" Have you attended to the instructions I gave you when I was last here?" inquired the General.

" Yes, sir," responded the lawyer, " and have to-day received two payments—one of five thousand, and the other for three thousand, and promises of an early settlement from the others. Shall I give you a cheque for the eight thousand dollars, General?"

"Never mind it this afternoon," said the General, "I will call again to-morrow."

When the General trusted a man, which was not very frequently, he trusted him absolutely. He had no doubt whatever of the integrity of his attorney. If questioned on the subject he would have spurned the very thought of Mr. Equity being a traitor to the trust he had reposed in him. He had been the General's attorney for several years, and the General did not doubt his being the soul of honor. In fact, until he perpetrated the deception mentioned in a former chapter, every act he had performed for the General had merited the confidence he had placed in him. But, overcome by a temptation, which was too strong for him, he had yielded to his desire for sudden wealth, and involved himself in such a manner, and to such an extent, that he knew his case was desperate, and unless he could devise some means whereby to raise the money he had unjustly acquired and lost, he must be disgraced and ruined.

The General and Captain Bland bade him good afternoon and left, to continue their ramble.

The attorney now sat down to think. He had already resolved, that come what might, he would not add another crime to the one he had committed. If he had robbed so much of the General's money, he was not vile enough, or coward enough, to steal more to escape from possible punishment. When he received the money for those two notes from the General he was absolutely certain, or thought he was, that he could easily restore it in a few days, and have a handsome surplus remaining. He had lost it; and if the worst came to the worst, he would throw himself on the General's mercy, and abide the issue.

But now a new hope dawned on him. This young man—this Captain Bland. He was convinced he had read his character aright. He was no doubt a nephew of Judge Bland. Both uncle and nephew were rich. Might he not openly confess his fault to the younger man, and ask his assistance. Could he not retrench his expenses, and with his rapidly increasing business, in a short time repay the advance if he received it. But would young Bland entertain his request? Had he money here, or failing that, would he influence his uncle, whose generous disposition was well known? He would make the appeal anyway. If refused, he was confident he would not be betrayed by Captain Bland, even to his friend, the General. Anxiety and suspense were wearing him away. The General had noticed it. He knew it himself. He would make the appeal, be the answer yea or nay.

And God help him.

CHAPTER XV.

SAN FRANCISCO.

Is my reader acquainted with San Francisco ? It is a wonderful city. In less than thirty years it has grown from a hamlet, with a few scattered habitations, to such proportions that it claims to be the eighth city in the Union. It has a wonderful his-history. A history without parallel in the record of cities, unless it be found in that of Melbourne, in the colony of Australia. Both owe their sudden and rapid rise to the discovery of gold. Both have become great permanent centers of population and large commercial emporiums. In both instances the establishment of the city led to an immense development of agricultural resources which were not believed to be possible, until long after they were far advanced in importance. Both in their earlier days witnessed scenes of such lawlessness and wasteful extravagance as has never been seen on such a scale in any other city. Sudden and easily acquired wealth in both afforded a wide arena for the exploits of gamblers, in which fabulous sums changed hands every hour of the day and night. In both the immense disparity in numbers of the sexes afforded opportunities for the exercise of influence and display of wantonness by reckless women, such as had never been witnessed in the world. In both men were known to light their cigars with hundred dollar gold bills, out of mere wantonness of waste. In the harbors of both fine vessels were left anchored in the stream, at the mercy of chance, deserted by officers and men, who had departed for the gold fields. In both the sudden and enormous influx of population caused many of the necessaries of life to rise to fabulous prices. This induced distant merchants to send large shipments of all kinds of stores, and so, in both, a plethora of the commodities so much in demand but a short time before, was the cause of consignors making heavy losses. In San Francisco much valuable merchandise was turned out on the city front, and left to the mercy of winds and weather, or to be carried off piecemeal by whoever chose to take them. The consignees had gone in search of gold, there was no one to receive the goods. The masters of vessels bundled them out upon the beach, and when they could return their crews, or obtain new ones, hastened away. Thus extremes ever follow each other, in national history, in human experience, and in commercial life. The weak, luxurious Charles s beheaded by the order of Cromwell. The stern puritanic rule of the Protector is succeeded by a court, the licentiousness of which has never been equalled. The wastefulness of the spendthrift of youth culminates in miserly hoarding in mature age ; the heirs of the great fortune scatter it to the winds. The merchant inflated by success overreaches his power, and is brought to destruction, to struggle upwards again if he can, to another fortune, which in turn is dissipated by his successors. The history of San Fraucisco is written in extremes. From its inception to the present day it has alternated and shifted from extremes of wealth to ex-

G

tremes of poverty. Now the gold is so abundant
that every man who has strong hands or an active
brain may obtain a share; the tide turns, and want
and privation are on every side; again the cloud
lifts and wealth abounds once more; it descends
and the cry of distress comes up on every hand.
How brilliant San Francisco's successful days have
been is attested by its numbers of splendid buildings; its banks, its churches, its palatial residences,
and its magnificent blocks of warehouses. Yes,
San Francisco is a wonderful city. But a more unfortunate site for its foundation could scarcely have
been chosen. The peninsula on which it is built is
mainly a mass of sand hills. Huge slices stripped
from them have been used to reclaim from the harbor all that portion of the city on which are
erected the wholesale and shipping warehouses.
The streets in this part of San Francisco, with one
or two exceptions, are narrow and badly paved, and
have unsightly and inconvenient wooden sidewalks,
which are continually covered with packages of
merchandise, giving the city a greater appearance
of business activity than it really has. These ob-
structions are left night and day upon the public
walks, with an utter disregard of the convenience
of foot-passengers. The city authorities are oblivious, or at least regardless of the fact. The streets
in many parts are dirty and ill-kept. Were it not for
the daily breeze which sweeps through the city from
noon to sundown, it would necessarily be most un-
healthy. Its climate is one of the least desirable in
the healthful and invigorating State of California.

An ordinarily cloudless sky is frequently obscured by a hazy atmosphere. The afternoon breeze sweeps clouds of dust along its streets, and thick mists coming in from the ocean at sundown on summer evenings, often settle down upon the city, rendering locomotion unpleasant to all, and injurious to the delicate.

Far differently situated is the beautiful city of homes, Oakland, across the bay, which is destined to rival, if not to surpass the parent city. Though only six miles distant from San Francisco, its climate is distinct as though it were in another land, being free from the prevalence of the daily strong winds and almost nightly summer fogs of San Francisco. Its streets are broad and numerous, are well-formed, and adorned by shade trees and by numberless charming homes surrounded by plats of verdant grass, and magnificent clusters of roses, geraniums, fuschias and other garden plants in infinite variety, the luxurious growth of which might well make glad the heart of any lover of floral beauty.

Regarding the climate of both San Francisco and Oakland, I may remark they have one peculiarity in common which I have never observed in any other part of the world—whilst the winter's cold is rarely if ever sufficient to produce snow—the summer heat is never excessive, and at its greatest never produces that lassitude so commonly experienced in the summer in the East and in other parts of the world. The climate is always invigorating.

CHAPTER XVI.

MR. EQUITY CONFESSES TO CAPTAIN BLAND.

Resolved to leave no stone unturned, and if possible to immediately make good the money he had so wrongfully obtained from the General, Mr. Equity determined at once to try the issue of his resolve; to appeal to the generosity of Captain Bland. He had gone through the account of fees due to him, which was a considerable one, and had found that two thousand five hundred dollars could be immediately collected. A portion of this sum he had received, and the balance would be paid him on the morrow. This still left him a defaulter to the amount of ten thousand dollars. Most bitterly did he regret his folly. But, regrets were vain. Leaving his office early he went home. He had determined that after he had dined he would go to the Palace and request a private interview with Captain Bland. To resolve with Mr. Equity was always to act. Deciding to walk to the Palace Hotel he set off immediately he had finished his dinner, pondering as he went, the difficulties of his position. He reflected that Captain Bland was an utter stranger to him, until that afternoon; and then he might not have money in San Francisco; and if he had, he might have use for it, or he might in any case decline to trust a man, who, by his own confession, had been unfaithful to the trust of another. Could he not make the request without assigning the object for which he required the money? In that case would not Captain Bland naturally inquire what security he could give him? and what answer

could he make ? His own health and a really pros-
perous business, were all he had to offer. Who
would lend a large sum of money on such security,
without knowing to what uses the money was to be
put ? No; he must tell the Truth, and take the
consequences. Win or lose his suit, there was only
one way to plead it. And again he cursed his folly
and stupidity, in allowing himself to be made the
dupe of a stock gambling trickster.

Inquiring for the Captain's room at the counter
of the hotel, he gave the number to the man in
charge of the elevator, and was landed on the desired floor.

Here he addressed the attendant in waiting: " I
want," he said, "to find Captain Bland."

" Yes, sah," said the negro, " I tink he is in ther
Judge's room, sah ; next his own. I'll see, sah."

" All right," said Mr. Equity, " tell him a gentleman would like to see him privately."

" What name, sah ? " inquired the waiter.

" Never mind the name," replied the attorney,
" I'll wait here."

In a few minutes, which seemed to Mr. Equity to
be hours (so intensified were his feelings), the Captain appeared.

" Ah, Mr. Equity," he said, "I am glad to see you.
The porter tells me you wish to see me privately.
Just step into my room."

The Captain noticed the anxious look on the
lawyer's face whilst taking a chair. Waving with
his hand an invitation to his guest to be seated also,
he awaited his pleasure to commence the interview.

Mr. Equity sat uneasily. The nervous motion of his hands and the pallor of his countenance betrayed it. Captain Bland, who observed the symptoms, saw there was trouble on the lawyer's mind, and with an undefinably anxious feeling awaited the disclosure he felt was coming, wondering why he could have been chosen as its receptacle.

At length the attorney spoke :—

"I have come to trouble you with a painful story of folly and crime. A man in San Francisco, who was struggling for a subsistence for himself and his family, his business barely supporting them, was found by a rich and benevolent gentleman, who gave him his encouragement and support. He not only entrusted him with his business, but directly and indirectly was the means of influencing others, who in turn employed the man. By this means he acquired a business, from the proceeds of which, had he been prudent and economical, he might have achieved a fortune. But he was foolishly wasteful and extravagant, and saved nothing. His benefactor, who was accounted by the world around him a hard, cold man, had used him as an instrument for the assistance of many deserving men, who were struggling to live honestly. One day a stock operator, whom the man believed to be a friend, came to him and assured him that by investing in a certain stock, he could double his money in a week. The man had no ready money, but succumbing to the temptation, committed a crime. He availed himself of the known generosity of his benefactor, and by false representations, obtained from him the sum of twelve thousand five hundred dollars, all of which he lost in the stock gamble recommended to him by his supposed friend, who got the money. He is now at a loss what to do. Whether to commit a further wrong, and run from the scenes of his folly and crime ; whether to take his own life, or to cast himself on the generosity of some friend to aid him until he can make good the defalcation. He has got together all the available assets he can realize upon. He is still ten thousand dollars short, which sum he hopes to be able to borrow. He knows, but few men would trust any man under such circumstances. He knows that he is not deserving of sympathy. He has, however, resolved to make an appeal to generosity, rather than commit another crime, and hopes speedily to make good the obligation from the proceeds of his business, which is considerable. He dare not approach his benefactor, who, with all his generosity, is so severely just that he would never pardon the offense, and might possibly ruin his business prospects forever. What can that man do ? What do you think of such a man, Captain Bland ?"

The captain, who had listened very attentively to every word the attorney had uttered, answered : "I think he is a weak fool and a scoundrel, Mr. Equity."

"That is so, Captain Bland," said the attorney, and then added firmly, "that man is myself, sir, and the benefactor your friend, General Sterne," and then he settled himself back in his chair, and, resting his elbows on his knees, covered his face with his hands.

This was a finale Captain Bland had not expected. Only that afternoon the General had spoken to him in the highest terms of the ability, perseverance and integrity of the attorney. Pausing for several moments, in which the lawyer suffered what seemed days of agony, he at length said :—

"Mr. Equity, this is a denouement I had not anticipated. I have no money here, beyond what I require for my own personal uses. With your permission, I will speak with my uncle on this subject. It shall go no further. I will see you in the morning. If you have no further observations to make I think we had better adjourn this interview. I am both shocked and grieved at the disclosures you have made. You have acted most wrongfully. I am, however, glad, that you have decided to go no further in crime. Good evening, sir. I will call on you in the morning, at your office."

Mr. Equity had risen. He noticed that Captain Bland did not offer him his hand, but he had promised to call on him.

"Good evening, Captain Bland," responded the lawyer. "I thank you for the courtesy you have shown me in listening to my story." And he went out, to carry home with him to a restless couch, his troubled thoughts, and a keen sense of the humiliation to which his own folly had made it necessary for him to submit.

Few young men in San Francisco had borne a higher reputation than Mr. Equity ; his intelligence, energy and good nature had made him a favorite in the circle in which he moved, and now his business success seemed to be assured he was regarded as one of the most promising and rising young men in his profession. He had kept himself free from many of the vices of a licentious city, and was highly esteemed. But a cloud had settled upon him which might burst at any moment, and involve him in disastrous ruin.

Would the the Captain influence the Judge, his uncle, in his favor? He had not promised to do so. In any case would the Judge entertain the thought of aiding a criminal to escape from well deserved punishment? Remorse, regret and speculations on the possible outcome of the Captain's conference with Judge Bland, and reflections on the next best course to pursue, if that failed, kept sleep from the attorney's eyes during the greater part of the night. He arrived at his office the following morning with such a worn and anxious look stamped on his features, that his clerk, to his infinite annoyance, greeted him with the remark :—

"You do not seem to be well this morning, Mr. Equity ?"

How easy it is to depart from the path of virtue. How difficult it is to make perfect the straight lines of Truth, when once broken by falsehood and deceit.

CHAPTER XVII.

THE NEW ARRIVALS.

Three days after the Commodore received the letters mentioned in a former chapter, a dispatch was handed to him, in which he read :—

OMAHA.

We shall be with you on Tuesday.   We are all well.

MAUDE CLARE.

It was evident the steamer by which his visitors had traveled had made better time than the one which had brought his mails.

The Commodore now examined the apartments he had selected, with a view of ascertaining if there was anything wanting, or anything he could add to increase their luxuriousness.   This, indeed, was nothing new.   From the time he had engaged them he had gone through the same performance several times every day, and on each occasion had adjourned to visit the marts which offered the best display of works of art and utility, the invariable result being some fresh additions in the form of statuette or painting, or some ingeniously contrived article which would increase the comfort of the rooms.   On such an errand bound, he now left the hotel, and proceeding down Market street, met Judge Bland, his nephew and General Sterne at the crossing from the Palace to Montgomery street.

" Good morning, gentlemen," said the Commodore, " I am glad to have met you.   I regret to say I shall be unable to attend the meeting of the Society to-night.   Affairs of importance to me will demand my presence elsewhere."

Again the Commodore made no mention of the expected arrivals. On this occasion he would have done so but for the presence of the General. His aversion to obtruding his family affairs on any one had restrained him hitherto, and now, knowing the General's idiosyncracy in regard to the fair sex, his innate delicacy of feeling positively forbade his making any mention of the subject in his presence.

" I am sorry," said the Judge. (I am afraid Judge Bland uttered a polite fiction, he felt relieved at the thought that they might postpone the meeting.) You are the keeper of our records, Commodore. It is true, ' my boy ' might perform the duties of Secretary, but I should like you to be present at the discussion. On the whole, I think it would be better to allow this meeting to lapse, and reassemble on our usual night next week."

Captain Bland also thought it would be best. (He admired the Commodore, whom he had met several times, and thought the meeting would be very incomplete without him.)

The General concurring, it was arranged that the Society should not meet until the following Tuesday.

The Commodore now separated from his friends, and continued his peregrinations. He made one or two purchases and returned to the hotel. Having lunched, he sought his room and laid those two treasured portraits before him. After a time, thinking this was not a fitting preparation for the duties of the evening, he resolved on a long walk. The Commodore was always a great walker. He would take a ramble which should occupy him until they should arrive, and return and receive them in their own parlor. He first, however, rang for his servant. When he entered he said to him :—

" Johnson, look at that portrait. Should you know that lady if you saw her ? "

" Anywhere, sir," said Johnson.

" Very well, Johnson ; I have had these rooms prepared for the reception of my sister, Mrs. Clare ; my daughter and her friend. They will arrive this afternoon by the overland ; I want you to cross the ferry and conduct the ladies to the carriage when they land, and assist my sister's servants with the baggage."

" Yes, sir ; is that all ? "

" That is all, Johnson; except that when they arrive here you may show them to their parlor, where they will find me waiting to receive them."

" I will attend to it, sir."

The Commodore now restored the portraits to his secretaire, and started out on his walk. He first climbed the heights of Nob Hill, descending on the other side, he proceeded as far as Lone Mountain, and returning by an easier route, arrived at the hotel at 4:45, just when the train, which he had ascertained was " on time," should reach the end of Long Wharf. He at once retired to his room to prepare himself to receive his family, and then repaired to the parlor which was to be Mrs. Clare's. He had not been there more than five minutes when Johnson, who was a well-trained English servant, born on the Commodore's estate, and strongly attached to him, knocked at the door. He announced the ladies, and retired, closing the door after him.

Rose knew her father instantly, by the portraits she had of him, and flew to the arms which were extended to receive her.

" My—dear—papa," she said.

"My darling, at last," murmured the Commodore, as he bent to kiss the ruby lips which, her head thrown back to look at him, were raised to him. Loosening her from his embrace, he held her with both hands, at arms' length, whilst with an artist's eye he took an inventory of the graces and beauties of her fresh young womanhood, and then gathered her to his breast again. Again releasing her, he drew forth his handkerchief, and under pretense of wiping his forehead, furtively removed the tears which had risen unbidden, and which he could not repress.

If the Commodore, in that moment, could have analyzed his feelings, he would not have known which preponderated, the intensity of his delight at meeting his child, the contempt he felt for his own display of emotion, or the thankfulness he experienced that there were no witnesses save his own family.

He now turned to his sister, who had been a delighted observer of the tender greeting her loved Rose had received from her father. Had she not been well versed in the peculiarities of his disposition, she would have been hurt at his not coming to meet them. She knew him well. A strong affection for each other had existed from childhood.

She was abundantly satisfied. Their meeting had called up a thousand tender reminiscences of the past in which memory, like a kaleidoscope, presented ever varying pictures of scenes from the early past to the present, all associated with their lifelong affection and mutual esteem. It was a revelation to both of them, of regret that so many long years had divided them.

Mrs. Clare now introduced to the Commodore the beautiful Geraldine.

"Welcome, to San Francisco, my daughter," said he, "if Rose claims you as her sister, I must claim you as my child," and taking both her hands in his, he kissed her with such fatherly kindness that Geraldine felt her proud heart swell with pleasurable emotion, and already began to realize that she should delight to yield to the Commodore the daughterly affection he seemed to desire.

The ladies retired to their rooms to remove their travel-stained garments and dress for dinner. They found that Annette, Mrs. Clare's maid, with the assistance of James Wily, had their trunks uncorded and everything in order for them.

The Commodore, left alone in the parlor, amused himself by comparing observations of his daughter and her adopted sister. In height and form there was a strong resemblance. In feature and expression there was none. Rose was as she herself had said, "fair." Her face was not one of those in which the rose and lily vie for the mastery, the lily was supreme, just tinted with a softened shade of pink, as if Aurora had touched her cheeks and left a faint reflection of her favorite color. Her hair approached the golden hue the poets love to sing of. Her eyes were blue and soft and calm; her mouth was small, but with full lips, which parted when she smiled and showed a set of teeth no human art could imitate successfully. When interested by conversation her face was a study. Every emotion, every feeling was indexed on it. The rich life's blood ebbed or flowed with every change, whilst the musical laugh which issued from her parted lips was full of happiness and spoke of perfect innocence.

Geraldine I cannot easily describe. She had a Grecian face which was statueque it its beauty when in repose, a calm and almost haughty bearing, which might have betokened pride and coldness. Her movements were measured and stately; more than one had watched her from afar, and admired her splendid beauty, and refrained from approaching too near, lest haply a closer acquaintance should destroy the pleasure the contemplation of her loveliness had evoked. And yet there was a tender heart within the proud beauty's bosom. She loved and almost venerated Mrs. Clare and all but idolized Rose. When in their society her eye could beam with tenderness, and whilst gracefully uttering the thoughts which emanated from a cultivated and powerful mind, her face would be transfigured by a warm, glowing beauty the superficial observer had never dreamed that she possessed. Such a transfiguration had occurred when the Commodore so warmly welcomed her to San Francisco.

Had Mrs. Clare wished to choose a foil to en-
hance the charms of her neice, she could not have
done better. But in lieu of the plainer face and
less beautiful form so often selected for such purpose, here was another beauty equally perfect, and
yet so distinct, that in the nature of things they
could never clash. Mrs. Clare, who dearly loved
them both, and regarded them with an all but maternal pride, fully appreciated the difference of feature and of mind, would not unfrequently speak of
them as her Red and her White Rose, or as Pleasant
Sunshine and Grateful Shade.

The Commodore had never imagined the pleasure he was to receive from the society of his
friends. Already he began to regret that he had
not gone to his sister and his daughter, or drawn
them to himself long ago. Already he was reckon-
ing on the many pleasant hours he should pass
with them, and calculating how he could prolong
their contemplated stay; or failing that, whether
he could not return with them to France. How
short is the distance human foresight can penetrate into the future. We build our castles in the
air and complacently admire them. But even as we
look upon them, a passing gust, a tiny puff, bears
them from our sight and they are gone forever.

CHAPTER XVIII.

AN EVENING AND A DAY.

When the Commodore entered the dining-room that evening with a handsome and stately lady, apparently little less than his own age, leaning on his arm, many were the expressions of surprise, for the Commodore was known to be a single man. Nor was the surprise in the least mitigated when the two distinguished and beautiful girls followed them up the hall, and seated themselves with the Commodore. There were but few tables at which the questions: " Who are they ? Where do they come from ? " were not asked. No one knew. As we have already stated, the Commodore had informed no one save his servant Johnson, of their coming; and even when engaging apartments for three guests and two servants, he had not named their sex. Not a few, therefore, on leaving the hall proceeded to the office and examined the hotel register, where they read: " Mrs. Clare," " Miss Pye," and " Miss Stanley, all of France." The Commore did not fail to notice the sensation his guests. created, and was far from displeased at it. In fact, whilst he was to all appearance, utterly oblivious to the notice his party attracted, he quietly observed it and experienced a feeling of gratified pride such as he had not realized for many years.

As they quitted the dining hall they met General Sterne, who was entering as they passed out. He noticed the Commodore, nodded, and was about to speak when, perceiving that the three ladies were

H

with him, he moved hastily forward.   In passing
the two younger, his eyes rested involuntarily on
Geraldine.   It was but for a moment, but her face
and form were photographed on his memory, and
to his great annoyance, through the entire time he
sat at the dinner table, the picture would continue
to present itself.   " What," he asked himself, "have
I to do with ladies ?   But, who is she ?   What do I
care who she is ?   She is superbly beautiful.   What
is that to me ? "   His interest was excited and re-
belled against his will, and thus his thoughts were
like a shuttlecock flying between the two battle-
dores; now the will was in possession and again excited interest held sway.   And so his thoughts
went on.   " A pure, proud face," suggested interest;
" Woman is naturally false," said will.   " She would
make a splendid model for a Diana," observed interest.   " What do I care if she would ? " answered
will.   " A face and figure that would grace a royal
diadem, murmured interest.   " Let them grace it,"
muttered will.   " What is her relationship to the
Commodore ? " inquired interest.   " I do not know
and do not care," declared will.   " Is she making a
long stay here ? " inquired interest.   " Let her stay
or go, it is all one to me ; I will dismiss the subject
from my mind," growled will.   But let him reason
as he would, memory would keep holding up her
likeness before him.   He finally determined to go
to the theater as soon as it opened, and divert his
mind by contemplating the amusements in progress
there.   He certainly did not wish to know the
ladies.

It is a matter of wonder that men who reject the teachings of divine Truth should often become fatalists. It is a thing to surprise us that the great Napoleon, when he rejected all belief in the Deity, deified fate. The man whose will and skill triumphed over so many obstacles, had to acknowledge a power mightier than himself. He did not recognize that power as God, nor its operations as the exercise of eternal justice, but as the fulfillment of the decree of destiny. If there be such a thing as destiny, it is a result following a cause. It is a consequence, pursuing action. It is the fulfillment of the fiat of infinite Truth which, when violated, places the subject in a position from which he must be redeemed and restored or inevitably destroyed.

The General had allowed his mind to become warped and embittered by his unfortunate early experience. Strong as was his love of justice, he had allowed the error of one foolish woman to so influence his mind as to make him absolutely unjust in thought, speech, and action, to the entire sex. He had robbed himself for years of the untold pleasures which the society of educated and cultivated woman affords to pure and healthy masculine minds. The destiny of which we have spoken had now opened before him a possibility. He saw it—he felt it. He strove with all his might to push it from him. But the fact remained that the time had come in which he was to be redeemed from the evil which had overshadowed his life, or he was to remain under its influence forever,

The Commodore, meanwhile, had retired to the privacy of his sister's drawing-room, where it had been arranged that the family should pass the first evening of their re-union, undisturbed by other presence. Three hours passed in social interchange of reminiscences and experiences, and passed so rapidly that the Commodore could scarcely believe his senses when he discovered that it was half-past ten. Knowing that the ladies must be wearied by their journey, he now suggested that they might wish to retire.

Rose and Geraldine bade the Commodore an affectionate good night, and sought their rooms. Mrs. Clare remained for an hour longer with her brother. She had much to say to him which she did not care to mention in the presence of the younger ladies. She informed him of the attentions that had been paid to Geraldine and Rose. On the voyage they both had numerous admirers. One an Englishman, a Mr. Frank Carleton, had come on with them to San Francisco, and would probably call upon them. He was a fine young man, possessed of a good property, and had been very attentive and obliging to them all throughout the journey.

The Commodore felt his airy castles for the future begin to totter. He was relieved when his sister continued :—

" He greatly admires Geraldine, but I do not think he has told her so. Nor do I think it will result in anything but disappointment for him if he does. He is cheerful and gay in disposition and manner, and decidedly amiable. But I do not think Geraldine will accept him. I know she likes him, but only as a friend. If she marries, I think it will be to some one who has high intellectual attainments. Her nature will demand that she shall venerate as well as love her husband."

Mrs. Clare continued :—

" On our voyage, Rose received an offer of marriage from an American gentleman, who had accompanied us from Liverpool. He was at least twenty years older than Rose. He was the head of a great mercantile firm in New York, and reputed to be very wealthy. Rose shed some tears over the subject. She had no idea his attentions meant, on his part, marriage. She had looked upon him as old enough to be her father, and was much grieved and really sorry. She said she greatly esteemed, but did not love him. He sought to persuade her that love would follow esteem, but all in vain. She remained immovable. After we landed in New York we saw no more of him. Instead of remaining a day or two, as we intended, we came on next day."

Again the Commodore's castles began to totter. He realized the fact, that in all human probability some other hand would be stretched forth more successfully, and would pluck from him his newly-restored Rose.

When his sister had retired, he thought long on the subjects of their conversation. He hoped he would not lose Rose too soon. He resolved, how-

ever, that no selfish desire of his should interfere
with her happiness.

The following morning the General closely
watched the Commodore's party as they walked up
the room. His seat was so placed that he could
see all that was going on. He now observed that
Mrs. Clare was a splendidly preserved woman. He
noticed the sweet, simple freshness of Rose; and
then his eyes rested on Geraldine, nor could he resist the fascination which seemed to control his will
and draw his attention to her every movement.
At last, disgusted and annoyed at himself, he left
the table. He had made no inquiry concerning the
ladies. He had made no remark about them. Nor
would he make, either. He would avoid the Commodore. And now he would go down to Pine street
and prosecute his studies of the ways of the stock
operators, and mature his plans by which he proposed to entangle Trackem & Cinchem in their own
net, and restore to Wily his properties.

The Commodore, who had ordered his carriage to
be in waiting at half-past ten o'clock, accompanied
the ladies for a drive through the park. Though
yet in a crude and unfinished condition, the San
Francisco park already gives evidence of coming
beauty which, as the years roll on, will undoubtedly
mature.

About an hour after their return, the Commodore
having joined the ladies in their drawing-room, a
waiter brought him two cards. They were those of
Judge and Captain Bland.

The Commodore explained to his sister that the

Judge was one of his closest personal friends and that Captain Bland was his nephew. She therefore gladly assented to his request to be allowed to invite them to call upon him there.

The waiter shortly returned and ushered in the gentlemen, who had no knowledge of the presence of the ladies until they had entered the room.

The Commodore introduced his friends. Judge Bland was surprised that he had had no intimation of the expected arrival of the Commodore's family.

The Commodore explained that they had arrived much earlier than was expected, and that he had proposed to inform the Judge of their coming, and should have done so had a favorable opportunity occurred.

Judge Bland was satisfied, and turning and bowing in such a manner to the ladies that the action applied to them all, he said :—

"Allow me to assure you that this pleasure is not less real for being unanticipated; and that I esteem my worthy friend the most fortunate man I know. I have seen many beautiful ladies in San Francisco, but I know of no one gentleman who has such a galaxy of grace and loveliness under his protection."

" I must suppose, Mr. Bland,' said Mrs. Clare, "that you were educated in *la belle* France. We have received no such compliment since we left home."

" Nay, madam," responded the Judge, " I was not so fortunate, although I spent several years in that country, and always admired the courteous and

deferential manner observed by educated French-
men when addressing a lady."

The conversation now became general. The
Judge was brilliant, the presence of beautiful and
accomplished women always had a more exhilarat-
ing effect on him than the choicest wine could produce.   Speaking on this subject he would often remark : " Female loveliness flavored with intelligence
is the real champagne of life."

Gradually the company resolved itself into pairs.
Captain Bland appropriating Geraldine—Judge
Bland carrying on an animated conversation with
Mrs. Clare, whilst Rose, who had drawn to her
father's side, to the great content of both, sat chat-
ting with him, neither observing that from his seat
across the room Captain Bland, who was also greatly
interested in his gifted companion, very frequently
shot furtive glances at the lovely Rose. whom he
thought the sweetest looking girl he had ever seen.

The Commodore pressed his guests to stay and
dine with him.   When they prepared to leave for
the dining-hall the Judge gallantly offered his arm
to Mrs. Clare.   The Captain tendered his escort to
Geraldine, and the Commodore brought up the rear
with his darling Rose.

The General, who was in his seat when they entered, observed the attentions of the Captain, and
as dinner progressed, allowed none of their movements to escape him.

When he left the hall for his own room he remarked to himself: " I do not think I like that

young Bland, he does not improve on acquaintance."

This was an unreasonable change in the General's
mind—what could have effected it ? Certainly no
lack of courtesy to him on the part of Captain
Bland.

CHAPTER XIX.

CAPTAIN BLAND CALLS ON MR. EQUITY.

When Mr. Equity left the rooms of Captain
Bland, the Captain sat for some time reflecting on
the revelation the attorney had made to him. He
anticipated an appeal for aid on behalf of the delin-
quent, but he did not expect the final denouement
which showed the attorney himself to be the defaulter. His own observation of the man, and the
General's commendation of him, had combined to
make him entertain a very high opinion of Mr.
Equity. Hence, when the attorney declared himself the culprit, whose sin he had so unsparingly
depicted, the Captain was filled with equal amazement and regret.

Honorable himself in all his actions and dealings,
he could scarcely comprehend how any man could
so far forget the principles of Truth and right as to
pursue such a course as Mr. Equity had confessed
he had pursued. Careful, though never parsimoni-
ous, always abundantly supplied with money, and
having only his own expenses to meet, Captain
Bland could hardly be expected to realize the
temptation the prospect of immediate gain offered

to a man who was extravagant in his habits, and had at the same time a wife and family dependent upon him. His first feelings were those of repugnance, and almost of contempt, for the man who could be so weak as to be so led away by the prospect of gain, and who could break faith with his benefactor in the way Mr. Equity had done, and his following thought was to tell him that he must find some other way to extricate himself from the net in which he had been caught by his own greed of gain and unrighteous action.

He had deferred his decision in order that he might reflect upon it, and although he intended to confer with his uncle on the subject, he felt fully convinced that his answer to Mr. Equity in the morning would be :—

" You have done a great wrong. You must devise the means yourself whereby to escape the consequences. I will not betray you, but I cannot help you."

But now the attorney was gone, and Milton sat alone, meditating on all he had heard. He began to ask himself, " If in the course the attorney had taken, in humiliating himself to confess his wrong-doing, there was not an evidence of higher and better principle than might have been expected from one who had been guilty of so great a breach of faith ? Might he not have added greater wrong to the wrong he had already committed, and by such means have had more wealth in his possession than he was now likely to have for years to come ? Did it not require more strength of purpose, and did it not show more nobility of soul to confess a wrong than to perpetrate a second to cover it? Was it not evident that, however reprehensible Mr. Equity's conduct might have been, his punishment was already terrible, and his repentance sincere? Might it not be his duty to aid him to return to the path of rectitude, and to help him to cover his sin? The lawyer had learned a lesson he would never forget. He implored assistance; he wished to retrace his steps and do what was right. Could he refuse that assistance, having it in his power to render it? Was it his place to judge the repentant man and to condemn him for the fault he had so fully confessed?" No. He would go to his uncle at once. He would consult him on the subject, and decide what was best to be done.

Returning to the Judge's room, he briefly related to him the secret divulged by Mr. Equity.

"It is a serious matter, my boy," said the Judge, "in which I do not know that I should care to interfere. A man who could betray one who has been so generously good to him as General Sterne has been to Mr. Equity, by his own confession, would be equally likely to deceive either you or I. At the same time, I am distressed to think of his having yielded to this temptation. I have known him for some time, and have esteemed and respected him."

"But, uncle," said Captain Bland, "if he had been irrevocably bad, would he not have added wrong to wrong,,and obtained the money from the General, ostensibly for some other purpose, and by that means have covered his present delinquency?"

"Undoubtedly he might have done so, my boy," replied the Judge, "but perhaps he had not the courage. Wrong-doing requires almost as much courage as the undeviating pursuit of virtue."

"But, uncle," asked Captain Bland, "does it not require more courage to confess a wrong done than to supplement the first by a second evil deed? May we not accept the confession as evidence of sincere repentance of the wrong done, and of a determination to pursue the path of rectitude for the future? My first impressions were that I should have nothing to do with the matter, but my maturer reflections lead me to the conviction that it is my duty to take a hazard on his future integrity, and to advance him the money."

"Perhaps you are right, my boy," said the Judge. "Have you the money here?"

"No, uncle, but I can draw on New York for it. I have more than the required sum lying there on demand."

"Well, never mind that," said the Judge; "in the morning I will give you a cheque for the ten thousand dollars, and you can go and make such arrangements for its repayment as you see fit. I would suggest that you ascertain how much a month Mr. Equity can pay, and take from him consecutive notes for the amount, and be sure not to allow him to make them for a greater monthly sum than he can easily meet."

"Thank you, uncle," said the Captain, "I will now retire; good night."

"Good night, my boy; God bless you," replied the Judge.

True to his promise, Captain Bland sought the office of Mr. Equity the following morning. He noticed how pale and ill the lawyer looked. Passing through the outer office he entered his private or consulting room. Captain Bland closed the door, and turning to Mr. Equity he said:—

"When you were with me at the hotel yesterday evening, I did not think I should see my way to aid you in this unfortunate matter. With my uncle's assistance I am able to do so. We equally deplore the wrong you have done, but we do not wish to see you disgraced. We wish to save you for better things. Judge Bland has given me the money to make good your deficiency."

"Thank God and you both!" ejaculated the attorney, whilst he experienced a feeling of relief, the nature and extent of which can only be realized by such as have escaped dishonor worse than death.

"And now," said Captain Bland, "about the repayment; how much per month can you afford to pay in abatement of the sum Judge Bland will advance you?"

"I have about five thousand dollars owing to me, and my business averaged during the past year about one thousand dollars a month. The moneys due me can only be collected by degrees and may take some time to get in. I could, however, repay fifteen hundred the first and second month, and one thousand a month until the money is fully paid."

"Do not attempt too much, Mr. Equity. Draw

for me twelve notes, the first two for one thousand dollars, and ten for eight hundred dollars each, payable the first in one month, the second in two months, and so on to the last."

" I do not know how to thank you for your generous goodness, Captain Bland," said the attorney, as he proceeded to fill the blanks of the required notes.

" No thanks are required, Mr. Equity," answered Captain Bland, " allow my uncle and myself to see that there are nobler qualities in you than might be predicated from your late action. Let us see you do your duty, Mr. Equity, and we shall be rewarded. At the same time, if you should be able to take up your paper earlier than its face calls for, it is for many reasons desirable for you to do so, but not on any account to crowd yourself to accomplish it."

Captain Bland received the notes, handed to the attorney the cheque, and left the office, the restored lawyer thanking him with tears in his eyes, and assuring him of compliance to the utmost of his ability with the wishes expressed and the advice given.

One hour later General Sterne entered the office and received a cheque from Mr. Equity for twenty-four thousand five hundred dollars, the amount now collected, together with a statement of his account, with a memorandum attached, stating the times at which the different borrowers had promised to take up the balance of the notes.

We shall occasionally see more of Mr. Equity in his legal capacity, as the story progresses ; it may therefore be well to state here that he from this time greatly retrenched his expenses, and followed his profession with redoubled energy, that he preserved and henceforth deserved the confidence and esteem of General Sterne, and was so fortunate as to receive a large sum he had considered lost, which enabled him to redeem all his notes within a few weeks, to the contentment of Judge and Captain Bland, in whose esteem he rose and continues to hold a high place. Does any one think that the attorney too easily escaped the consequences of his crime? If so, I repeat to him the words of the prophet of Nazareth:—

"Let him who is without sin amongst you, cast the first stone at him."

CHAPTER XX.

TRACKEM & CINCHEM IN THE TOILS.

Wily was faithful to his promises. He regularly called on the General every evening, and he abstained from the too free use of intoxicating liquors. The General not only made his own observations, but privately made various inquiries; the result satisfying him that he was not mistaken in his estimate of the man he proposed to benefit.

Trackem & Cinchem were not a little surprised at the change which had come over Wily, and asked each other and themselves, What does it mean?

As the days went by, he continued to frequent their office as much as ever, though he never brought in a customer, but then he was expecting, from day to day, to bring in General Sterne, so they took no particular notice of him, supposing him to be devoting all his time and energies to his work of securing the General, which thing accomplished, they assured themselves of a good haul, as the General was new to the business, and would be easy to pluck. It was enough for them that the General proposed to invest a large sum of money, and that they would receive the main order. Under such circumstances it would be strange indeed if they could not make big money out of it. Whether their orders were to buy or sell short was a matter of no moment to them, they could easily play him anyway.

Meantime, the General pursued his own course, conversing with different stock operators, and searching, examining and comparing the information he received from the various sources. He discovered that the favorite mode of creating a deal was by the formation of a pool, that is, an arrangement and agreement was entered into between certain large operators and capitalists to buy and sell on joint and common account, the stock in a certain mine. He ascertained that it was not an unusual thing for nine-tenths, and sometimes more, of the capital stock of a mine to be thus aggregated, behind which a large subscribed sum was placed, wherewith to buy up the remaining stock of the mine, or as much as was necessary to force the market price to a given figure. The effect of such operations (which were kept as private as possible, and their very existence positively denied by the parties chiefly interested), was ordinarily to induce the public to believe that there was a known but undeclared development in the mine, consequently many persons were induced to invest, with the hope of realizing early dividends, as well as a profit from the stock.   He also found that the members of such pools, or at least the managing portion, employed a number of irresponsible men who were busily engaged in circulating rumors of rich discoveries in the mine, which it is needless to say were, in the majority of cases, false.   If he could judge from the entirety of such rumors, circulated with regard to the Comstock mines during the past three years (no mine on the line, saving the Consolidated Virginia and the California, having yielded one single dividend to the stockholders, despite the numberless encouraging reports circulated regarding first one and then another of them during that time), then these reports were undoubtedly lies.   He had also ascertained that it was not an unusul thing for some member of these unholy alliances to play the remainder, thus, when the subscription of stock was made, he would retain a portion of his own stock, and borrow as much more as was possible, and finally sell it out to the pool, that is, to his partners in the deal, at high figures.   To say that the General was disgusted with the discoveries he made would but faintly express the indignation with which he contemplated them, or the horror with which his mind revolted from the subject he had undertaken to examine.   But he had entered on the work, and he

i

would probe it to the very bottom. He never had neglected a duty because it was unpleasant, and he would faithfully perform the work he had agreed to accomplish for the information and enlightenment of the "Society in Search of Truth."

In the midst of his reflections on these subjects Wily approached him, and drawing him aside from the watchful stock gamblers congregated about the entrance to the Boards, said to him :—

"I have got the information you wanted, General. Things could not be more suitable for your purpose. I have ascertained that a body of low grade ore has been struck in the Alta mine. It may not amount to anything, and probably will not. Nothing is known of it save by one or two of the directors. A pool is now being formed by the big holders, and Trackem & Cinchem are short on the stock two thousand shares, at an average of about eight and a half dollars."

"Do Trackem & Cinchem know anything about the discovery, or the pool ?" inquired the General.

"No," answered Wily, "I have ascertained that they are quite in the dark."

"That will do," said the General, "meet me here in half an hour."

The General left Wily and proceeded to Trackem & Cinchem's office. It was the noon recess. Both partners were in. Cinchem was delighted to see the General, and called his partner, Trackem, and introduced him.

"I should like a few moments' private conversation with you, gentlemen," said the General.

The partners would be most happy. Would General Sterne step into the private office ?

Mr. Cinchem led the way for the General, Mr. Trackem following and closing the door.

" Do you think, gentlemen, you could contrive to short a considerable line of Alta for me ? I have no faith in the present market, and think I should like to be short on it, and have selected Alta. It has had a number of assessments. The assessments are collected by the short seller from the buyer, I believe ? "

Mr. Cinchem thought of their own lines of shorts, and cast a significant glance at Mr. Trackem, and answered :—

" That is so, General. I have no doubt we could accomplish what you wish. How many shares would you like to short ? "

" I was thinking of about five thousand shares," replied the General, " could you do it this afternoon ? "

Mr. Cinchem answered : " I think not, sir ; if I may advise, I should say leave it till the morning session, it will be more favorable."

" Very well," said the General, " what is the price of the stock this morning, Mr. Trackem ? "

" Eight and a quarter."

" That will do," answered the General, " I will now write you an order and will call on you to-morrow morning and will give you what money you require. You do only a commission business, I believe ? "

" Only a commission business," answered Mr. Cinchem.

When the General had left the office, Cinchem turned to Trackem and said : " Nothing could be more fortunate. This afternoon, Trackem, you must increase our shorts to at least double—make in all say four to five thousand. In to-morrow's session you can break the stock with the General's commission, to half the present price, and we can fill and make an easy gain of from ten to twenty thousand."

" Has the General put any limit to his order ?" inquired Mr. Trackem.

" None whatever," answered his partner.

" Well, he is good enough for the risk," said Mr. Trackem, " I have ascertained that he is worth a million anyway. I will attend to the short business, Cinchem."

" You must do it carefully," said Cinchem, " it will shake the market, but it will only convince the General he is right. Ha ! ha ! this is the best streak of luck we have had for months."

Mr. Trackem now left the office, gave his instructions to his satellites, and before night was short four thousand five hundred shares, all told.

If Trackem & Cinchem were well satisfied, the General was even more so. Things had shaped exactly as he foresaw and desired. He instantly devined the object of the delay and it enabled him to approach his second move with confidence. He now returned to Wily.

" Come with me," he said, and they proceeded to

the General's bankers, where he drew a cheque for ten thousand dollars, " place this," said he, handing the money to Wily, " with five different brokers—choose the most reliable, if you know of such—three in the San Francisco and two in the Pacific Board. Give each two thousand dollars, and tell them you want to buy stock to a much larger amount. You will tell them what stock hereafter; also say that you will make good the amount of your purchases to-morrow at twelve o'clock. You will then proceed to buy Alta shares and distribute your purchases as evenly as you can amongst the different brokers. Be careful that Trackem gains no clue to your movements, he will certainly sell short this afternoon. Do not touch them until they are well under eight, and then buy all you can, but not eagerly. Be careful that the market is left no stronger than when you start in. That is for to-night. You have a great deal to do, and a good deal of machinery to arrange to accomplish it. You had better begin at once."

Wily, to whom every move was familiar, performed his part to admiration. He closely watched Trackem, and succeeded in buying, through the three brokers he had selected (Budd, Wattles, and Brooks), two thousand shares of him, and twelve hundred in smaller lots from other brokers and dealers, who watched and followed Trackem's lead. The result was thirty-two hundred shares bought at an average of seven and three-quarters, but so apparently scattered were the purchases that no suspicion of the Truth crossed the mind of any of

the sellers or even the brokers who were acting for
Wily. He reported his success to General Sterne,
who commended his tact and activity, and appointed ten o'clock the following morning as the
time at which Wily should meet him, and receive
the balance of the money to pay for the stock.

Early the following day the General returned to
the office of Trackem & Cinchem; both partners
were in.

" Do you think you can do my business to-day ?"
inquired the General.

" I have no doubt of it, General," answered the
broker.

" Have you done anything for me so far ? " asked
the General.

" No, not at present, sir; I will accomplish it this
morning," said Mr. Trackem.

" Kindly allow me to see the order I gave you
yesterday ?"

It was produced by Mr. Cinchem.

" Ah," said the General, " I see that the stock has
declined somewhat since yesterday," and folding the
bill of instructions and placing it in his pocket-book,
he added : " I do not think I should care to sell
short at the present price."

The partners looked at each other in dismay.
What did it mean ?

Whilst the General said : " Good morning, gentlemen." and left the office.

Mr. Trackem seized his hat and rushed to the
Stock Board.

Wily had been there before him some time; he

had received fresh moneys to deposit, and fresh instructions also, he had entered the San ·Francisco Stock Board himself and employed a trusty friend in the Pacific. They had bought all that came forward, the total only making fifteen hundred shares· The price now asked was eight and three-quarter dollars. As Trackem, the heavy seller of the day before, now entered the Board room, many eyes were turned on him to see what action he would take. It was no use ; he was heavily short; he must break the market at any hazard. Seeing a director in the hall he asked him :

" Is there anything new from the mine ? "

" Nothing," said the director.

Rushing to the center he cried : " Sell a thousand Alta at eight and five-eights,"

" Take them," said Budd, and they were booked to Wily.

" Sell a thousand more at eight and three-quarters," he shouted.

" Take 'em," said Wattles, and again they were booked to Wily, and this time Trackem noticed Wily standing by the buyer.

" Sell a thousand more at nine," he yelled.

" Take 'em," said Brooks, and again they were booked to Wily, and Trackem looking at the purchaser, saw him speaking to his old victim. Then the Truth flashed on him. He was now seven thousand five hundred shares short. Frantic with rage he rushed from the hall.

CHAPTER XXI.

THE GENERAL DRAWS ON THE STACK.

When Mr. Trackem rushed, in his impotent rage, from the Stock Board, he wanted air and time to think. He fully realized that his dupe had been used to dupe him. The recognition of the fact almost choked him with rage, hence his sudden exit. Out in the fresh air, he tried to calmly survey his position. It was true that his contracts at the present time, could he fill them at the market quotation last made, of nine dollars per share, would only show a loss of four or five thousand dollars. But would the Nemesis that was pursuing him stop there? What would be the result if the thing went no farther? But a trifle; no more than he had often lost before. But would it end there? He did not doubt but the General had possessed himself of Wily's history, and that Wily had enlightened him as to the action of the firm in the matter of the Savage venture, or that he had learned that the firm were short on Alta, or that the General had provided the funds to avenge them both. What could he do against General Sterne, who had at least ten dollars to the firm's one? But then he might be mistaken. Anyway, he reasoned, it was not likely the General would place his money in the hands of a man so recently, if not now so habitually, addicted to liquor that he was known to be intoxicated almost every night of his life. No; things could not be so utterly bad as he had momentarily feared. He would return to the Board. Several thousand shares of stock the firm must have for immediate delivery. There was nothing in the mine. The stock would, in due course, fall back. The firm would be all right, and possibly make a profit out of the apparent disaster. Anyway, he would not give up for the present. They had several thousand shares of customers' stock they were carrying for them, through their bankers, on fifty per cent margins; he would use that stock as far as it would go, to tide over present difficulties, and buy just enough to supply the deficiency for immediate delivery, and await results, and see what was to be done afterwards. But now he must have one to two thousand shares to supplement the stock they were carrying. He would return to the Board and purchase them on the best terms he could.

When Trackem left the Board room a temporary lull occurred, and a number of individuals who knew Wily, and had observed his movements, crowded round him, and in turn privately asked him how it was he was buying so largely. To most of them he declined to give any answer, but to two or three whom he knew could not retain the information, he imparted the fact that a body of ore had been struck in the mine, and that a combination was already formed to make a big deal in the stock. The statement he made (as he had foreseen) flew through the Board room like wildfire, and every man who was short hastened to fill, and not a few purchased for a rise. The consequence was that when Trackem re-entered the room, after an absence of twenty minutes, fifteen dollars was bid for the stock, and little offering at any price.

Meanwhile Wily, pursuing the instructions the General had given him, commenced to hunt up the customers of Trackem & Cinchem, and gave them the information he had imparted in the Board, and at the same time intimated that Trackem & Cinchem were short on the stock to such an extent that it was extremely improbable they would be able to fill without an enormous loss, which must prove very disastrous to them. The effect of this information was immediate.

Cinchem, hearing how the market was going, had sent round to all his customers holding the stock, advising them of the rise, and intimating the advisability of disposing of it, hoping by this means to weaken the market. This advice, crossing the information given by Wily, had exactly the contrary effect to what Cinchem intended. Some sent down the balances due from them to Trackem & Cinchem, and demanded their stock. The remainder decided to transfer their accounts, and gave to other brokers orders on the firm for their shares, which were presented in due course, with the balances due upon the respective accounts to Trackem & Cinchem. The consequence was that Cinchem found that, in order to make the deliveries of the day, he must have four thousand shares of stock. He had tried every available source, but could not borrow a share.

About the time the formal session commenced,

Cinchem dispatched a note to Trackem, which read as follows :—

"Win or lose, we must have four thousand shares of Alta to-day."

Trackem read and re-read the note, wondering what it meant. Consternation and dismay were depicted on his every feature. Scarcely able to give any attention to the preceding business, he waited for the call of Alta. Determined to make one more effort, and as yet knowing nothing of the reported development, he sprang to the floor the moment it was called and offered five hundred shares at fifteen. They were instantly taken by a broker who sat in the outer ring. Turning to look at him, Trackem saw that Wily, who stood behind him, was the buyer. He now turned his back on his fate, as such he regarded Wily, and commenced to buy. He purchased in all two thousand five hundred shares, which averaged him nearly eighteen dollars. When he returned to his seat he footed up his morning's work, and came to the conclusion that the result was a loss of a little over twenty thousand dollars, and the firm were still short five thousand five hundred shares.

Trackem did not wait for the call of the remainder of the stocks on the list, but immediately returned to his office. Entering in great haste and excitement, he called his partner into the private office, where he impetuously demanded of Cinchem :

"What is up with Alta—what the ——— does this rise mean ?"

"It is reported," said Cinchem, "that a large

body of ore has been cut, and that the stock is closely pooled."

" Why the ———— did we not know it before? We have been played with a vengeance. We shall be lucky if we are not ruined, Cinchem."

" How so ? " inquired Cinchem.

" How so ? " mimicked Trackem, " why we have dropped over twenty thousand on Alta this morning and we are still short fifty-five hundred shares."

" Fifty-five hundred shares ! " repeated Cinchem, " how is that ?   Did you not fill this morning, when I sent you that memorandum ?"

"Memorandum be ————," said Trackem, " how could I fill ?   I bought twenty-five hundred shares which averaged seventeen and a half, and makes us a cool loss so far of over twenty thousand."

" Well, how are we fifty-five hundred shares short? That only leaves two thousand deficient,' said Cinchem.

" How are we ?   Why, when I went into the Board this morning I saw Blank, he is a director, and asked him if there was anything new in the mine ?   He told me no.   Eight and three-quarters was asked. I wanted to break the market, so I offered a thousand at five-eighths, which were taken.   Not to be beaten, I next offered a thousand at three-quarters, which were also taken.   I then offered a thousand at nine ; they were taken too. Then I left the Board room.   When I returned, it was only a few minutes after, fifteen was asked.   I determined to wait for the regular call, and when Alta was called I made one more effort, and offered five hundred at fifteen, which were at once taken. Then I turned to buy; you know the rest."

Cinchem was now a picture of mingled consternation and rage. Turning fiercely to his partner, he said :—

"You are a fool, Trackem."

"A fool, am I?" answered Trackem. "Who was the fool who saw such a splendid thing in that cursed General Sterne's order? Who saw such a magnificent haul to be made so easily by doubling our shorts? A fool, am I? Why you must be a cursed fool. You have had Wily here every day under your eye, and yet you have let him play you and beat you. Wily has been behind this move, and General Sterne has been behind Wily. D—— them. They may put Alta to a hundred, for aught I know."

This was confounding news indeed to Cinchem. He stood a full minute dumb with amazement. At length he recovered himself, and said:—

"This is a bad business, we must pull through as best we can."

"That is so," answered Trackem, "you must take up the customers' margin stocks which are in bank and use them for present delivery."

"We haven't any," said Cinchem.

"Haven't any?" repeated Trackem, "why there must be over two thousand shares."

"Not a share," answered Cinchem, "they have all been taken up this morning."

"What, all of them, Pheby's and Bradley's and— all of them?" inquired Trackem.

"Every one of them," replied Cinchem.

"Wily, again," muttered Trackem, and he rushed from the office. In his haste to reach the Board room, he nearly tumbled over the diminutive man who has a nut stand near the corner of the street, and plumped into the arms of the stalwart female curbstone broker, who is known as Mrs. Galloper. Freeing himself from her embrace, he hurried forward. On his way he bitterly realized the fact that ne was caught in a net which had been cast for him by General Sterne and Wily. He felt the meshes closing round him, and knew that the General, with a strong hand, was drawing in the slack.

CHAPTER XXII.

SENTIMENT AND WOMEN'S RIGHTS.

We left the Commodore and his family with their guests at the dinner-table. Dinner concluded, they returned to Mrs. Clare's room.

The Judge now requested the ladies to favor him with some music, of which he was a passionate lover. They cheerfully assented to his request, and Mrs. Clare, who was a brilliant pianist, was gallantly escorted to the piano by the Judge, who declining the proffered services of Captain Bland, waited by her side and turned the leaves whilst she executed a sonata of Beethoven with admirable skill and exquisite taste. Nor did he leave his position when at her request Geraldine came to her side to sing, escorted by Captain Bland. The music or the splendid woman beside him held him enthralled. Had not the Judge been known to be a universal admirer of beauty, it might have been assumed that he was captivated by Mrs. Clare, who, though at least forty years of age, had retained her charms of personal appearance, to which were added many graces of mind and manner, the result of careful self-culture and constant association with the elegant refinement of the best society of France.

It is certain that Judge Bland thought her one of the most perfect specimens of mature womanhood he had ever seen. But we must waive our reflections and hear Geraldine's song.

THE NEGLECTED.

Oh, what is love?
A passing thing;
A fleeting dove
Upon the wing,
Oh, what is woman ? But a toy
To man; who wantonly deceives her;
To win, he will his arts employ,
But having won, how soon he leaves her.

The silent tear,
The mournful sigh,
To see or hear,
He is not by.
In solitude she sits alone,
Her lord is absent on his pleasure;
His love, his beautiful, his own,
She sits alone and waits his leisure.

For she is his ;
He owns her now;
The virgin kiss—
The marriage vow
Which with a simple faith she gave,
By her in holy trust were given.
Her home may be a living grave,
She will not break the vow to Heaven.

The artist who composed the music of the song, had caught to perfection the author's meaning. Its strains seemed to double the force of every thought

expressed in the words.   It was rendered by Geraldine with a complete appreciation of both music
and sentiment.   Her rich contralto voice, now full
of fire and again tremulous with tender pathos, had
the effect of holding her audience spell-bound until
Captain Bland had led her to a seat, when the
gentlemen, recovering, as if from the effect of an
enchantment, led by the Judge, made the room resound with applause.

When it had subsided, the Judge, walking across ·
the room to Geraldine, said to her: " Thank you
very much, Miss Stanley.   That is a beautiful song,
expressive of woman's devotion and man's indifference and neglect, and the music is charmingly appropriate to the words.   You have a wonderful talent for music."

Geraldine smiled and bowed her acknowledgements.

Mrs. Clare answered: "Both my daughters (she
always spoke of them as her own) completed their
musical studies in Italy, where I procured for them
the best masters Florence and Venice afforded.   We
resided in Italy two years, only returning to France
last fall.   Some evening, when you shall have a
leisure hour, we shall be happy to entertain you,
Mr. Bland, also Captain Bland, with a concert."

Both gentlemen expressed their thanks, and assured Mrs. Clare that they would find the leisure
any evening it might suit her convenience to be
troubled with them.

" I think, Geraldine," remarked the Commodore,
" that song of yours, with all its beauty, will

scarcely be appreciated in San Francisco, at least by the ladies."

" Why not, papa ? " (Geraldine had already adopted the Commodore.)

" Because," said the Commodore, " the sentiment expressed is at variance with the practice of the people. It belongs to another world and another order of men and women.

"Explain your meaning, brother," said Mrs. Clare.

" My meaning is," replied the Commodore, " that whilst I do not doubt the fact of the picture of man's inconstancy and neglect being applicable to a very considerable extent to San Francisco husbands I have my very grave doubts concerning the devotion and resignation of its women under such trying circumstances. I do not doubt the existence of loyal wives who, in their lonely homes bemoan their husbands' coldness and neglect, but I am convinced that in a great number of instances the effect of such neglect as you described is seen in doubly deserted homes. The husband seeks his own pleasures, the wife hers, and the end is found in the divorce court."

Here the Commodore thrust his hand into the breast-pocket of his coat and drew forth a memorandum book, the pages of which he turned over, evidently seeking for data. He continued :—

" If my memory is correct I have here some figures I clipped from a recent paper, in which it was stated that during the preceding year there had been three divorces to every five weddings in this

J

city, and a very large number were for the cause
described in your song—neglect. The average Californian woman of the present day believes she
has equal rights with man, and claims the privilege of exercising them. The marriage rite is fast
degenerating into a simple civil contract—in which
the vows are made between man and woman ; the
accompanying vows to heaven, which were universal with our forefathers, are fast becoming old-
fashioned, and bid fair to be obsolete ere long. Our
women for the most part reason in this way : That
which is my husband's is mine. If it is my place to
stay at home, his place is beside me. If he spends
his leisure hours from home, so will I. If he leaves
me too much alone, I will leave him. And, regardless of all consequences, she not unfrequently seeks
and regains her freedom through the divorcr court,
but to repeat her former experience."

" This is a painful subject, Commodore, but I fear
your statements are the Truth," said the Judge, at
the same time rising to bid his adieu. He had
been informed by the Commodore that he had engaged a box for the evening for the ladies and himself at the charming theater which forms the central part of the Baldwin Hotel. It was now time
for Judge and Captain Bland to retire. The
Captain felt as if he could have lingered there forever.

" Well, uncle," said he when they had left the
room, "what do you think of Commodore Pye's
family ? "

"Think, my boy," replied the Judge, " why I

think they are the most delightful trio I ever met. Three such charmingly amiable and accomplished women are rarely found in one family. It made me remember my advancing years. I could almost wish I were young again. By the bye, you seemed to be intensely interested in Miss Stanley—you scarcely left her side from the moment you met her. She is beautiful, and I do not doubt she is good. As I saw you so happily seated beside her, I could but think of those lines of Campbell :

> " The world was sad, the garden was a wild,
> And man, the hermit, sighed till woman smiled."

" Does she smile on you, my boy? Are you hard hit?"

The Judge, who had never married himself, was nevertheless desirous to see Milton settled in life. He had often told him that, could he live his time over again, he should marry at the latest at thirty ; but he was too old now.

Responding to his uncle's question, Milton answered : " Not at all, uncle ; I was about to ask you the same question. Your attentions to the Commodore's sister were so marked and so corteous that I began to think that after having stood the siege of nearly half a century, you were about to succumb at last to the charms and graces of the handsome widow."

" Nonesense, my boy," said the Judge, " Mrs. Clare is a splendid woman, cultivated and refined, beautiful and amiable, and though I suppose that she must be forty, she appears that she might carry another twenty years or more without being *passee*, but there it ends. Now I have been candid with you. Tell me what you think of the Commodore's adopted daughter Geraldine ? "

" I think," said Milton, " she is a model of classic excellencies. She combines the beauty of Venus, the purity of Diana and the wisdom of Minerva."

" Bravo ! my boy," said the Judge, " not at all gone, eh ? "

" Not in the least, uncle. Do you not find the charming and amiable and beautiful and acccomplished Mrs. Clare occupying a large share of your thoughts ? "

" Well done, my boy, a good retort," said the Judge, laughing heartily, but he added : " at fifty years of age I am too old to marry."

" We shall see, uncle. We have not spoken of the Commodore's own daughter, Rose. What do you think of her ? "

" A fair, pretty, graceful girl, but she was sitting with her father all the time, and so I scarcely spoke to her."

" Neither did I," said Milton.

Here both uncle and nephew lapsed into reverie. As they walked home, each seemed so well pleased with his own thoughts that neither noticed the other did not speak.

CHAPTER XXIII.

WOMEN AND WINE.

The succeeding morning Geraldine and Rose having intimated their wish to do some shopping, the Commodore's carriage was in waiting for them. Mrs. Clare, who had decided to spend the morning at home, instructed her butler-courier, James Wily, to accompany the carriage as footman to the young ladies. Thus attended they left the hotel to investigate the various establishments on Kearny and Montgomery streets which deal in the numberless commodities that seem to be necessary to perfect the comfort and beautification of the fair sex.

These shopping excursions have always been a mystery to me. How so many ladies contrive to fill the major portion of one or two days in every week with this to them apparently most important duty, is one of those inscrutable things, the key to which I have never found. There must be secrets connected with the female toilet of which the ordinary run of unsophisticated masculine humanity has no conception. Here were our two young friends, Rose and Geraldine, just arrived from London and Paris with a dray-load of the productions of the finest costumeries of both cities, and yet forsooth, on the third day after their arrival in San Francisco, they must needs go shopping.

I verily believe that if a cargo of ladies were wrecked on the domains of the King of the Cannibal Islands, ere three days had elapsed this inordinate propensity would so strongly assert itself in some of their bosoms, that parties would be organ-

ized at all hazards "to go shopping." To be just to
our young friends in the present instance, I must
admit that they did not cause the dry goods clerks
to turn over half the contents of t e establishments
they visited simply to gratify their curiosity, whilst
they purchased nothing, a feat which is so often
accomplished by regular shoppers, that I have arrived at the conclusion that those specimens of the
genus homo who have been predestined to the occupation of dry goods clerks are especially endowed by a beneficent Creator with peculiar qualities fitting them for the occupation, or they are
lineal descendants of Job, and participate not only
in his blood, but his sublime virtue, patience. It
appeared that one or two trifles had been neglected
or forgotten. These they asked for, and having
procured them, proceeded to inspect the windows of
such establishments as were engaged in the sale of
works of art. They were both admirers of the
beautiful, in painting and statuary. During their
residence in Italy, Mrs. Clare had taken considerable pains to educate their taste and develop in each
of them a high order of appreciativeness of art.
They lingered some time over several paintings of
the grand scenery of California, which were admirably executed. Rose's attention was finally attracted by a painting of a mountain scene, which
was most striking and effective. A blending of
forest trees, mountain heights, with rugged rocks,
down which a stream was leaping, sparkling and
foaming as it descended, step by step, the ladder of
stone, which the artist had depicted on the canvas.

It was evidently a fancy sketch. The quick eye of Geraldine detected an impossible position in an angle represented in the descent of the stream. The defect had escaped the notice of Rose, who exclaimed :—

" How beautiful !"

They neither of them observed a tall, dark gentleman who stopped also, apparently to look at the paintings. He stood so close to Geraldine that he almost touched her. He heard Rose's exclamation and awaited Geraldine's answer.

" It is very attractive," she said, " but if you examine the streamlet you will find that the painter has made a mistake which destroys the merit of his work ; and then," she added in a low tone, as if speaking to herself, " nothing is truly beautiful that is not true."

The gentleman glanced at Geraldine. It was a look in which he seemed to concentrate all the energy of a strong nature. As if by the force of his own will he would penetrate the inner sanctuary of her life, and read the hidden mysteries inscribed upon the tablets of her heart.

Still unobserved by her, he moved on, murmuring to himself as he went: " Nothing is truly beautiful that is not true."

Rose, who looked up when Geraldine spoke, noticed the tall stranger beside her, and saw the keen glance of scrutiny with which he regarded her sister. When he left the window she said to Geraldine: " Did you see that tall, handsome gentleman standing beside you ? He looked at you so earnestly that I could not help thinking that he was under the impression that he knew you."

"It is impossible," said Geraldine, "we know no one in San Francisco save papa's friends whom he introduced last night," and she renewed her contemplation of the paintings before her.

To be admired was nothing new to Geraldine; though her bearing was such as might seem to indicate pride, she had not a vestige of vanity. What some supposed to be pride was the outward expression of conscious worth, or the result of a training which had inculcated dignity of character and action, and of moving in society, in which from her debut to the present hour she had always been one of the central figures. It was distinct in nature and essence from that vulgar thing which is found in the circles of shoddyism, and is the outward manifestation of an over-estimate of the importance of wealth, or some other equally deplorable misconception of the basis upon which human esteem should be founded.

She did not give another thought to the General, for it was he, but shortly afterwards re-entered the carriage with Rose, and after continuing their drive for a time, returned to the hotel.

General Sterne meantime had arrived there before them. How many times whilst on his way he repeated to himself the words of Geraldine: "Nothing is truly beautiful that is not true," he never could tell. "Am I haunted?" he said to himself. "First the form and features, now the voice and words, of what—a girl—a lovely girl, it is true—

but after all these years am I to be drawn into the society of woman, which I have shunned and avoided so long?" His interest was excited to such a degree, that to solve the problem of his fascination was an imperative necessity. He determined it should be done, and flattered himself it would be easily accomplished. "Beneath the surface," he reasoned, "all women are alike. But what is the secret of this attraction which is drawing me against my will towards this lady, to whom I have never spoken a word?"

He retired to his room, and in a few moments rang the bell and dispatched his card by the waiter to Commodore Pye.

The waiter returned, "Commodore Pye is in his room, sir, and will be glad to see you. You know his number, it is——

"Yes," said the General, "I know his rooms." In a few moments he was there.

The Commodore heartily welcomed him; always a genial man, Commodore Pye's nature seemed to have expanded during the past few days. He had frequently found himself verging on the borders of enthusiasm, and strange to say, it no longer annoyed him, he was conscious of the fact.

The General had come on an errand he did not like. He was sure its nature was unsuspected by the Commodore. Strong man though he was, he expected that he should be very awkward in his approaches to it. He therefore felt relieved when the Commodore said:—

"Why, this is a treat, General; you rarely favor

me with a visit to my den.   Try one of these cigars,
they are real Cubans.   I imported them myself.
They were selected for me by an old sea-going
friend of mine, who has for some time past been
resident in Cuba."

The General lighted a cigar.   He was glad to
smoke.   It gave him time to think.

What cowards men often are when the heart becomes only a little involved.   The sailor, who will
run his ship under the nose of an ironclad; the
soldier, who will lead his men into the jaws of
death; will blush and hesitate and stammer when,
being in such circumstances, he is required to utter
the word " woman."

' And now," said the Commodore, " I want you to
try this wine.   It is of California growth.   I think
it very fine.   I have drank still Hock in England,
and in many parts of the continent of Europe, for
which I have paid one and a half to two dollars
a bottle, which was not any better."

The General tasted and praised it.

" Yes," continued the Commodore, " that is fine
wine, and many of our full-bodied wines, our Ports,
Tokays, Mountain Vineyard, and other varieties,
vant but age to make them better than any imported, and our champagnes, such as Eclipse and
Private Cuvee, and some few others, are far superior
to any ordinary imported brands."

" That is so," replied the General.   " The fools are
not all dead yet.   They buy inferior imported wines
at much higher prices.   They think there is virtue
in them because they come from a distance."

"Very true," said the Commodore. "This State of California ought to be supplying half the countries of the world with wine. If I had the ordering of its affairs, in a few years such would be the case."

"How would you accomplish it?" asked the General.

"In the first place," said the Commodore, "I would appoint a commission of, say four men, two of whom should be geologists, and the others experienced vine-dressers, who should examine the soils upon which are grown the various descriptions of grapes used in the production of wine in all the best wine-growing countries of Europe, and also the kind of grapes suitable to each soil, and the various modes of culture and processes of utilization. I would publish the information so obtained, and place it within the reach of all vine-growers."

"I am afraid, Commodore, you would get into trouble. You would be charged with being concerned in getting up a job the instant you named a commission."

"Possibly so" replied the Commodore. "But if I could succeed in stimulating an already important industry to such proportions as it might, with knowledge and well directed energy, be made to assume, I would endure the obloquy with satisfaction. California is the natural home of the grape. Some of its wines are not to be excelled, but there is much misapplied capital and unskillful labor in the industry of wine-growing. Thus, grapes are frequently grown in rich valleys which would be

better fitted for the production of wine if grown on
the poorer hillsides, and in many other ways the
industry suffers through lack of knowledge, which
it is the interest of the people of the State to supply to those who follow it.   I am satisfied that with
a little fostering care on behalf of the Legislature,
the wine-growing industry may be raised to an
importance which is not dreamed of to-day.   I
have here a collection of facts and figures (divin;
into his pocket for the inevitable memorandum
book), which I think you would find interesting."

"The subject is a very important one," said the
General.

Here the Commodore suddenly remembered that
General Sterne might have called with some special
object, and remarked :—

"I must really apologize, General, for taking up
so much time.   You possibly called to see me on
some other subject ?"

The General was in for it now.   For one moment
he hesitated.   He then replied :—

"Yes, Commodore, I have.   It is to ask you to
do me the favor of introducing me to your sister
and daughters."

The General had ascertained who the ladies were;
so far his former resolutions had given way.   If when
the General made his request a thunderbolt had fallen
in the room, or a bombshell entered the window, the
Commodore could not have experienced greater
amazement.   A resident of the hotel, reputed to be
very wealthy, a Mr. Boldwinner, had previously
asked the same favor.   The Commodore had

referred the matter to the judgment of his sister, who said that she had heard so much of the gallantries of Mr. Boldwinner, she regretted to say she must decline the honor of his acquaintance. But such a request from General Sterne was altogether another thing, and totally unexpected.

For several moments he looked at the General in blank astonishment, then rising to his feet, he walked across to him and held out his hand.

"My dear General," said he, "I should have requested this pleasure long ago, but—but—"

"You thought I was fool enough not to desire it. Certainly, no apologies are due to me, Commodore. If there be fault in the matter, it is all mine."

Let us then adjourn at once to my sister's drawing-room. I know she is in. The young ladies are out taking a morning drive," said the Commodore.

"I saw them," said the General.

The Commodore led the way, still wondering. General Sterne followed him.

CHAPTER XXIV.

THE GENERAL ON THE ROAD TO CONVERSION.

They entered Mrs. Clare's drawing-room together.

"Allow me, sister," said the Commodore, "the pleasure of introducing to you my most esteemed friend, General Sterne."

"General Sterne, Mrs. Clare."

It was with a strange feeling of novelty that the General realized the fact that he was standing opposite a magnificent, well bred lady, in her own splendidly appointed appartment. The room, indeed, was not in any way superior in costliness to his own; it was not so full of choice works of art, but it had an easy elegance about it—that graceful charm with which refined woman invests the abode she owns or shares—a something which all the wealth of the Bonanza firm could never impart to a bachelor's apartment. So long self-ostracised from the society of ladies, a conviction now flashed upon his mind that, not the sex he had schooled himself to despise, but he, had been the loser.

To a man less habitually calm and self-possessed, the position would have been a trying one, and even to the General it was an ordeal, although the pleasure he experienced prevailed over a somewhat oppressive feeling of strangeness. Had he been even less at ease, the tact of the kind-hearted Mrs. Clare would have drawn him to self-forgetfulness. Self-abnegation and kindly sympathy with others were prominent features of her character. Many years ago she had abandoned sorrowing for her husband of her youth because she thought it savored too much of selfish regret, and had devoted her life to the culture of the two lovely girls left to her care. She thought she saw a hidden sorrow in the General's grave manner. He speedily found himself conversing with her with a pleasurable content he would not have believed possible when he entered the room. Their conversation, in which the Commodore joined, ranged over a variety of subjects, embracing comparison of the customs and habits of various nationalities, and impressions of different places on the continent of Europe, which all three had visited at different times. As the conversation progressed, the General realized a fact, which, from isolation from the sex he had almost forgotten, that the observations of an educated and refined ·lady add a piquancy to discussion which cannot exist without her presence, and are to it what fragrance is to the rose, or boquet to the juice of the grape.

The door now opened and Rose and Geraldine entered, accompanied by Mr. Frank Carleton, whom Rose introduced to her father, explaining that they found him walking and had taken him with them for a drive. She then waited for the introduction of the stranger, whom she instantly recognized as the tall gentleman she had seen at the picture store.

"General Sterne," said the Commodore, "allow me to introduce you to my daughter, Miss Pye, and my adopted daughter, Miss Stanley, and also," he added, " Mr. Carleton."

" Mr. Carleton, General Sterne."

Did the younger man catch in the eagle eyes of the General, which were turned upon him, a glimpse of destiny ? Did the General foresee that their paths were to cross. It is certain that each at that moment had an intuitive foreboding of a coming antagonism, though neither could foretell when, or how, or why it was to come.

Rose and Geraldine retired to remove their wraps. When they had passed from the drawing-room Rose exclaimed :—

"Why Geraldine, that is the gentleman who was looking at you so earnestly as we were standing at the window admiring the paintings. You remember I spoke of it."

"Yes, my dear, I remember. Do you mean it was General Sterne ?"

"Yes, I recognized him in a moment. Do you not think he is a very handsome man ?"

"Really, Rose, I hardly noticed him ; but what observation I did make was not altogether pleasing to me."

"Why Geraldine, I am surprised. If I might use the expression of a young lady in the dining-room at breakfast time, I should say, 'he is most perfectly splendid.'"

"Don't use it, dear Rose, mamma would not like it. She always objects to superlative terms of admiration or dislike, and would think it unbecoming."

Mrs. Clare had devoted her life to training the two motherless girls, and had taught them both to call her mamma.

"I won't use it again, Geraldine, but you were not favorably impressed with General Sterne. What did you see in him you did not like ?"

"It did not amount to that, Rose dear. It was only an impression ; I may be mistaken, but if I rightly read his character, he is a proud, cold, haughty and unforgiving man. I hope I am wrong, dear."

" Oh! dreadful, Geraldine; I hope you are wrong, too. If you are not, he must be a Satyr, or a Blue Beard. Why, I should be afraid to go near him if he were not one of papa's friends."

" I don't think he will hurt you, dear," said Geraldine, laughing at the mimicry of horror which Rose had assumed. " We are not always accountable for our likes or dislikes ; with me they are intuitive. Sometimes they are prophetical, and sometimes unjust."

" What do you think of San Francisco, Mr. Carleton ?" inquired the Commodore, when the young ladies had left the room.

" A question, sir, I have scarcely settled in my own mind yet. I have wandered, I think, all over it since I have been here. I have seen handsome buildings that would grace the West End of London, or the Boulevards of Paris, and I have seen dirty streets and ill-kept pavements which would disgrace the smallest town in England, or in western Europe. I have seen in the same streets indications of magnificent opulence and careless neglect. In fact, I have amused myself by marking contrasts. But on the whole, considering its youth, and its rapid growth, it is one of the most astonishing cities I have ever seen."

" Your observations are just," said General Sterne, " there is too much culpable neglect in the management of the public thoroughfares on the part of the city authorities, and there are some things which are difficult for them to control. For instance, this city is mainly built on a number of sand hills, and the wind blowing in from them drifts the sand down the streets. And then the pavements are laid in sand, which is continually working up. Of course the city authorities might remedy the inconveniencies arising from these evils by the employment of scavengers and copious water. But here a new difficulty presents itself; the city does not own its water supplies, which every city should do. The waterworks are owned by a monopoly, consequently the supply of water for public uses is a continual bone of contention between the authorities and the Water Company, and the convenience and comfort of the people are neglected, on the ground that they are too costly to purchase."

Just at this time Rose and Geraldine returned. The General placed a seat for Rose between himself and the Commodore. Mr. Carleton, rising from the sofa on which he was sitting, invited Geraldine to share it with him, to which she gracefully assented.

" Did you have a pleasant drive, my daughters ? " inquired the Commodore.

" Very, papa," responded Rose, " it was particularly so after we met Mr. Carleton. He is an old friend now, and it always adds to our pleasure to meet old friends. I saw you, General Sterne; you were standing beside my sister when we were looking at some paintings."

As Rose uttered these words she looked up at the General with an air of apparent awe, whilst a smile which contradicted the assumed fear played about the corners of her mouth.

Geraldine, looking across at her, saw the acting on Rose's part, and did not know whether to smile at her reminder of the conversation in the bedroom, or to feel vexed with her. She never could be angry with Rose ; her sunny smile and perfect good nature would chase away every thought of anger almost before Geraldine could realize that she felt it.

"I saw you," answered the General. "There were a number of specimens of local talent in that window. What did you think of the exhibits of American art you saw ?"

"Some of them were fine, spirited paintings," said Rose, "and appeared to me to be very skillfully executed. When we were in Italy, mamma was at great pains to make us connoisseurs of art. I am afraid she was not successful with me ; I know the effects which please me, but I do not regard them with the critic's eye, as sister does. She detects a fault in an instant."

"Which I observed," said the General; "she pointed out to you a defect in the artist's portrayal of a mountain cataract which spoiled what would have otherwise been a very beautiful picture, and she told you a great Truth when she remarked : 'Nothing is truly beautiful that is not True.'"

As the General made this remark, all eyes were turned on Geraldine. Rose arched her brows and assumed a look which seemed to say, "I told you how closely he observed you." The General gave a penetrating glance, which appeared to ask, "What further have you to say in defence of such a proposition ?" The rest of the company waited in silence for Geraldine's response, which they knew would come.

For a moment Geraldine appeared as if she might have been invoking the spirit of inspiration. Looking up, she said :—

"Is it not so, General Sterne? Are not Beauty and Truth always allied? When Truth departs from Beauty, is not Beauty marred? What is it in the great oration that thrills our souls? Is it not the Truth well told? What is it in the poet's song that moves our tenderest sympathies? Is it not the Truth well sung? What is it in the sculptor's art that wakes our admiration, and brings forth our praise? Is it not the truthful portraiture of God's creative skill? What is it in the painting that en-thralls our gaze and makes the picture truly great? Is it not the Truths of greater nature truly shown? Take Truth away, and poet, painter, sculptor, and the orator have lost their power. The secret charm is gone. There is no Beauty without Truth."

" As Geraldine spoke, every eye was fixed on her as she proceeded. It appeared as if her whole soul was in the thoughts she uttered, and the cold, calm beauty of her face was changed. It was full of tender, thoughtful sweetness. When she ended, a gentle blush seemed to indicate a consciousness of having said more than she had intended.

Mr. Carleton drank in every word she uttered with eager, admiring interest.

General Sterne, looking still at Geraldine, said to himself, " How unjust I have been," and then aloud,

"You are right, Miss Stanley; nothing is truly Beautiful that is not True."

"General Sterne and Mr. Carleton," said Mrs. Clare, "we anticipate the pleasure of the company of Judge Bland and Captain Bland to-morrow night. We propose to have a musical evening. Your presence will afford us additional pleasure."

"I shall be delighted to come," responded Mr. Carleton.

"Thank you, madam, I will avail myself of your kindness," said the General.

CHAPTER XXV.

RE-UNITED BROTHERS.

It must not be supposed that General Sterne had allowed his mind to be so much diverted by the events we have related as to cause him to neglect the duties he had undertaken on behalf of the Society in Search of Truth, or to lose sight of the speculation in which he had embarked, in hope of restoring to Wily the properties of which he had been unjustly deprived.

That his mind often dwelt on Geraldine he could not deny, but not to the exclusion of the engagements upon which he had entered. His own feel-feelings towards her he had never yet analyzed. He had greatly admired her from the time of his first observation of her on the night of her arrival. He had felt an interest which he did not care to admit even to himself. An interest which was intensified whilst he listened and observed her when she so firmly and beautifully illustrated her strong belief in the essential beauty of Truth. He had noticed that Mr. Carleton appeared greatly enchanted, and he did not doubt but Milton Bland was equally impressed with her beauty and genius. They were both much younger than himself, and probably Geraldine regarded one or the other with a feeling of greater favor than himself. He did not know that it made any very material difference if such was the case. It was nevertheless a fact that he did not like to witness the bestowal of any mark of favor by her to either of them. But yet, so far he had regarded her much as he would have regarded a beautiful statue, or painting, or poem, the ingenious construction of which he wished to analyze. He had not, therefore, been diverted from the pursuit of the labors he had planned. As soon as he perceived that Trackem & Cinchem were fairly caught in the net of their own trickery and greed, he at once sought his attorney, to whom he said :—

" Do you know the firm of brokers of Trackem & Cinchem, Mr. Equity ? "

Mr. Equity did know them to his sorrow. The greatest trouble he ever had experienced, which had nearly overwhelmed him, had come through their good offices. He almost trembled, fearing the General had made the discovery, and was about to tax him with it. Assuming as great an air of unconcern as he possibly could, he answered :—

" Yes, General, I know them very well."

Great was his relief when General Sterne said : "That is well. Do they know that you are my attorney ? "

" I think not, General; I have never mentioned the circumstance to them, and they are too busy with their stock operations to notice or think of it, if I had done so."

" That is better; they are not personal friends or clients of yours, I suppose, Mr. Equity ? "

" Neither, General; I may say I do not wish to have them in either capacity."

" You are right, sir," said the General. Here he handed to the attorney a slip of paper. " You will find here a list of properties. The first is a ranch which is situated in Alameda county; the description is here. The other three are San Francisco properties. I want to purchase all four—Trackem & Cinchem own them all. They are just now in trouble, and I think they will have to dispose of these properties very soon, if not immediately. I want you to let them know that you are a buyer of real estate, and seeking for investments. You have there the prices they paid for them. I have no doubt the urgency of their necessities will enable you to acquire them at the prices there named, which I am willing to give. Take this in hand at once—do it directly, or through an agent, as you see best. You will probably be able to complete the commission inside of seven days. Do not let me be known as the buyer. I will call every day to see what progress you are making."

" I think I had better employ an agent."

He remembered that Trackem & Cinchem were well aware that he had been stripped bare by his losses in stocks.

"Very well," said the General, rising to go, "I leave it with you."

The General never forgot that his attorney's time was his capital, and therefore never lingered in his office when the business for which he called was ended.

In the meantime Wily had gone to the Baldwin Hotel in hope of finding the General. Crossing the entrance toward the elevator, he met a man he did not know, but whose face seemed strangely familiar. He looked at him, walked past him, and again returned close to him, attracting the stranger's attention by the earnestness of his scrutiny. Wily had no bashfulness. His experience on the street had taken away from him every semblance of such weakness, if he ever had it. Now, walking up to the stranger, he said :—

"I think I know you, sir ; what is your name ? "

The stranger looked at him at first with an expression which seemed to say, " You have plenty of cool impudence," but as he continued to observe Wily's face, which was full of anxious expectancy, he answered: "My name is James Wily, at your service."

"I thought so," said Wily, "and you were born at Exeter, in England, and went to France with Mr. Pye and his little girl. Let me see, it must be all of eighteen years ago. You had a brother, a little bit of a chap, about twelve years old. He ran away from home and went to sea shortly after you left England; his name was—let me see—yes, his name was William. Do you know what became of him?"

"No, sir; I do not," answered James Wily, "we never heard any more of him. We made a good many inquiries about him, but never could hear anything of him after the ship, in which he went to New York as cabin-boy, got there. We suppose he is dead."

"Well, he was a worthless, harum-scarum young dog, anyway," said Wily; "it was not likely he would come to any good anywhere."

"Indeed, sir," said James Wily, "he was a good and affectionate boy, but fond of adventure, and wanted to go to sea, and when father and mother would not hear of it, he made his clothes into a bundle and was gone before they knew anything about it."

"Are your father and mother living?" inquired Wily.

"Yes, sir," said James, "but they are getting very old."

"They must be," said Wily, "and I suppose they were never able to save anything for their old age?"

(Wily thought of what he might have done for them had he so desired in the days of his prosperity.)

"Very little, sir," said James. He did not mention the fact that he sent them every month a portion of his earnings, which alone had kept them out of the poor-house.

"Ah!" said Wily, (his reflections were not pleasant; his self-condemnation was great.) After a little he inquired: "Have you no hope of hearing from William again? Why if he is living, he must be nearly thirty years old by this time."

"Yes, sir; that would be his age next December; but we have long ceased to expect to hear of him."

"And yet," said Wily, "I think he is alive. I am sure I saw him in San Francisco not many months ago."

James now regarded Wily with earnest attention.

Wily looked intently at his brother for a few moments, then he said: "James, don't you know me? I am the little runaway Will."

We will draw a veil over the interview of the brothers. I could do but scant justice to the feelings of the faithful, honest attendant of Mrs. Clare, who thus by mere accident of circumstance had met and recovered his only living relative of his own generation. I confess myself unequal to the task. If my reader has stood alone in the world, and has received as from the dead some loved one whom he has long mourned as lost—whom he has taken back to his affection as one returned from the tomb, then can he paint for himself the feelings of James Wily in thus finding his brother.

Or, if he has been a voluntary exile, self-isolated from every living tie, neglectful of every family duty, and has been received into the arms of love, where love was justly forfeited, then can he realize what were the feelings of William Wily, as he thought of his parents' poverty, of the wealth he had had and lost, of his thoughtless neglect, and of the tender affection with which his brother now received him.

Suffice it for me to say that they sat in James' room until the night was far advanced, recounting their past experience and their present prospects. That William Wily made earnest resolves that, when he realized the prosperity which he saw the General was working out for him (though he did not dream of its extent), his old father and mother should never lack comforts whilst he had a dollar to give them, and that he would never fail to keep in communication with both them and James. He learned to his great surprise that the American Commodore Pye, for some years resident in San Francisco, was his brother James' old English master. That Mrs. Clare, whom he also remembered as Miss Pye, was staying at the Baldwin Hotel, and with her the baby Rose, whom he last saw on the day his brother James left England with Mr. Pye, who was taking her to his sister in France. That his brother had ever since remained in the service of Mrs. Clare, who was still a widow, and for whom James had that respectful affection which can only be found among servants of the higher orders of the old countries. William told his brother his experiences before he reached California, his subsequent success, and later ruin, and of the new dawn of prosperity. When they had repeated many things again and again, they at last parted for the night, both thanking God that they were reunited.

CHAPTER XXVI.

CAPTAIN BLAND AND FRANK CARLETON VISIT THE CHINESE QUARTER.

When General Sterne and Mr. Carleton left the room of Mrs. Clare, the Commodore, who had resolved on a walk, accompanied Mr. Carleton down Market street. He was pleased with the frankness as well as the appearance of the young man, and determined to seek an opportunity to introduce him to Judge Bland and his nephew, entertaining the belief that he would be a pleasant companion for Milton, who had, as yet, but few opportunities of making the acquaintance of young men in San Francisco. The Commodore had formed a sincere regard for Milton. Predisposed in his favor by the oft repeated eulogiums of the Judge, he had been further impressed by his own observations, which had resulted in a belief on his part that Milton was one of the most excellent young fellows he had ever met. His sister's favorable remarks concerning Frank Carleton caused him to desire to bring them together. He thought he would not wait for the introduction which would necessarily occur in Mrs. Clare's apartments the following evening, but seek an opportunity to give it at once. Calling at the Palace, he met the Judge and Captain Bland, who were just proceeding to lunch. Having introduced Mr. Frank Carleton to them as an English traveling companion of his sister and daughters, both accepted the cordial invitation of the Judge to join him at lunch, and the Commodore saw with satisfaction that Milton and Frank appeared to make a favorable impression on each other. Milton, of course, knew nothing of Mr. Carleton's supposed attachment to Geraldine, and Frank was equally oblivious of the fact that Milton was credited, at least by his uncle, with being considerably affected in the same quarter. Had Mr. Carleton had any such suspicion, he might not so cordially have met the advances which Milton Bland freely extended to him. It is said that love is blind. In one respect it is well it is so, inasmuch as, for this reason, it fails to see many of the imperfections of the loved one; but in another regard it is a misfortune, seeing that it is only too frequently unable to see any virtue in a rival. Both unaware of the proclivity, which in the instance of the one really existed, and with which the other was credited, their fraternization was easy and simple. Before lunch was completed they had resolved to spend the afternoon together, inspecting some of the sights of the city.

The conversation at table naturally turned on the Commodore's family, the pleasant hours passed in their society the preceding evening, and their anticipations of enjoyment of the musical treat in store for them on the evening of the coming day. The Judge was, as ever, enthusiastic.

"Commodore," said he, "how have you lived alone for so many years, when youth, beauty and cultured intellect were waiting your call, to surround your life with sunshine and happiness?"

"Really, Judge," replied the Commodore, "I have asked myself the same question many times. I could not have believed that the presence of my sister and daughters would have been productive of so much pleasure to me."

"And to your friends," added the Judge. "Had I such a family, I should be the happiest man alive. The young ladies, sir, are the admiration of every one, and I may add that Mrs. Clare is a model of perfect womanhood, not only in physique, but in mental development and kind-heartedness."

Here Captain Bland gave his uncle a glance, which the latter understood to mean: "Not all hit, eh? Quite a mistake. Did I not tell you so?"

The Commodore replied, very gravely:—

"My daughters are all I could wish them to be, sir, and my sister is one of the most estimable of women."

The young men now left the table to undertake the ramble they had decided on. At the suggestion of Milton Bland, they walked in the direction of Chinatown, which he had decided to investigate, and had already engaged the services of a detective to accompany him.

On their way they heard a pistol shot. The sound proceeded from a house by which they were passing. The policeman leaving them, darted into the house, remained a few minutes, and returned, elbowing his way through the crowd which had congregated on the sidewalk, and rejoined them.

"What is the trouble?" inquired Milton.

"Only a man suicided," said the policeman.

"Did you ascertain the cause?" asked Mr. Carleton.

"Oh, yes," replied the detective, "it was the old

trouble. He left a note, saying he had lost all his money in stock gambling, and did not wish to live. It's a frequent thing here; sometimes it is done with a pistol, sometimes with poison, and sometimes they jump off one of the ferry-boats. They have money, and when it goes, they go after it."

"Is the man dead?" inquired Milton.

"Dead as an Egyptian mummy," said the detective. "He's blown the roof of his head off."

They were soon in the Chinese quarter. At first they were amused and interested with what they saw. It presented the appearance of a foreign city transplanted and flourishing in the centre of another city. They noticed that the first floors were all small stores, in which the celestial inhabitants retailed their wares, and pursued their industries with untiring perseverence, and a stolid look, such as we have seen on an old cart horse's face, who for years has answered the gee-whoas of his driver, and has come at last to the condition of an automaton, whose sole occupation is to throw his shoulder on the collar, or his weight on to the breeching, when directed by whip or rein or word of mouth.

They noticed the novelties of the scene around them; they observed not only the peculiarities of the articles of wearing appeal, but also of food, especially the vegetables that were offered for sale, many of which were distinct from anything they had ever seen; and although cultivated in suburbs of the city, are used exclusively by the Mongolian inhabitants. So far their observations had been both amusing and interesting, but they were to witness a variety of phases of Chinese life. Their guide led the way into what they supposed was a cellar. To their supprise, they found it was an underground room of about ten by twelve feet. It was an opium den, about which was scattered in various attitudes some eighteen or twenty Chinamen, and one white man, all of whom were more or less under the influence of the powerfull narcotic. They presented a diversity of appearances, which varied from that of the half-intoxicated man to that of the idiot. Disgusted with the pestiverous odors of the place and with the spectacle, they hastened away. The detective next led them to the Chinese hospital (if such it may be called) for lepers, where they observed a number of sufferers from that most fearful disease. There were patients in all stages, some newly entered, in whom the disease had but recently developed itself, and others from whom its ravages had obliterated a'l semblance of the former being. They hurried from the scene; they had been disgusted in the opium den; they were horrified at the exhibition presented in the lepers, hospital, and thankful to escape and once more breath the purer air of the street. Their guide now introduced them into a lodging house, which had once been one of the first hotels of San Francisco. It had been divided and sub-divided on the first floor. The height of the room had been split by the introduction of an intermediate floor. Their guide informed them that nearly four hundred Chinese occupants tenanted the space in which there could not have been wholesome breathing room for more than fifty people. He next conducted them to a house occupied by Chinese women—here they would not linger. The evils of which they declined to be spectators it would ill become me to present to my readers. They left the house, paid and discharged their attendant, and were satisfied that they had seen all they ever wished to see of Chinatown.

"How is it' inquired Frank Carleton of Milton, "that the laws of health and the safety of a city like San Francisco are allowed to be endangered by the presence of such evils as we have witnessed to-day? Has the city no sanitary laws, or are there no appointed authorities to put them into force?"

"Both laws and authorities exist," answered Milton, "but for some unexplained reason the evils are not remedied, although I have been told that some of the newspapers have been ventilating the subject for years. Some affirm that they are owing to the negligence of the Board of Supervisors and the Board of Health, whilst others do not hesitate to say that both Boards, and also the police force, are in the pay of the Chinese, from whom they levy large contributions, in consideration of which they close their eyes to the evils and dangers which exist in their very midst."

" But are the constituted authorities so dead to all sense of honor and official duty as to be capable of such things?"

"Of my own knowledge I cannot say, but I fear in some cases it is so. There is much to be said on both sides of the Chinese question, which is agitat-

I.

ing the minds of the residents of the Pacific Slope to-day. It is certain that many works of public utility and many industries have been established and carried on successfully, to the increase of the commerce and importance of San Francisco, which could have no existence without the presence of the labor of the Chinese. It is also true that the time did exist when domestic help would have been all but unprocurable without them; and it is difficult to make any manufacturer understand that he should pay half as much again for the services of a white man as he can get the same work performed for and equally well by a copper-colored one—who can live on food upon which a white man would starve, and kennel (I will not say house) himself in a space little larger than a full-sized coffin. But on the other hand, the white laborer seeking employ-ment feels himself hardly used, when he finds the various fields of labor occupied by his yellow-skinned neighbor to his own exclusion, and declines to attempt to compete with him, because he affirms, and perhaps justly, that such competition would cut him off from hope. It would be 'starvation for life with hard labor.' And there is another evil that is greatly felt, not only by the laboring man, but by the thinking portion of the well-to-do orders of San Francisco, which is, that the festering plague spot of Chinese occupation in San Francisco, with all its foul corruptions, continues to spread and grow. A central portion of the city, once its most important part, has been entirely absorbed by the Mongolians, and as wealth and respectability continue to withdraw from their vicinity, so does the hidious octopus stretch forth its tentacles and wrap them round another house, and another block, which, once polluted and befouled by their presence, never again are tenanted by white men. Civilization with its cleanliness recedes before the foul, offensive advances of barbarous hordes of unclean idolators. What wonder, then, that a cry has arisen in San Francisco, the echoes of which are heard through the length and breadth of the Union, demanding a remedy for the evil which threatens the very existence of San Francisco as an American city?"

CHAPTER XXVII.

THE SHADOW OF DEATH.

Milton Bland was so well pleased with his new acquaintance that he pressed him to dine and spend the evening with him, to which Frank, having no other engagement, readily agreed. During the evening they became confidential to each other, Milton recounting his collegiate and military experiences. Frank in turn informed him that he had left college only one year ago. His education was commenced under the instructions of a private tutor, from whose care he was removed to Eton, where he went through the preparatory course, after which he removed to Oxford, where he remained four years. He received the B. A. degree, and was well satisfied with his progress, as was also his father. The latter had ad-

vised him to spend one year in travel, and then
to return home and attend to the duties of his estate which he had inherited from a maternal uncle.
He had spent nine months on the continent of
Europe, and was tired of rambling. He was returning home, when on the boat which conveyed him
from Calais to Dover, he met and was introduced
to Mrs. Clare and her daughters. He called on
them twice at the Langham Hotel, in London,
where they stayed, and finally decided to accompany them in their westward journey at least as far
as New York. He went home, saw his friends, and
made his arrangements to rejoin Mrs. Clare's party
at Liverpool, and had finally accompanied them to
San Francisco. His admiration of Mrs. Clare was
almost unbounded. He thought her in culture and
breeding as near perfection as it was possible for a
human being to be. And her niece, Miss Pye, he
considered an unaffected, amiable girl, in fact, she
had all the good qualities one might expect to find
in a young lady reared under the watchful eye and
affectionate care of so cultivated a lady as Mrs.
Clare.

Milton listened with unaffected pleasure to the
praises of Rose, and scarcely noticed the fact that
Miss Stanley was only alluded to by Frank.

In the course of the evening the Judge joined
them.

"Ha! my boy," said he to Milton, "got a new
friend, have you? I am afraid the poor old uncle
is destined to be neglected and forgotten. I am
getting jealous, what with your fair friends at the

Baldwin Hotel, for whose society ' my boy ' abandons me once or twice every day, and now yourself, Mr. Carleton, I suppose I must content myself with the remembrance of Byron's experience, who tells us :—

> ' Love bears within itself the very germ
> Of change; and how should this be otherwise;
> That violent things more quickly find a term
> Is shown through nature's whole analogus.'

" Thus the old gives place to the new—the old uncle is deserted for the new young friends."

" Not so, my good uncle," answered Milton, " Byron measured the delinquencies of men and women by his own degeneracy, and was vainly egotistical enough to estimate mankind and womankind also by his own standard, which was a morally defective and practically corrupt one.

" Well, 'my boy,' I forgive you; I suppose you were discussing your fair lady friends at the Baldwin ? "

> "And when a lady 's in the case,
> All other things of course give place."

" I was speaking of Mrs. Clare," said Frank, "and of the pleasant hours I had passed in her society during the past month. She has a fund of knowledge, derived from study as well as observation of the world. Her society is delightful at all times."

Judge Bland had a shrewd suspicion, not that Frank had not been speaking of the lady in question, but than the younger ladies had been the more absorbing topic. He answered thoughtfully :—

·' Mrs. Clare is a most estimable lady."

" She is, sir," said Frank. " I was just about to

tell Captain Bland of the pleasant horse-back rides
I had on two occasions when in London, with Miss
Stanley and Miss Pye. Our English ladies are
many of them great equestriennes, as you are doubtless aware. Both of Mrs. Clare's daughters are excellent horsewomen."

"I noticed the fact of which you speak when in
England," answered the Judge, "and have seen
ladies ride fearlessly over hedges, walls, and streams
which daunted many of the gentlemen hunters.
During my stay in England I attended the meet of
the hounds in various parts of the country, and was
not a little surprised at the hardihood and daring of
many of the lady hunters. Equestrianism is little
pursued in San Francisco. You will frequently
hear persons speak of riding, by which they usually
mean what the English would call driving. But if
you desire to afford the young ladies the pleasure of
a ride to the park, it is possible that you might
obtain Mrs. Clare's consent."

"Do you think she would give it, uncle?" eagerly
inquired Milton.

"Faint heart never won fair lady, 'my boy,'" said
the Judge. "Try her; you may remember for your
encouragement that Mrs. Clare has none of the San
Francisco prejudices concerning horseback exercise
for ladies."

The young men thus encouraged determined to
wait on Mrs. Clare in the morning and ask the desired permission, and the pleasure of the young
ladies' society.

Early on the following day they ascertained

where good and reliable saddle-horses could be obtained, and then sauntered to the Baldwin. The young ladies were pleased with the proposition; Rose was especially delighted, and Mrs. Clare graciously consented to their united wishes, only stipulating that James her servant should ride behind the party and attend on them. She charged the young men to take good care of her two roses.

At eleven o'clock the horses were at the door of the hotel, and the young ladies, who had watched their approach from Mrs. Clare's parlor window, descended to meet the gentlemen. Rose placed one tiny boot in the hand offered for the purpose by Mr. Carleton, and vaulted into the saddle, Milton affording the same assistance to Geraldine. The whole party were quickly mounted, and moved up the street followed at a distance of about fifty paces by James Wily, who also rode a good horse.

Mr. Carleton acting as the escort of Rose, led the party, and Captain Bland attending Geraldine, followed. This was not the arrangement either of the gentlemen desired, hence, when they had proceeded some distance Mr. Carleton slackened pace and Captain Bland and Geraldine drew into line with them, and when they again pressed forward a transposition had taken place. Mr. Carleton took the lead with Geraldine whilst Milton followed, accompanying Rose. They were now on the outskirts of the town and approaching the park.

"Are you fond of horseback exercise, Miss Pye?" inquired Milton.

"Very," answered Rose. "It is so invigorating;

so different to reclining indolently in a carriage. I
learned to ride almost as soon as I could walk. I
had a little pony, and James used to hold me on
and lead Taffy (that was my pony's name) round
the park. When I grew bigger James used to ride
beside me, holding Taffy by a leading-rein, and
afterwards when I could manage him myself, I used
to scamper all over the country, James riding behind me to see, as mamma said, that I did not get
into any mischief. Then when sister came to live
with us we had each a beautiful riding horse. Hers
was jet black; she called him Misrour. Mine was a
dappled grey, with a clear full eye, with which he
would look at me as if he wanted to speak to me.
I called him Araby. When mamma bought Araby
for me I superannuated Taffy. I have still got him;
he is old and almost blind; he has never done any
work since mamma gave me Araby. In summer
time he is out in his baddock; in the winter he has
a warm, snug box, and eats, and nods, and sleeps.
Poor dear old Taffy."

As Rose uttered this ejaculation there was a tender look in her eyes called up by the remembrance
of the old companions of her childhood's happiness.
Poor dear old Taffy, he had a place in her affectionate nature which Araby, with all his fire of action
and graceful beauty, could never fill.

Milton, gazing at her, thought, "How beautiful
she is; how full of sympathy must her heart be
which has such warm affection for the dumb friend
of her girlhood."

" You were very fond of Taffy, Miss Pye ? " he said.

"Oh, yes !" answered Rose, "and he was equally fond of me. He would come to my call anywhere. I used to take him a slice of bread and a lump of sugar every morning. Sometimes I would pretend I had not got them, and hold them in my hand behind me. Taffy soon understood my tricks, and would walk round behind me and nibble them as I held them in my hand. At such times he would look at me as if he wanted to say: ' I know all about it, and I intend to find it.' And then when I was going for a ride, he would stand perfectly still until I was upon his back, then he would scamper away as if he enjoyed the fun as much as I did. Oh, those were happy days !"

"But are not the present happy days, also ?" inquired Milton, who was feeling that this was one of the pleasantest he had ever spent.

"Certainly, Captain Bland," she answered; "but so different. Can any days ever be so happy as those of childhood?"

Milton did not answer. He was thinking what happy days he could have with her by his side, when suddenly a large dog dashed from the shrubbery of the park which they had just entered, and bounded under the nose of Rose's horse, which leaped high in the air, and then started at a headlong gallop. To lay whip to his own horse and follow in pursuit, in hope of arresting the frightened animal, was the work of a moment. James Wily, who had witnessed the performance of the startled horse, struck his spurs into the sides of the powerful beast he rode, and thundered in the wake of Captain Bland. It was but a few seconds. Mr. Carleton and Geraldine, who were in advance of them, had turned a corner. Rose bravely sat the alarmed animal, grasping a rein in each hand, her body thrown back, and her whole weight on the bit. She was just turning the corner, Milton was about ten paces behind her; James Wily was within half a length of Milton, when, to their horror, they saw a carriage with a pair of horses rapidly wheeling toward her, and knew that a collision was inevitable. Both instantly reined in their horses. At that moment Rose's horse struck the carriage, and rearing, fell heavily over on its back, its head, in the fall, almost touching that of Milton's horse. So sudden was the shock that Rose was precipitated backwards through the air toward Milton. Quick as thought he stretched out his right arm, and catching her, arrested her fall, and held her until James, leaping from his saddle, took her inanimate and apparently lifeless form from his arms and laid her upon the green sward beside them. Had Milton been six inches more forward or backward he could not have arrested her fall; it would have been impossible. It was well, indeed, that James was beside him, for had not James seized with one hand the reins of Milton's horse, whilst with the other he steadied him in his seat, he must have been borne to the ground by the shock. As it was he was terribly shaken. Regardless of his own pain, he leaped from his horse. To James he said :—

"Ride instantly to the nearest stable and procure a carriage."

To Mr. Carleton, who now joined them :—

"Return, my friend, to the Baldwin Hotel and inform them of this sad accident. Break the news gently."

To Miss Stanley, who was calm and self-possessed, her pallor alone betraying her anxiety, he said :—

"Loosen such garments as may oppress her breathing, whilst I go for water."

"Sir," he said to one of the occupants of the carriage, "take my horse and ride as for your life, and bring me wine or spirits."

The instructions were given rapidly, but were unquestioningly obeyed. Hastening to one of the faucets, he returned with water which he had drawn in his hat, and kneeling by the side of Rose, bathed her face and hands. This he continued to do for some minutes, at the same time watching for the re-appearance of the gentleman he had dispatched for stimulants. When, at last, ten minutes had passed and Rose showed no signs of returning life, still kneeling, he contemplated her in sad silence. Then, forgetful of all other presence save that of the unfortunate girl, he murmured :—

"So lately have I found thee, and must I let thee go so soon? My love! My beautiful! And thou art dead!"

And then, whilst tears streamed down his cheeks, he stooped and tenderly kissed her pure white forehead.   Geraldine, who sat on the other side of Rose, holding one cold hand in her own, amazement now added to her agony of grief, regarded him with wonder, not unmixed with awe.

CHAPTER XXVIII.

THE GENERAL WINS THE GAME.

Mr. Equity was very much surprised to find that General Sterne knew so much of the affairs of Trackem & Cinchem, as was evidenced by the instructions he had given.   What could the General have to do with the firm? and why did he wish to buy those particular properties?   Mr. Equity was of opinion that there were equally good and perhaps better investments to be had.   There must have been some dealings between the parties, of which the attorney had no knowledge.   In that case, had Trackem & Cinchem mentioned his business with the firm?   It was not likely.   Dishonest men do not ordinarily speak of their tricks to men like General Sterne.   Was the firm really embarrassed?   If so, how did it happen, and how did the General become cognizant of the fact?   What was it to the General?   These and many other questions he asked himself, without finding any solution, and then reflecting that he would gain more knowledge by setting in motion the business entrusted to him by the General, he went out and deputed a real estate agent, with whom he was well acquainted, to make the desired approaches to Trackem & Cinchem.

This the agent did at once, and in less than an hour reported to Mr. Equity that any or all of the properties were under offer to him, stating the various prices, which Mr. Equity found corresponded very nearly with the amounts named by the General; the sum total as written down by him being sixty-five thousand dollars, the amount asked by Trackem & Cinchem being sixty-seven thousand five hundred.

"You found Trackem & Cinchem anxious to dispose of the properties, as I told you they would be, Mr. Snipacre ?"

"Well, yes," said Snipacre; "they were willing to sell any or all of them, and want the transactions closed quickly. Their business is so large, so Cinchem said, that they can better employ their capital in it than letting it lie idle in property."

"Very good," said Mr. Equity, laughing (he was human enough to feel complacent whilst contemplating the pressure and possibly final ruin of his betrayers), "that is easily understood. We will not give them sixty-seven thousand five hundred. You may take your time, Snipacre, and offer them fifty-five thousand, and if you find it necessary, you may give twenty-five hundred more. Remember, it is a cash purchase, which, if I am correctly informed, will be a great inducement to them just now. But take care that the properties do not slip through your fingers."

"There are plenty more as good if they do," said Snipacre, "but I will look closely after them."

The same afternoon Mr. Snipacre returned and

reported to Mr. Equity that he had completed the purchase of the properties for fifty-seven thousand five hundred dollars, and handed to him the duplicate of a contract of purchase and sale between himself (Snipacre) and the firm, and informed him that the title deeds were in the hands of Trackem & Cinchem's bankers, to whom they had been pledged as a collateral. The bankers had countersigned the contract, and to them the money was to be paid. He also presented a request on the part of Trackem & Cinchem that the preliminaries might be hurried through as quickly as possible.

General Sterne entered the office soon after the departure of the agent, and learned with great satisfaction the success of his plan. He directed Mr. Equity to use dispatch in examining the various abstracts of title, and making the conveyances.

Mr. Equity informed him that he had ascertained that the abstracts had been written up within the past week for Trackem & Cinchem's bankers, and observed :—

"The conveyances will be made to yourself, of course, General ? "

" No, Mr. Equity; not to me, but to William Wily, of San Francisco."

The General was now satisfied. He did not wish to run Trackem & Cinchem to the earth. He did wish to make them disgorge the properties of Wily. So admirably had his plans, aided by fortuitous circumstances and Wily's tact, succeeded, that he stood to win, on an outlay of about seventy thousand dollars, enough to pay for the re-purchase of

Wily's properties, and have a large surplus remaining. The rise on the market, started by the purchase of some eight thousand shares of Alta on his account, had continued. The stock was now selling for twenty-five dollars. With peculiar satisfaction, he regarded the circumstance that Trackem & Cinchem would certainly lose as much as they had swindled Wily out of, and that by an indirect process it would come into his bank account, and be employed by him in re-establishing Wily in his rights.

He now sought Wily, and having found him, directed him to commence to unload the stock he held.

"This I shall leave entirely in your hands," said the General, "and I have no doubt you will display as much ability in making the sales as you did in effecting the purchases. It is not necessary for me to direct you. You are aware that so much stock as I hold cannot be realized in one session of the Board without breaking the market. This I do not wish, if it can be avoided. You will call on me as usual after dinner."

"Certainly, General," answered Wily.

Passing through the throngs gathered about the entrances of Stock Boards, he noticed, with his usual interest, the characters by whom he was surrounded. There were men who were dressed in suits, the patterns and styles of which were the newest; with massive chains and sparkling diamonds; whose bearing seemed to convey the impression that each esteemed himself "The glass of fashion, and the mold of form." These were men who had newly made a raise, and were airing their freshly acquired adornments in the presence of their less fortunate brethren. Beside them were others, whose greasy coat collars and dilapidated continuations indicated that the wheel of fortune had long turned the wrong way for them. Rushing through the crowd were the runner boys and dealers who, on any change in the price of the stock of any mine, fly across Pine street, to the imminent danger of their own necks, to convey the news to their employers, or to make a turn on the market—their precipitancy being so impetuous that one might imagine it was the last moment for the closing of the final account, and they rushing to obtain the sole chance of an entrance through the closing gates of heaven.

And there was the ubiquitous Mrs. Slow, the curbstone brokeress, of whom it is said that she, some years ago, obtained five hundred dollars to invest in mining stock from a female client, and invested it so securely that the lady never spent it afterwards, because she could not get it. After many attempts to re-possess herself of her own, she ultimately sought the assistance of the courts. When put on the witness stand, Mrs. Slow was required to state what she had done with the money. She said she had invested it in stocks.

"You have invested it in stocks, have you?" inquired the counsel for the plaintiff, "In what stocks?"

"You don't suppose I have eaten it, do you?" said Mrs. Slow; "this is the stock."

The attorney said he would not answer for the fact of her not having eaten it, whilst she handed to the court five certificates. This is a copy of one of them.—

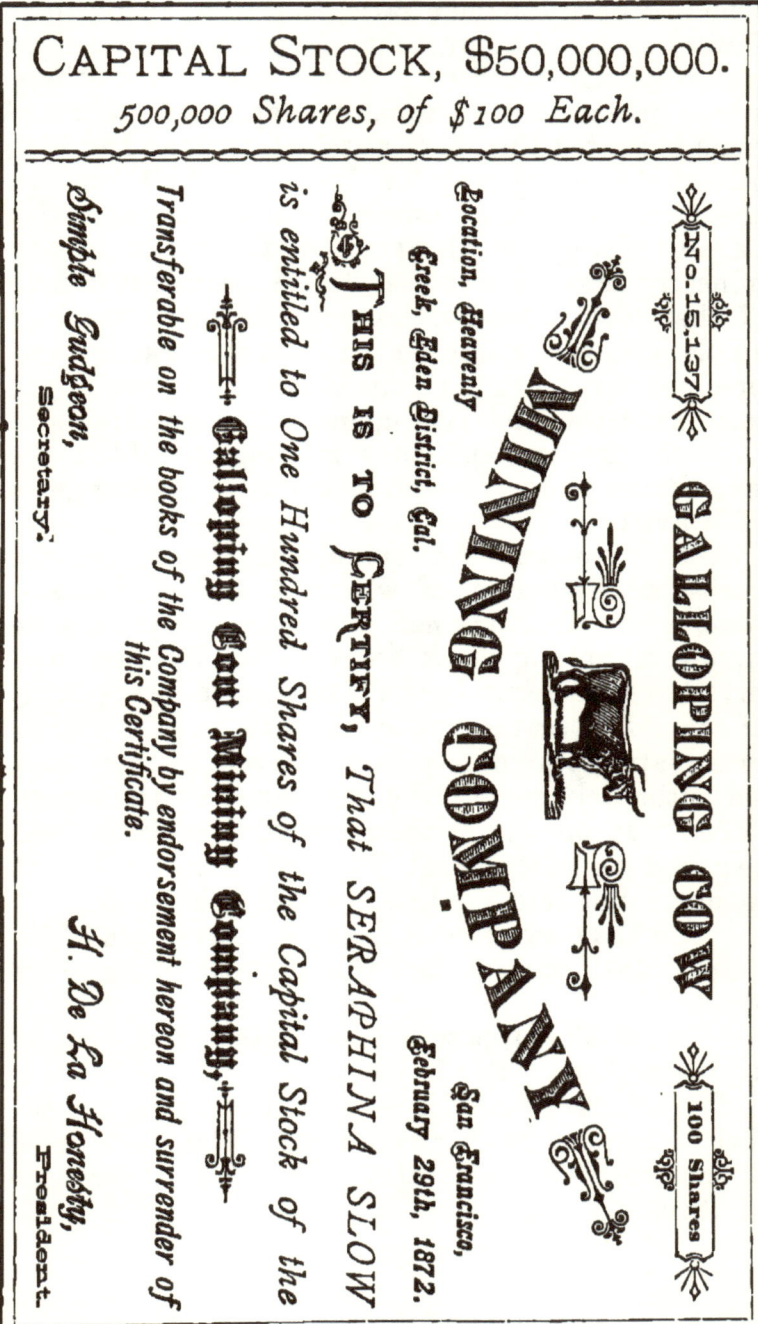

CAPITAL STOCK, $50,000,000.

500,000 Shares, of $100 Each.

No. 15,137

GALLOPING COW

MINING COMPANY

Location, Heavenly Creek, Eden District, Cal.

THIS IS TO CERTIFY, That SERAPHINA SLOW is entitled to One Hundred Shares of the Capital Stock of the

Galloping Cow Mining Company,

Transferable on the books of the Company by endorsement hereon and surrender of this Certificate.

San Francisco,
February 29th, 1872.

100 Shares

Simple Gudgeon,
Secretary.

H. De La Honesty,
President.

M

Passing hastily by Mrs. Slow, who had learned by
some means that he was a large holder of Sierra
Navada, and was preparing to introduce herself and
her talent to his notice, the General made his way
back to the Baldwin. He was full of thought.
Many men would have felt proud and vain of
the success so rapidly achieved. He experienced no
elation and uttered no self-congratulation. He
recognized the fact that he had been used as an
instrument by destiny, or by the never failing
justice of the immutable Ruler of the Universe, to
compel restitution and deal out retributive punishment. Now the work was all but accomplished.
Whilst he viewed with pleasure the prospect of re-
claiming and rehabilitating Wily, he began to inquire of himself, had he not allowed his justly
provoked anger and displeasure against Trackem &
Cinchem to carry him too far? He had planned the
measures by which they were compelled to relin-
quish Wily's properties. So far he had no regret,
but the thing did not end there, and he was not
quite satisfied that it was his duty to be the judge
and executioner of the delinquents beyond that
point. On one thing he had firmly resolved : after
he had appropriated enough of the funds to cover
his own outlay and make payment for Wily's properties, he would not use one cent of the balance;
he would distribute it amongst the various charities,
and even that should be done anonymously. He
did not want the money, and he would have felt it
to be beneath himself to possess one dollar which
had been acquired, not by honest industry, but

by a favoring circumstance, in a system, that of stock gambling, which he believed to be corrupting in its nature, and debasing to its votaries. Nor did he credit himself with any ability in the accomplishment of his purposes. He had seen enough to know that such operations as he had engaged in would nineteen times out of twenty result in great financial loss. This had turned out a succcess because destiny willed it. Full of these thoughts, he entered his room, and opening his organ and placing before him the " Oratorio of Israel in Egypt," he played with spirit and power that triumphant song of Moses and Myriam, in which the Israelites, having escaped from the Egyptians, justly attribute their escape and the overthrow of their jois to the omnipotent arm of Jehovah. It was a habit with General Sterne when strongly moved to seek his piano or organ, and the music he produced at such times would, by its correspondence with his feelings, serve as an index by which the listener might learn his moods.

At seven o'clock, according to appointment, Wiley entered the General's room, and reported to him that he had disposed of seventeen hundred shares of stock at an average of a little under twenty-five dollars a share, and that he had carefully scattered the stock through several brokers' hands.

" That is well, Wily," said the General, " continue to sell them quietly until you have disposed of them all."

Wily looked disappointed, and remarked : " Don't

you think you had better hold on, General ? I do not think the deal has more than begun yet ?"

" No !" said the General firmly, " I think I have accomplished the purpose I had in view ; I now wish to close the transaction as early as possible. By-the-by, Wily, suppose you had your ranch and other properties, and were out of stocks, and situated as you once were, do you think you would wish to gamble again ?"

" Not much, General," answered Wily ; " I would sooner cut my right hand off !   A man may make a winning now and then, as you have just done, but if he goes on he will be busted sure."

" You must understand, Wily," said the General, " that I only went into the venture to try an experiment, and have no intention to make any more in the same direction ; and that reminds me, Wily, of a circumstance I wish to name to you, to which you must on no account make any allusion : There is in San Francisco at the present time a company of several gentlemen who meet once a week.   They are all members of a society, the existence of which is known only to themselves. It is called the ' Society in Search of Truth.'   I want you on Tuesday evening to attend that meeting with me as a visitor and give some evidence on stock operations ; you can go from here with me if you choose."

" Only too happy," answered Wily.

And then he added : " I did not tell you of a surprise I had the day before yesterday.   Mrs. Clare's man-servant proves to be my only brother, who had not seen or heard of me for eighteen years; never since I ran away from home to go to sea, when I was a little fellow about twelve years old."

" I am afraid you were very neglectful of your family, Wily; was he pleased to see you ?"

"More pleased than I deserved. It was a pleasant surprise to both of us," responded Wily.

" I am very glad to hear it. By the way, I want you to meet me at my attorney's (Mr. Equity's) office; you know it—at two o'clock to-morrow. I think there will be another pleasant surprise to meet you there."

CHAPTER XXIX.

WILL WILY HAS EMOTIONS.

The brothers Wily spent much of their time together. The duties of James were very light, and William now gave all the spare time he had to his brother. He also made the acquaintance of Annette, Mrs. Clare's French maid, whom he thought the smartest and brightest little woman he had ever met. She was, in fact, just like hundreds of other French girls in her position. She was pretty because there was no especial feature which forbade the application of the term to a bright, cheery, dark-eyed girl, who was always brisk and lively, and who intensely amused William by the quickness of her movements and the pertness of her sallies.

William looked to see her every time he called,

nor was he often dissapointed. Sharp little women
of a little over twenty can ordinarily contrive to
manufacture a few moments in which to speak to a
man they like to meet, no matter how pressing
their other duties are.   And then she was really a
good-hearted girl, and probably thought that William liked to see her very much, and so out of the
very kindness of her heart she could not bear to
disappoint the poor fellow.

William had already begun to think that if he
had the old home which once was his, how pleasant
it would be to have a bright little woman like her
to preside over it.   But then his home was gone,
and it would be many a long day before he had
such another.   He knew the General was about to
give him a new start, but he did not know in what
way.

"James," he said to his brother, as Annette left
the room in which she had remained with them for
a few minutes, " that is one of the smartest little
women I ever saw.   If I had my old ranch now, I
would ask her to be my wife to-morrow.''

"And you might do much worse, William," answered James, "Annette is a good girl; she has
been with Mrs. Clare six years; she was only sixteen when she came to us; first she was parlor-
maid, and since has been lady's-maid to Mrs. Clare;
I don't know what Mrs. Clare could do without
her."

" Oh, that's got to come anyway," said William,
" she don't expect to keep her forever.   But there,
its no use my talking, I haven't enough to buy a

broom with, let alone a wife to look after it."

This conversation took place on the evening of the day in which the events transpired that are mentioned in the last chapter. The following morning William Wily was astir betimes, and from the opening of the business of the day, was watching the stock market, and was successful in reducing the number of the general shares. During the noon recess he collected the coin due for the stock sold as he had been directed, and deposited it to the General's credit at his bankers. It now wanted only a few minutes to two o'clock. Wily therefore proceeded to Mr. Equity's office, where he found General Sterne in consultation with the attorney. In a few moments Trackem and Cinchem entered, accompanied by the cashier of the bank they used. The clerk ushered them into the private office, and requested Wily to enter also, which he did, wondering what it all meant. As he entered he observed that a considerable bundle of papers lay in front of Mr. Equity, and that he held in his hand a check, which he could see bore the bank mark of certification.

"Gentlemen, please be seated ; we are all ready. I hold in my hand a certified cheque for fifty-seven thousand five hundred dollars. This document," laying his hand on a lengthy manuscript before him, "is an absolute conveyance of the following properties :" enumerating all the pieces of real estate which had been conveyed, piecemeal by Wily to Trackem & Cinchem, "which you, Mr. Trackem and Mr. Cinchem, as owners, and you, Mr. Goldnote,

as mortgagee, are required to sign, conveying all
the joint and several interests of you all to Mr.
William Wily, his heirs and assigns. The deed is a
long one; do you wish me to read it ? "

Trackem now looked at Cinchem, and Cinchem
returned the look with interest. It was but a
glance, but there was accusation on the part of the
former, and recrimination on that of the latter. It
was understood by both—each knew what the other
meant : " Here is the man that we ensnared and
plundered, and all our labor is lost," and whilst
Trackem signaled : " It is your fault," Cinchem re-
buked it on Trackem. Either of them could have
danced with rage. But there were witnesses. Their
banker, Mr. Goldnote, was there ; General Sterne,
whom they now both feared and hated, was there ;
the General's attorney, whom they had also swindled, was there ; and then Wily himself was present, and might they not plunder him again as they
had done before ? Mr. Trackem, catching at the
hope, rose and approaching Wily, held out his hand,
saying :—

" I congratulate you, Mr. Wily, on the recovery
of the property you were so unfortunate as to
lose."

He was instantly followed by Cinchem, who
said :—

" I always told you the tide would turn with you,
Mr. Wily."

If Trackem & Cinchem were amazed, Wily was
even more so. He did not know what the reconvey-
ance of his old estates to him meant. He therefore

bowed his head in acknowledgment of the congratulations offered by the now obsequious brokers, but not one word did he utter.

The General and Mr. Equity watched their movements. They estimated the congratulations at their true value.

Mr. Equity now repeated the question : "Do you wish me to read the document, gentlemen ? "

Mr. Goldnote answered : " I do not think it is necessary, Mr. Equity ; our attorney has perused it, and is satisfied."

Trackem and Cinchem replied simultaneously : " It is not at all necessary."

" Then, gentlemen, I will ask you to append your signatures."

The three names were appended in due order. Mr. Equity handed the certified cheque to Mr. Goldnote, and the three retired, both Trackem and Cinchem shaking hands with Wily and requesting him to call and see them very often.

Mr. Equity handed over the documents to Wily, and said to him : " Mr. Wily, I have much pleasure in giving you these papers, which restore to you your properties," after which, having business to attend to elsewhere, he excused himself and retired.

When he was gone, Wily rose from his seat, and approaching General Sterne, said :—

" What does all this mean, General ? I do not understand it. I can never repay you the fifty-seven thousand five hundred dollars you have advanced me."

" You have nothing to pay me, Wily, that is your share of our Alta venture."

" Why, General," said Wily, " it is more than half of what you stand to make, and you risked seventy thousand dollars to make it, whilst I hadn't a dollar to risk."

" You make a mistake, Wily," answered the General, " I did not risk my money to make money for myself, but to regain for you your rights, and punish the men who swindled you, and who would do it again could they find an opportunity. Already they are plotting to accomplish it."

" Which they never will," said Wily, " so long as God gives me my senses. Never will I gamble in stocks again. But, General, it is wrong for me to take this money from you; I have not earned it, and I have no right to it."

" Wily," said the General, "again you make a mistake. This is your money, which I have been the instrument in causing Trackem & Cinchem to disgorge. It is right for you to keep it—it is your own. It would be wrong for me to keep it. Of the balance that may come to me, I may say it is already disposed of. I will not retain one cent of the money gained in a business so stained with iniquity, nor should I like to see you take a single dollar more than your own, even from the men who robbed you. And remember, I hold you to your promise to quit stock gambling."

" You need not remind me of that, General," he said, and then sat down to think. Wily sat in silence some minutes. The General did not interrupt his thoughts. All his life, in that short time, like a moving panorama, passed before him. He saw the happy home of his careless boyish days. He saw his old father and mother weeping for the loss of himself—the runaway boy. He saw the scenes and places in which he labored, whilst working his way to California. He saw his own homestead, of which he was the contented owner. He saw himself intoxicated with the madness of stock gambling. He saw himself a ruined, desperate man, recklessly rushing towards a drunkard's grave. He saw his brother taking the prodigal into the arms of love. He saw Annette no longer in the far, unattainable future, but his, when he could win her. He saw his old father and mother in their poverty in the distant cottage home, and was thankful he could help them now. He saw General Sterne as an angel of God who had saved him from self-destruction and made a man of him again. His heart was too full for utterance. Reverently taking the General's hand into both his own, he pressed it to his lips, and turning slowly, walked out of the office.

CHAPTER XXX.

CAPTAIN BLAND FINDS HIMSELF A HERO.

When the young ladies left Mrs. Clare, she had no foreboding of evil. They were both good horsewomen, and under the care of Mr. Carleton and Captain Bland, with James Wily in attendance, she had no doubt but they would have a pleasant ride and greatly enjoy themselves. Loving Rose and Geraldine as she did, their pleasure and enjoyments always gave her satisfaction ; and having a sincere regard for both Mr. Carleton and Captain Bland, she had trusted the young ladies to their care without any hesitation. After they were gone, she amused herself with reading and music. She did not leave her drawing room. Mrs. Clare's nature was one of the kind which may be said to be self-contained. Though always charming, and sometimes brilliant, when in society, it was never from a love of display. The charm of her manner was the result of culture and refined society on a mental organization naturally contemplative. She could always find pleasure in her own society. Her mind rarely lost its poise. Great however was her consternation, when in less than an hour after the party had left, Mr. Carleton entered her room alone. She saw the troubled look on his face, and instantly divined some accident had happened.

"Mr Carleton," she said, "you are the bearer of bad news ; do not hesitate, but tell me at once what it is."

"I am grieved, madam, to have to inform you that Miss Pye has been thrown from her horse in the park."

Mrs. Clare's anxiety now became terrible. She rose and rang the bell for her maid.

"Is she seriously hurt, Mr. Carleton ?" she asked.

"I hope not, madam," he replied; "Captain Bland, who was just behind her, caught her in his arms as she was thrown backward from her saddle."

"Annette," said Mrs. Clare to her maid as she entered, "see if my brother is in his room; if so, ask him to step here at once. Then order his carriage for me, and tell Johnson to have it at the door as quickly as possible, and prepare to accompany me. Now, Mr. Carlton, tell me how it happened."

" A dog rushing from the shrubbery startled Miss Pye's horse," answered Frank ; " it bolted, and struck a carriage turning a corner. I did not witness the accident. James, who saw it, gave me the particulars. I will now return."

" Do, Mr. Carleton ; I shall not be far behind you."

*　　*　　*　　*　　*　　*　　*　　*　　*

When Milton had uttered his sad lament, and pressed that first kiss on the brow of the unconcious Rose, he continued to kneel beside her, still gazing at her, and was apparently unaware of the presence of Geraldine, who sat watching her, and occasionally glancing up at Milton, whose countenance bore the expression of such unutterable woe, that, still wondering, she began to realize that poignant as was her own grief, he was a yet greater sufferer. The clatter of horses' hoofs was now heard ; glancing along the drive, she saw the gentleman on Milton's horse running with the stimulant he had directed him to procure. At the same time she heard a carriage approaching in an opposite direction. James Wily, in defiance of the park commissioners' regulations, was urging a pair of horses to their utmost speed, whilst the owner of the carriage followed behind on James' horse at an equally rapid pace. Milton did not stir ; his whole thought and care were concentrated on Rose, from

whom he did not raise his eyes even for a moment.
He thought he saw a slight heaving of her bosom,
and the faintest tinge of color slowly mounting to
her cheek, and then he heard a sigh, so soft that no
other ear than that of a lover or a tender mother
could have caught it.   Leaning over Rose, he
touched Geraldine, and in a low tone, in which his
whole soul seemed concentrated, he said :—

"Thank God, she lives !"

Subdued as were the accents, Rose heard them,
and opened her eyes.   She looked at Milton, then at
Geraldine, and asked :—

"Where am I?   What has happened ?"

As she murmured the second question, she turned
her eyes again to Milton.   As she looked up at him,
a flush spread over her face and died away.

What was it ? Did she read in those glad, tender
eyes the tale of love he had uttered beside her inanimate form ?   Did she notice the tears still linger-
ing on his cheek ?   Did she feel the kiss which he
had pressed upon her brow ? or had her spirit told
her wakening heart of the scene which it, not she,
had witnessed ?

Geraldine answered :—

"You were thrown from your horse, dear, but you
did not fall to the ground.   Captain Bland, who
was just behind you, caught you in his arms."

Again that momentary flush, and Rose said :—

"Yes, I remember; my horse struck against a
carriage.   Where is he now ?"

"He is here, dear," replied Geraldine.   She did
n)t tell her he was motionless, and getting cold and

stiff. The blow he had received when he struck the carriage had killed him.

"Do you feel hurt, Rose, dear? Have you any pain?" she asked.

"I scarcely know," replied Rose; "I think not. I feel shaken and weary, but I don't think I have any pain."

The carriage and the horseman were both waiting. Milton now sprang to his feet, and bringing the wine which the stranger had procured for him, poured out a glass, which he passed to Geraldine to hold whilst he tenderly raised Rose into a sitting posture, and then handed her the glass, saying :—

"Drink this wine, Miss Pye. It will revive you."

Rose took the wine, and said :—

"Thank you, Captain Bland; I think I can get on my horse now."

"No, Miss Pye," said Milton, firmly, "that must not be. I have procured a carriage for you, and James shall drive you home; and, with your permission, I will accompany you."

Instructing the stable man to take charge of the saddle horses, and directing James Wily to drive, and to avoid shaking the carriage, as far as possible, he assisted Rose, and afterwards Geraldine, into it, and then, having thanked the gentleman who procured the wine, entered himself.

They had not gone very far when they met Mr. Carleton, riding as hard as his horse could pelt. In his headlong haste he passed the carriage, and would have gone on, to find the dead horse sole occupant of the spot where he left his friends, had not James hailed him from the box. He quickly wheeled round and rode up beside the carriage, where he was delighted to find that Rose, though looking pale, was apparently not seriously harmed by her perilous adventure. He informed the party of the approach of Mrs. Clare, and then putting spurs to his foaming horse, dashed forward to meet her and impart the pleasing intelligence.

Annette had quickly returned to Mrs. Clare's room, ready to accompany her, and informed her that the Commodore had gone out. Mrs. Clare descended to the carriage at once, and Johnson, acting on her instruction, took such a pace out of the the Commodore's bays as they had never been required to exhibit since they had come into his possession.

The suffering of Mrs. Clare on that journey was such as she had never experienced since those long by-gone days of her early widowhood. The uncertainty and suspense were terrible. Mr. Carleton had doubtless told her what he believed was true, but then by his own account Rose was insensible when he left her. She might be dead, and at the thought a groan burst from her which alarmed Annette, who as yet knew nothing of the cause of their hurried journey. Mrs. Clare recovered herself, and thought of her dear, loving child. She thought of her as the all but helpless infant she had received from her brother's arms and promised to love and rear in such manner that she should never know the loss of her dead mother's love. She thought of the winning ways and merry laughter of the romping prattler; she saw her in her demure propriety, when, a little child, she first allowed her to go to church; she remembered how she had watched over Rose in sickness, and how she herself (when the victim of suffering), had been tenderly nursed by the loving girl; she remembered how, through all the stages of budding womanhood she had loved and cherished her, and now, when the fruition of her labors was an hourly delight to her heart, was she to lose her thus? If so, what would her brother do? Already he idolized her. She dare not think of it.

Happily her suspense was soon to end, for Mr. Carleton, dashing up to the carriage, his horse reek-with foam, informed her that Rose had recovered from her faint, and was now on the way with Miss Stanley and Captain Bland, and would soon meet her.

More thankful than words could express, grateful also to Mr. Carleton for his attention to herself, and truly glad that the Commodore had been prevented by absence from sharing in her anxiety and alarm, she still hurried forward. She could not rest until her own eyes had seen the loved girl, and her own ears heard from Rose's lips that she was unharmed. When the carriages met, she at once left her own and entered the one occupied by Rose and Geraldine and Captain Bland, and taking the seat beside Rose, vacated for her by Geraldine, she tenderly embraced her, inquiring :—

"Are you sure you are not hurt, my darling?"

"I think not, mamma," said Rose.

There was a tender, thoughtful look in her eyes —the 'boy god' had been busy with her heart during that short drive, and though thoughtful, she seemed happy. Her usual color had all but returned. Several times on the way when she had caught the eyes of Milton, full of gladness and affection, resting upon her, it had more than returned. Her young heart swelled with an emotion which was new and full of delight.

" But, dear mamma," she added, " I am so sorry you were informed of my accident. I know it made you very anxious, and all about nothing."

" It was all done for the best, my dear," replied Mrs. Clare. " It was very good of Mr. Carleton to come and inform me of it. It might have been so much worse. But I am glad your papa did not hear of it. Fortunately he had just gone out when Mr. Carleton arrived."

" Oh, I am so glad," said Rose, and busied herself with her own happy thoughts, whilst Mrs. Clare questioned and cross-questioned Captain Bland and Geraldine until she had elicited every particular of the circumstances attending Rose's peril and escape. When the story was complete, she held out her hand to him and said :—

" I do not know how to thank you, Captain Bland. You have undoubtedly saved Rose from dreadful injury, perhaps from death."

Rose glanced across at Milton, a shy, grateful pleasure in the look, which thrilled him with an answering joy.

" I fear, madam, I have been much to blame for

selecting the horses we procured this morning. I was assured by the owner that the two ridden by the young ladies were perfectly quiet and reliable. I fear I was not sufficiently careful."

"Do not Blame yourself, Captain Bland," said Mrs. Clare, "but accept my gratitude, which I know will be shared by my brother, for the gallant act which probably saved dear Rose's life. As to the accident, it was to occur; it might, and probably would, have happened with any other horse under similar circumstances. The disaster was dreadful. To you we owe the escape of Rose from, possibly, death."

When they arrived at the hotel, although Rose declared she was entirely recovered, the Commodore insisted on sending for a doctor. He then requested a full account of the accident. When it was concluded, he said to Milton :—

"You have laid me under obligations, Captain Bland, which I shall never be able to repay to you."

"I trust not, Commodore," he replied, momentarily glancing at Rose, who read his meaning : that some day he would ask the Commodore for her.

The Commodore's expressions of gratitude to Milton were supplemented by Mrs. Clare and Geraldine. Milton would have been less or more than human if in such circumstances he had not experienced some elation at finding himself " the hero of the day."

CHAPTER XXXI.

THE NIGHT OF THE MUSICAL PARTY.

When the physician who answered the summons of the Commodore was told the circumstances of the case upon which he was called to attend, he " looked wise."

General Sterne, who chanced to be present, subsequently remarked : " I have observed that doctors almost invariably do look wise ; and that some have so ably cultivated the art of looking wise, and have arrived at such perfection, that I have felt inclined to apply to them the adage, 'solemn as a ——.' I am not very sure whether it is a judge or a jackass ; anyway, it is immaterial, seeing that the line of demarkation is in some instances so extremely narrow that it is often difficult to discover the difference between the two animals But it is not their fault ; the donkeys cannot help themselves, for nature made them so, and the judges I alluded to are scarcely to blame, for (though they had no knowledge of law or general fitness for the positions they occupy), not themselves, but the popular vote made them judges.   Now, with regard to the wise look of some of the followers of Esculapius it is otherwise.   Their wise looks are the result of study and practice. The masks they wear, by long use, have become a part of their faces —it a species of humbug.   But then it is humbug which pays.   It is an absolute necessity to some doctors : they could do nothing without it.   Nor is the humbug confined to looks. It is humbug to write p'escriptions in hieroglyphics and Latin, when plain English would be much better. But then a prescription written thus—

> ℞ Sodium chloride, 3i,
> Aqua distillata, Oss.,
> ℳ S. 3i. ter die.
>   X. Y. Z.

looks so very much wiser, and is consequently so much more advantageous to both doctor and chemist than it would be if written as follows :—

> A pinch of salt.
> Half a pint of cold water.
> Take a teaspoonful three times a day.

But even here the doctor is less to blame than his patients. The solemnity of his face and the mystery of his prescriptions are to the unlearned evidences of his wisdom. This he knows, and upholds the humbug, because humbug pays.

To the credit of the worthy doctor called in by the Commodore, notwithstanding the temptation of having a rich patient on his hands, after some questions, and careful observation of Rose, he declared that she was convalescent; but remarked that as she had received a severe shock, which had resulted in a swoon, he thought it desirable that for a few days she should be quiet and avoid strong exercise and excitement, when, he said, he did not doubt she would be perfectly restored.

When the doctor had left the room, Mrs. Clare suggested the postponement of the musical party which was to meet in the evening. The proposition was strenuously opposed by Rose. A compromise was finally effected, Mrs. Clare stipulating that Rose should use the couch during the evening, and on no account take part in the musical performances. At eight o'clock, Judge Blank and Milton, accompanied by Mr. Carleton, arrived, and were immediately followed by General Sterne.

Milton had told his uncle of Rose's misfortune, but he had not mentioned the fact that he had arrested her fall, nor given any intimation of the pain which he had suffered from the shock. When Milton received the whole of Rose's weight on his right arm, he thought the arm was going with her. Athletic and muscular as he was, the wrench was so severe as to cause him much pain for some days after. He was, therefore, very glad to draw a chair beside Rose's couch, and to claim exemption from contribution to the musical exercises of the evening. This he did on the plea that he must be in attendance on Miss Pye; for the couch on which she reclined, he said, might possibly prove as treacherous as the horse she rode in the morning

Rose, during the intervening hours, had been examining her own heart. She had a vague impresison of words of love uttered by Milton, and of warm lips pressed to her forehead whilst slowly returning to consciousness. She had seen the looks with which he had regarded her. She had heard the tones of fervent gratitude with which he had uttered the words, "Thank God, she lives," and she had rightly read every look he gave her, and noted the tenderness of his every word and action that had reference to her on that journey home. She could not be mistaken He loved her, and would tell her so. Her pulse quickened at the thought, and a glad, happy smile played on her sunny face. But then she had known him only a few days. Might she not be mistaken What if all the sympathy and kindness of to-day were but the result of friendly pleasure at her escape from death? Perhaps, after all, he did not love her She, admiring his noble, manly presence and his gentleness to her, had let her heart go to him. She could not recall it. Perhaps he did not want it Then he should never know her love for him She could die with shame, if she thought he believed she was putting herself in his way She would school herself. She would guard her actions and her looks. Nothing would she say or do to betray her love to him. But he had been very kind to her. He had saved her from serious injury, probably from death. She could not be rude to him. She could not be unkind to him. What should she do? Had there been anything that was definite which she could have stated, she would unhesitatingly have divulged it to Mrs. Clare. But there was nothing to tell. And then their acquaintance was so very recent. She could seek no counsel. She could do nothing but guard herself and wait. She finally resolved that she would treat him with all the friendly kindness which he, as her preserver, deserved at her hands; but no word or look should betray the love he had awakened.

Milton, sitting beside her and conversing with her, felt that there was a change, and sought to analyze it. She had seemed so near to him a few hours ago,

and now a barrier had risen which appeared insur-
mountable. What was it ? Had he offended her?
It was impossible. Was she a coquette? He looked
at the pure, truthful face beside him and scorned
the thought. What was the change ? She was not
less amiable. In her present condition of a semi-
invalid she seemed more beautiful. But she was
different. The voice that spoke to him gave forth
calm and measured accents. The eyes that looked
at him were full of kindness. But the love-light
which in the morning had beamed a joyous response
to his own fond glance was gone. What did it
mean ?

Did she love another ? Had she, in the moments
of gratitude to him for saving her life forgotten
that other love? and now, after hours of reflection,
returned to the sense of duty? If so, God help
him. He felt sure no power of his could swerve
her from her loyalty to duty and Truth. All these
thoughts passed through his mind as he sat beside
her, he questioning, and she answering him in a
gentle, quiet way, but with no sign or token of the
love he had fondly hoped had been awakened for
himself alone. And so the evening passed by, and
when at its close Milton left the room with his
uncle, he thought her farther removed from him
than on the first day he met her. What was this
something that had come between them ? Rose's
actions were distant from those of the common flirt
or coquette, whose smiles are shams, whose frowns
are masks, whose mind is too selfishly small and
shallow to love or to hate in earnest, who pursues

her own wiles to gratify her own vanity and self-love without regard to any other thing than self-gratification. No; Milton felt and knew that her heart was too pure and her nature too noble to trifle with the hopes or happiness of another. Her disposition was such that she could not bear to inflict suffering on any living thing. Sooner would she suffer, herself, than be the cause of suffering to others. She delighted in knowing that everybody who knew her loved her, and in seeing everybody and everything around her happy. She had been to Milton, all through that evening, as kind as she could be, but it was the kindness of a sister, calm, gentle and unimpassioned. He had looked in vain for the warm, answering glances of love, and the tell-tale blush which he was sure were given, and all for him, in the morning.

Rose had seen the troubled look which occasionally crossed his features during the evening, and had asked herself: What was the cause of it? Had he in her society been recreant to duty? Had he some other tie which honor bound him to respect? If so, herself alone should know the sorrow of her heart. The knowledge of her love should live and die with her. Oh, she thought, that woman had man's privilege! How speedily would she solve the mystery. But no, it must not, could not be. She must wait; and if heaven willed it, she would suffer, and no human ear should ever hear a murmur from her lips.

Rose's couch had been placed at the opposite end of the room to the piano, consequently Milton and herself had been left all but to themselves, as the rest of the party congregated around the instrument.

Commodore Pye told Judge Bland of the part of Milton in the morning's adventure which Milton had concealed. The Judge listened with intense interest and satisfaction to the words of praise and expressions of gratitude with which the Commodore spoke of "his boy."

"Commodore," said the delighted Judge, "it is like a chapter from a romance, in which 'my boy' is the gallant knight and your lovely daughter the lady fair."

And then both were silent, the Judge thinking to himself: This is the secret, then. It is not the magnificent Geraldine, but the fair-haired Rose, 'my boy' is seeking to win. I daresay he is right. I must observe her more closely.

Meantime the Commodore was trying to solve a problem: Was Captain Bland to be the man who was to rob him of his newly restored Rose ? If he won her love and asked his consent, what could he say ? Nothing. In birth, education and fortune he was her equal. In mind, manners and appearance he was all he could wish for as a son-in-law. But he did not want a son-in-law; at least, not yet. He could not bear to think of losing Rose so soon. And then he looked at both of them. He saw the calm, even manner of Rose ; he flattered himself that he had no cause for present alarm. As to the future, it must care for itself. God grant his darling might be happy, anyway.

The evening's music was a great success, General Sterne and Mr. Carleton both aiding Mrs. Clare and Geraldine, thereby greatly adding to the enjoyment of the circle.

During the evening the General had many opportunities of studying Geraldine. Nothing so much charmed him in her as those gradual transformia- which invariably occurred when her spirit was stirred by the sentiments she heard or uttered, either in conversation or in song. It then appeared to her observers as if she were some sublime effort of the statuary's skill, which was then and there endowed with soul and life by the word of Truth or the harmony of sound. The transitions were waited for and watched for by the General, who soon learned to know as by intuition, when to expect them.

Nor was the General less a study to Geraldine, who had already expressed her opinion regarding him, which so far she had in no wise changed. Her keen, penetrating mind sought to find a solution to that certain something in his bearing which at their first interview had repelled her. If she had been unjust in her strictures, she would like to know it. She could be severe in her expressions, but she could not knowingly be unjust. She was destined to have given to her by the General the key to much she could not understand.

Placing a chair by hers during an interval in the music, he said to her :—

"It may appear strange when I tell you that this

is the first evening in eighteen years that I have spent in a lady's drawing-room."

"Such being the case, General Sterne, we should esteem ourselves greatly honored by your presence," said Geraldine. "Will you tell me why you have for so long a time avoided the society of ladies?"

For a moment the General searchingly regarded her. Did his ear detect a covert of sarcasm in the first portion of her remark? No; her look was expressive of interest, certainly, not of sarcasm. Should he answer her question? and if so, how? What if he were to tell her his story? which he never yet had told to living man or woman. He would like to watch her whilst she listened to the tale of his youthful sorrow.

"Miss Stanley," he answered, "I will reply to your question. It is a story no other being has ever heard from me. When I was quite a boy my parents died, leaving me in the charge of my uncle, a Virginian gentleman, whose estates adjoined those bequeathed to me by my father. My uncle had a daughter, who was two years my junior. My cousin Belle and I grew up together, and when but boy and girl, we promised each other we would marry when we were old enough. Belle's disposition and moods were as variable as the shadows of the forest trees when swayed by the breeze. She was a lovely girl, and I allowed my pleasures to give way to hers at all times. When I was seventeen I left my uncle's home and went to Harvard, only returning to spend the vacations in Virginia, always finding Belle more lovely than before. When I was twenty and she was eighteen we were formally engaged, with my uncle's consent and approbation. I believe he was delighted with the prospect of our union. I returned to college, and having completed my studies, arrived at home in time to celebrate my twenty-first birthday. Belle and I were to be married one month later At this time she was radiantly beautiful, and seemed perfectly happy. Again I left home for New York, to procure fitting bridal gifts for my Belle. I returned two days before our appointed wedding day. I found blank faces on every side. The truth was soon told to me. The preceding day she had fled her home with a worthless neighbor of ours and was married to him. Her father's anger was terrible. He would have killed her husband could he have found him then. I counselled him to leave them to the punishment of heaven. I then sold my properties, and from that time to this I have been a wanderer, and, I had almost said, a vagabond, on the earth. I schooled myself to hate the very name of woman. That is why, Miss Stanley, I have constantly avoided social life for so many years."

" I fear, General Sterne," said Geraldine," " that I have thoughtlessly given you pain by requesting this recital from you ? I am truly sorry."

" Not at all, Miss Stanley, I have lived down the pain and grief long years ago."

" And what became of your counsin, General ? "

" She lived only a short time. The brutality and

neglect of her husband killed her before she had been a wife a year.'

"And her husband?" said Geraldine.

"He became a ruined and desperate man. I do not even know if he lives. It is many years since I heard of him."

"This," thought Geraldine, when the company was gone, and she had retired to her own room, "is the secret of that dark look which I so misread and mistrusted. I have been most unjust. Will he ever be really happy again? or is that gone from him forever? Poor General Sterne! I am truly sorry for him."

CHAPTER XXXII.

WHICH CONTAINS A PECK OF TROUBLE.

The morning after Mrs. Clare's musical party a dispatch was received by Captain Bland, the contents of which were as follows :—

WASHINGTON.

CAPTAIN BLAND,

Palace Hotel, San Francisco :—

I am directed by the War Department to recall your leave of absence, and instruct you to proceed at once to Oregon, and there to raise such forces as you can, and protect the settlers against the Indian raiders.

—— —— ——,

Colonel ——- Reg't.

True to the call of duty, Milton's first thought was to consult the papers. He found that a steamer was advertised to sail that day at noon. He next went to his uncle's room and informed him of his sudden departure.

"It is too bad, 'my boy,'" said the Judge; "but," he added, "duty must be attended to."

The Judge spent an hour with Milton, aiding him in procuring such things as he required, and getting everything in order to start, and then, having a little time to spare, they resolved to call on their friends at the Baldwin, and apprise them of Milton's intended departure, and bid them good bye.

Judge and Captain Bland sent up their cards. The ladies were at home, and would be pleased to see them.

The Commodore was in Mrs. Clare's parlor with his sister and daughters when they entered.

Milton had just taken Rose's hand in his when the Judge said: "We have come on a farewell visit, Mrs. Clare: 'my boy' has received orders to go direct to Oregon and assist in putting down the outbreak of the Bannock Indians. He sails to-day at twelve o'clock."

Rose had caught the word "farewell," and listened with eager interest to each succeeding word. Her hand remained in Milton's; she did not withdraw it. She seemed unconscious of the fact. She stood with parted lips and bated breath, waiting the conclusion of the Judge's remark, and then all the resolutions of the preceding evening vanished from her mind; Milton was there—he was going away to fight the treacherous Indians—he was go-

ing now. Perhaps he would be killed; but if he
lived she would be gone to France before he could
return. Looking up into his face whilst the rising
tears suffused her eyes, and almost choked her utterance, she said :—

"It is the end. We shall never meet again."
How can I portray Milton's feelings? How
place before my reader the varied emotions of
which he was the subject? Last night he had all
but arrived at the conclusion that his love was
hopeless. This morning he had been almost relieved to think that he was to be engaged in the stir-
ring scenes of active warfare. And now, before the
sun had reached meridian height, the Truth had
flashed upon him, and the mournful wail of Rose's
loving heart, breaking forth in the words she uttered : " It is the end. We shall never meet again,"
had filled his very being with such mingled joy and
sorrow—joy in knowing she loved him; sorrow
at the knowledge they must part; that he, holding
firm her hand in his, stood dumb and motionless,
whilst inclination waged a war with duty. It was
a fearful struggle. What to him were honor, duty,
name, or fame, compared with Rose? But could
he offer her a sullied name? Could he, with such
a prize in view, prove recreant to duty? No. So
duty triumphed. Then he spoke :—

"I will return to you, nor time, nor space shall
hinder. Dear Rose, farewell."

"May God preserve you, Milton." That was all
she said, and glided from the room.

Captain Bland now hastened his adieux.

"Come back to us soon," said the Commodore, "we do not forget the debt we owe you."

"We shall miss you and look for your return, and pray for your preservation," said Mrs. Clare.

"I feel," said the proud Geraldine, "as if I were losing a brother. Remember what you have spoken, and soon return." She laid her hand in his as she spoke.

"I will return; I will remember," said Milton, "God bless you, my sister." This last was spoken in a low tone, and was unnoticed by the rest.

Geraldine read and understood him aright, and for love of Rose gave him a sister's love.

"She loves you," she said; "be true."

"True unto death," he answered, and he left the room, his uncle following him.

They now hurried down to the Palace Hotel. Milton's luggage was got together, and the Judge accompanied him to the boat. He noticed that Milton was silent and sad. He said:—

"You do not like this duty 'my boy?'"

"Uncle," he said, "it is true. Last night I should have been glad of it. This morning I rejoiced at it. And now, if honor did not demand my going, I would decline to go. I have a foreboding of evil; may God avert it. You have been a second father to me; to you I must open my heart. Uncle, I love and am loved by Rose Pye; only this morning have I learned her love for me. Watch over her, uncle; she is all the world to me. Write to me often and tell me of her. I leave her to your care."

"Are you betrothed?" inquired Judge Bland.

O

"We are, and we are not," answered Milton. "Last night I was a fool—I was blind. I mistook her maidenly reserve for indifference. This morning I know that my love is returned, and I am the happiest and most miserable fellow living ; my heart bids me linger here ; duty calls me away—you, now, dear uncle, know at what a sacrifice I obey the call of duty. God grant my forebodings prove untrue."

"Amen, 'my boy,'" answered the Judge, "but can you not remain ? Why not throw up your commission ? You do not need it. Why should you sacrifice yourself ? "

The Judge, alarmed for the safety of his nephew, had allowed himself to be carried on to the utterance of words he would never have expressed in his calmer moments.

" It may not be, uncle," said Milton ; "can I, a soldier, quit my post, or turn my back on duty because inclination says remain ? No ; never could I esteem myself worthy of Rose ; never could I regain my self-respect if I failed to obey my country's call in the hour of need. I go. The issue is in higher hands."

" You are right, ' my boy,'" said the Judge. Go, and may the good God preserve you and bring you back to us in safety."

The Judge accompanied Milton on board, inspected his cabin, received Milton's commission to apologize to General Sterne and Frank Carleton for not calling to say good-bye, which he would have done had time permitted, and his reiterated instructions regarding Rose, and then, when the third bell rang, he regained the wharf and watched the vessel out of dock and down the harbor. Then he re-entered the carriage that was waiting for him and returned to the hotel. It was now only eleven days since his boy arrived, but his departure left a void—a blank—in his life which he did not know how to fill. He did not like the mission on which Milton had gone. If he had had his own company behind him, who knew and relied on him, whilst he knew and trusted them, it would have been bad enough, but to have to raise a new company, whom he did know, and which, all undisciplined, he was to lead against a foe wily as a tiger, and treacherous as the waves of ocean, was altogether too bad. Had Milton been called upon to enter the arena of ancient Roman sports, and do the duty of a gladiator, in his opinion, it would not have been worse. The Judge had allowed his affection and anxiety for his boy to carry away his judgment. The facts were few and simple. Milton was no carpet soldier. He had requested more than once, that in event of any emergency arising, he might be put in active duty, and now there was need for his services, he was near at hand; his leave of absence was cancelled, and he directed to go to the front. The Judge would have seen little hardship had the instructions been dispatched to any other man, but his kind heart was stirred by anxiety for and sympathy with Milton, which warped his judgment and made it unjust. The command was given. Milton had received and instantly responded to it. He was gone, and his good old uncle wandered about during the day without a motive or object, solely because he was too restless to be still,

In the afternoon the General called to see Mrs. Clare. Geraldine was with her; Rose was not present; she was weary, she said, and would go and lie down in her own room. She had much to think of. She was quite sure now that Milton loved her—the thought made her happy. But then came the remembrance that he was gone—gone to fight those Indian savages. He might be mutilated—nay, worse—he might be killed. No mutilation could change her love. He might come to her maimed, or lame, or blind—only let him come. A dreadful fear oppressed her that she would never see him more, and so she lay and thought, and thought.

General Sterne was surprised at himself; he could but wonder at the pleasure he experienced when in the presence of Commodore Pye's family. These calls, which were now of daily occurrence, were to him what the oasis in the desert is to the weary, thirsty, dust-choked traveler. Mrs. Clare was greatly interested in the General, whose observations were generally laconic, who had never paid a compliment in her presence, and whose remarks were often tinctured with a racy vein of satire which was fresh and original, and sometimes very amusing to her, though always uttered with the greatest gravity by him. And Geraldine, since that revelation of last evening, felt for him the kindest sympathy, and received him very kindly.

My reader must not suppose that in the growth

of friendly relations there was anything on the part of General Sterne or of Geraldine which approached love. The General had never entertained such a thought, and it had not so much as entered the mind of Geraldine. Their meetings were therefore free and unconstrained, nor did the presence of Mr. Carleton, whom he often met in Mrs. Clare's drawing-room, and whose attentions were always freely bestowed on Geraldine, appear to excite any special attention on his part; in fact, it might have been supposed it was unobserved by him. Mr. Carleton now entered the room.

"So General," said he, when he had made his salutations to Mrs. Clare and Geraldine, "our mutual friend, Captain Bland, has left us; his uncle informs me he received a dispatch from Washington this morning directing him to proceed to Oregon to aid in the suppression of the Indian outbreak."

"Indeed," answered the General, "I had not heard of his summons or departure. Indian troubles are a necessity. Their occurrence is periodical and their effect salutary."

"How so, General?" inquired Mrs. Clare.

"We have an institution, madam," replied the General, "which is known as the Indian Bureau, and another which is known as the United States Army. An occasional scare is good for both those institutions."

"But how about the people, General, is it good for them?" asked Mrs. Clare.

"That, madam," answered the General, "is another question. I have almost arrived at the conclusion that the people were made for the institutions, and not the institutions for the people."

CHAPTER XXXIII.

THE SOCIETY IS AGAIN CALLED TO ORDER.

It was the evening on which was to be held the third meeting of the "Society in Search of Truth." The Judge had had his room put in order for the reception of his guests. He looked around with entire, satisfaction until his eye rested on the chair which he had prepared for "his boy." "Will he ever fill it again?" he murmured. "Will he return to me, or will he perish in the far off wilds of Oregon?" He remembered Milton's forebodings of evil. Ever since he left him the Judge had felt very anxious, and to-day he had been quite depressed, by an undefinable fear of evil, for the presence of which he could not account, and which all his philosophy could not expel from his mind. From whence comes that partial prescience of coming evil, which, not always, but sometimes, foreshadows the trouble that approaches us? Does the angel of destiny whisper to our spirits the secret of the future? or does he, pausing to look at us in sympathy, knowing our coming woe, leave the shadow of his presence on our souls, from which we strive to free ourselves without avail? It is a mystery we cannot solve. But this we know, that sometimes sorrow comes upon us unawares, whilst at other times it "casts its shadow before," and we sit beneath the shadow and feel its gloom whilst we wait, in doubt and fear, the final outcome. The Judge remembered now that he had duties to perform, and that he must be ready to discharge them.

Just then his eye caught and rested on the Venus and Adonis, with the flying Cupid, which adorned Milton's chairs. He asked himself, "Was that thought of mine prophetic? And how will it end?" Poor Rose! He had learned, during these few days of Milton's absence, to love her as his own daughter There was an earnest, pleading look in her eyes when she spoke to the Judge, which seemed to say: " Oh, bring him back to me!" Her light, joyous laugh was now but seldom heard. She, too, seemed to be under the influence of that shadow of destiny. His heart yearned toward the lovely girl, whose sorrow for the absence of "his boy" seemed greater than his own. But now he must put away these thoughts. It was eight o'clock. His guests entered together, the Commodore and General, and with them Mr Carleton and William Wily.

The General spoke:—

"I have taken the liberty, Judge Bland, of introducing these two gentlemen, Mr. Carleton and Mr Wily, as visitors. Mr. Wily will give us the benefit of his observations on the subject now under discussion."

"I am pleased to see you, gentlemen," responded the Judge. "I presume General Sterne has informed you that it is requisite for you to take the oath of secresy. It is necessary to preserve inviolably secret the existence as well as the proceedings of the 'Society in Search of Truth' for the present. Mr. Secretary, please administer the oath."

Both the visitors subscribed the oath, and the Judge, adopting his usual formula, arose and said:—

"Gentlemen and members of the Society in Search of Truth: I regret that we have this evening one vacant chair (pointing to Milton's seat, which remained unoccupied, two other chairs having been placed for the visitors). 'My boy,' that is, Captain Bland, has responded to the call of duty, and is probably fighting in his country's cause against the hostile Indians in the north. May the God of battles watch over him."

Here each of the gentlemen bowed his head, thereby intimating that they joined in the prayer.

"Whilst we," continued the Judge, "are assembled here in the interest of a cause not less noble, the cause of Truth. Truth is an attribute of the Deity. Truth is stamped on every work of his creative power. The sun, moon and stars, moving in their orbits through revolving ages, have proclaimed the Truth of Him who said, 'This is your work, to give light unto the day and the night. Perform ye it.' The seasons following each other in their courses, declare the Truth. He appointed them their labors, and maintains their order. The trees yielding their fruits and the plants shedding their fragrance, exemplify the Truth. He declared they are good, and has made each produce and re-produce its kind for the refreshment and delight of man through cycles of time. Truth is written on every tree, on every plant, on every flower, on every blade of grass, and every grain of sand; it shines in every star, it glistens in every drop of dew. It is the stamp of God, who cannot lie.

"I recently heard that celebrated lecturer, Henry

Ward Beecher, at Oakland, in his lecture, 'The Wastes and Burdens of Society.' Speaking of the examination of witnesses, when under oath, by attorneys, he said, 'Such a mode of examination would make God Almighty lie.' Gentlemen, God is essential Truth. The Deity cannot lie. The lecturer must have forgotten the reverence he owed to his master's name.

"The subject, upon the examination of which we have entered, viz: 'Stock Operations,' has so far proved a painful one to contemplate. I trust we shall be able to discover some more pleasing features than have yet been disclosed in the Society's meetings. If not, we must endure it patiently. We have sworn to seek the Truth, and the Truth alone. In the words of Butler, we will

"'Dare to be true; nothing can need a lie,
A fault which needs it most, grows two thereby.'

"Let us do our duty, and follow the advice of Herbert, who says :—

"'If Truth be with thy friend, be with them both,
Share in the conquest, and confess a troth.'

"With these brief observations, I leave the subject of 'Stock Operations' in your hands."

"Mr. President," said General Sterne, "I will now, with your permission, request Mr. Wily, who has had great experience in the conduct of stock business, to give us the result of his observations."

"We shall be glad to hear Mr. Wily," answered the President.

"The subject," said Wily, "of which I have to

speak is so large that, were I to give my whole experience, it would take me all the balance of this week to get through."

"And it would be very interesting, no doubt," said the Judge.

"Don't inflict too much, Mr. Wily," remarked the Commodore.

"Proceed, Wily," said the General, "and we will mark, learn and inwardly digest."

' It appears to me," continued Wily, "that stock gambling is a kind of madness. When people have long indulged in it, they rarely quit until they are dead broke, and then they often return to it when they make another raise by some other pursuit. I have known hundreds of men who sold out good mines and business and gambled in stocks until every dollar was lost. I have known scores of women who sunk homes and all they had besides in stock gambling, and then begged and borrowed wherever they could from their friends to pursue the infatuation. And yet most of these people knew that they were walking on the edge of a volcano, which might engulf them at any moment. Some of them made a little at first. By and by they lost; then they went on in hope of getting even, and ultimately they did get even—with the ground—completely bursted. And yet, every time they passed the Stock Boards they saw crowds of men loitering about the doors who were without a dollar, and utterly demoralized and useless for any other pursuit since they became infatuated with stock gambling.

"Gentlemen, I was one of those loafers, and should be now if it were not for the kindness of—"

" Wily," said General Sterne, "let that pass."

"Well, gentlemen," said Wily, "most people who deal in stocks know that nothing is done on merit ; they understand that the market is a gamble, and that stocks are put up and down solely for the purposes of manipulation. They know that it is almost impossible to learn the Truth about any mine on the Comstock. They know that the prices of stocks are raised or lowered all the time by wash (that is fictitious sales). They have good reason to believe that pumps have been purposely broken ; mills burnt down, and mines fired, solely to depress the market prices ; and that volumes of lies have been spoken and written to inflate them ; that assessments have been levied and dividends declared unwarrantably, for the same purposes ; and that the diamond drill, which is of great advantage to mining, is continually used to the detriment of outside stockholders ; and that these things are perpetrated in defiance of justice and right."

"Now, please tell us something about the conduct of brokers' business, Mr. Wily," said the General.

" The brokers and operators," said Wily, " are divided into two orders, the one which is known as bulls, and the other as bears. The bulls are those who are looking for a rise in the market ; the bears are those who are anticipating a fall. Some of them are persistent bulls or bears, others chop and change round. Many of the brokers profess to do nothing but a commission business. In most cases that is a humbug. They get drawn into speculation and go on. The transactions of the market are divided into regular, cash, long, and short. The regular transactions are the purchases and sales which are made to-day and settled within bank hours to-morrow. The cash transactions are concluded on the day in which they are made. The longs are purchases of stock to be delivered at a deferred date, which may be any time from two to ninety days. The shorts are contracts to deliver stock the vendor is not possessed of at from two to ninety days from date. In either case a twenty per cent. margin, or in other words, twenty per cent.˙ of the market value, is put up by the parties as a guarantee of fulfillment of contract. Long purchasers are buyers on time of stocks they have not the ready money to pay for. Short sales are sales of stock for future delivery, or of borrowed stock, which the seller must at some time replace.

"In order to encourage, not mining, but stock gambling, some of the banks, whose directors are interested in the gambling, advance fifty per cent. of the market price of certain stocks to the brokers. When the banks wish to inflate the market, they are very liberal with their advances. When they wish to depress it, they reduce the credit of their broker customers, and, by that means, force stocks in the market. The facilities afforded by banks to brokers places in their hands a large amount of power, which is often most unjustly used. Brokers by these means are enabled to make advances to their customers, whose stocks they are carrying, or are supposed to be carrying, for it often happens that they neither purchase nor sell when directed to do so by their customers. Thus, a customer deposits a thousand dollars and directs a broker to buy him two thousand dollars worth of Ophir. If the broker is dishonest and believes that Ophir is on the decline, he does not buy the stock at all. He takes the thousand dollars and uses it. He returns to his client a sale note at or near the highest quotation of the day and charges him interest from date on the one thousand dollars presumably advanced by him on the customer's account. Or, supposing he is short himself and is carrying a quantity of customers' stock in any corporation, he will not hesitate to sell out that stock to help weaken the market, although he knows he is using his customer's stock without his knowledge or consent, and is depressing its value and injuring him thereby. I will not say there are not brokers by whom these things are not done, but I have reason to think they are few in number. The system, as it is at present conducted, is rotten from stem to stern. When I first entered into stock gambling I had no knowledge of these things, and, as a consequence, I was soon stripped bare. General Sterne, taking advantage of such information as is rarely obtainable, and at a great risk, which the chances are a hundred to one would result in serious loss were he to attempt it again, has succeeded in catching a brace of scoundrels short, and in cinching them the worst way, and has most generously—"

" Mr. Wily," said the General, waving his hand to him to be seated, " I am much obliged to you for the information you have imparted. I request you to say no more on the subject of our private affairs."

The Judge now spoke : " I desire to mention to you at this time a conversation I had with the great banker, Mr. Highwater, who informed me of his views on the subject of stock operations. He gave it as his opinion that they were positively beneficial to the people ; he assured me that the Comstock lode had a number of good mines upon · it, which he, and his friends who control them, could open up as soon as, as—I think he said as soon as they were ready. And, I think, that if the management of the mines and the conduct of the operators and brokers were as bad as represented by General Sterne, in his remarks at our last meeting, and you, Mr. Wily, in this, that a man of Mr. Highwater's wealth and position in mining circles would endeavor to check and remedy such great evils."

" Not much, Mr. President," said Wily, " he is the boss schemer of the whole crowd, and in order to play his big tricks he lets the small fry make their little ones."

" I am sorry to hear it, sir," replied the Judge.

" I had hoped," said the Commodore, " to have proved by figures that there is a brighter side to stock operations than the one we have looked at ; I regret to say it is not in the figures."   Here the

Commodore hopelessly closed his memorandum book.

"Mr. President," said the General, ' I beg to offer the following resolution :—

" In the opinion of this Society, stock operations as at present conducted, are—
" Subversive of morality and Truth ;
" Conducive to frauds and trickeries ;
" Productive of disasters and distress ;
" Injurious to industry and commerce, and
" Disgraceful to many concerned."

The motion was put by the President and carried.

The Commodore begged leave to offer the following resolution, which was unanimously adopted :—

"That the proceedings of the ' Society in Search of Truth,' in relation to stock operations, shall be printed and circulated forthwith, and that they shall be

DEDICATED

TO ALL

THE LOVERS OF TRUTH

IN THE

GREAT AMERICAN NATION."

CHAPTER XXXIV.

A SUPPOSED MADMAN.

When Wily, overpowered by the generous transfer the General had made of his winnings in the
stock operation in which he had engaged, quitted
the office of Mr. Equity, he could not have spoken
to save his life.   That brief review of the past he
had taken whilst sitting in the room, had awakened
emotions which would have choked him had he endeavored to speak.   He knew it, and left in silence.
The General, reading and respecting his feelings,
let him depart alone.   Once in the open air, he soon
recovered command of himself, and then hastened
back to the Stock Boards to urge on to completion
the work of disposing of the General's stock to the
best possible advantage.   In doing this he had to
use a great deal of caution, for he was known to
represent a large interest in the Alta mine, and he
was closely watched and closely questioned by brokers and dealers scores of times every day.   Wily
was shrewd and careful.   He imparted no information save such as could do no injury to, and might
possibly advance, the General's interests.   Not a
few who would hardly have deigned to notice Wily
a fortnight ago, now treated him with deference.
How prone men are to worship wealth.   The ancient Israelites, taking advantage of the absence of
Moses, made for themselves a golden calf and bowed
themselves down before it and worshipped it.   In
all ages there have been worshippers of the golden
calf, and in this nineteenth century, with all its

knowledge and cultivation, and refinement, there are not a few men and women who never bow the knee to the majesty of heaven, nor render well deserved homage to human genius, or talent, or worth, but who will bow themselves to the very dust in humble admiration of a golden calf. It matters not that it is polluted with the filth of the gutter ; it matters not that it is vile with crime or foul with disease, they will gladly embrace it, and bow down before it, for it is a golden calf.

The stock business of the day concluded, Wily immediately sought the Baldwin Hotel, and went to his brother's room. James was in—he was writing to his old father and mother. William walked up and down the room ; he picked up a book from the table and turned the leaves over in a desultory manner, then laid it down and commenced to whistle a tune, still walking the floor. Then he hummed a snatch of a song, and at the end wound up by taking a chair in his arms and waltzing around the room, whistling the " Blauen Donau " as an accompaniment with all his might. James now laid down his pen ; he observed his brother earnestly. He had thought his conduct unusual and eccentric when he entered the room. Now he had not the slightest doubt but he was crazed. He turned to him and asked :—

"William, what is the matter ?"

William did not answer ; he only quickened his pace, and went flying around the room with such rapidity that James every moment expected to see some portion of the furniture come to irreparable

P

grief, but did not think it desirable at present to interfere with the supposed madman.

At length, tiring of his exercise, William set his chair down in front of his brother, and holding out his hand to him, he said : " I am going to get married, James, and shall settle down on my ranch, but before I fix myself on my property, I shall just take a run home to the Old Country and see father and mother, and do something for them."

James was quite sure now that he was mad. Only that morning, before he left him, William was lamenting the loss of his ranch, and had borrowed a dollar from James, so that he might not be without money. And now he was cutting up and indulging in the wildest antics, and talking about marrying, and settling down on the ranch, and traveling, and doing something for the old folks at home, as if he were a rich man. He watched him very closely thinking meantime what was best to be done. William was evidently very excited; he hoped he would not do himself a mischief. In the meantime it would be better. he thought, to humor him, whilst he considered what he should do for his safety, so he said :—

" You think you will get married, William; whom do you mean to marry ? "

" Whom ? " said William, " Why, Annette, of course ; the brightest, smartest little woman out. I will look after the cows, the pigs, and the grain-fields ; she shall look after the chickens, and ducks, and the garden, and by and by we'll have some chicks of our own, and we'll name the first boy after you, for a good old fellow that you are." As he said this he gave James such a hearty slap on his shoulder that he nearly sent him off his chair.

"He is certainly getting dangerous," thought James. He now rang the bell, and turning again to William, said: "It will cost you money to go to England, William, have you thought of that?"

There was a knock at the door. James backed up to it, keeping his eye on his brother.

"Go," said James to the porter, "and give my respects to Commodore Pye, and ask him to come to me immediately."

William began to whistle the moment his brother left him. Directly he returned he answered:—

"That is all correct, James, it will only cost a thousand or so, and I don't care about that."

At this juncture, Annette, who was passing along the corridor and heard the brothers' voices, opened the door and walked into the room. No sooner did William catch sight of her than he shouted, "Bravo! it is Annette," and springing from his seat, he cried: "Let's have a dance." Seizing her around the waist, he commenced whistling a schottische, and carried the half-amazed and half-offended girl around the room at what a sailor would call "the rate of knots."

In the midst of this terpsichorean exercise the Commodore arrived at the door, heard the noise, and walked in.

"What, Wily? Why, Annette," said he, as he recognized his sister's maid, "you are having a great time to-day. Did you send for me to witness it ?   Would it not be as well to send for Mrs. Clare and the young ladies also ?   They might possibly enjoy the entertainment."

The Commodore closed the door and stood with his back to it   Annette, blushing to the roots of her hair, looked in vain for a means of exit. James Wily's face wore a look of great concern.   William alone, though perfectly sobered by the Commodore's entrance, seemed quite happy.   The Commodore, taking in the picture at a glance, was intensely amused

"Continue your sports," he said : "I am really sorry, James, you have not invited more ladies, in which case I should have felt inclined to take a spin myself."

James was greatly distressed. "Commodore," he said, " I have taken the liberty of sending for you to ask your advice. I am greatly afraid there is something seriously wrong with my unfortunate brother William."

William Wily, at this announcement, opened his eyes in amazement, his lips moved as if to speak, but he did not utter a word.

" He has behaved so strangely since he came in, half an hour ago, that I am afraid his troubles have unseated his reason, and want to ask you what is best to be done."

As he ceased speaking Annette uttered a scream and sank down on a chair.

The Commodore steadily looked at William, who for a moment knit his brows, as if annoyed, and then burst into laughter, which was so far removed from that of the maniac, and so full of contented amusement, that the Commodore saw in a moment that James' fears were without foundation.

"Will you, William Wily, explain to me what cause you have given your brother to entertain the belief of which he has spoken ? "

"I really cannot say, Commodore, unless it was because I told him that I intended to marry Annette."

At this declaration Annette raised her eyes to those of William, at first with a look of fear, which gave place to one of pleasure as she looked into the clear, steady pair of optics which met and kindly retained her questioning gaze. Now blushing with womanly shame and joy, she covered her face with her apron, whilst eagerly waiting what was to follow.

"And has Annette consented to the arrangement ?" inquired the Commodore.

"I have not asked her, sir," replied William, "I came here this afternoon for that very purpose."

"That is where it is, sir," said James Wily, "he has not a dollar in the world. Only this morning he told me he could not think of marrying. And now he speaks of his ranch, that was his before he lost it, as if it were still his own, and of marrying, and traveling, as if he was a millionaire."

The Commodore again looked at William. Was he mistaken ? No ; that clear, calm, steady eye had no madness in it. There was a secret here which William had not divulged to his brother.

"And what does Annette say ?" asked the Commodore, addressing her, " to the man, who, having no money to support her, wants to marry her ? "

" I—think—we—can—manage—to—earn—a—living—between—us, sir," said Annette.

" Well, James, don't you think there are two of the company a little mad ? " smilingly asked the Commodore.

" I really don't know, Commodore," replied James, whose fears with regard to his brother's sanity were fast subsiding, though he was still greatly perplexed.

" And now, William, I think you have something to explain ; had you spoken it earlier, your brother would not have thought you mad. What is it ? "

" This afternoon, Commodore," said Wily, " through the kind generosity of your friend, General Sterne, I have received back all the properties I lost in stock gambling, and am therefore comfortably fixed."

At this announcement Annette looked up at William, tears springing to her eyes, which were full of joy and proud gladness.

" William," said James Wily, rising and taking his brother's hand, " forgive me for thinking you mad. I am very glad to hear of your good fortune. Commodore Pye, I am sorry I so needlessly disturbed you."

" Don't apologize," said the hearty Commodore, "I would not have missed this scene on any account. I am glad, James, to find that William's madness has a method in it. Annette," he added, " you must not forget to ask me to your wedding, nor your great friend, General Sterne, whose goodness, like still waters, runs deep. William, I am sorry to have interrupted your dance. Don't forget that I shall expect to dance at your wedding, and when a god-father is in order, if I am here you may call on me."

CHAPTER XXXV.

WHICH IS A RECORD OF PLEASANT HOURS AND OF A GREAT SORROW.

The friendship of General Sterne with the members of the Commodore's family ripened apace. The more he saw of the three ladies the more fully did he appreciate the charm of their society, and something approaching regret grew upon his own mind, that he had allowed the disappointment of his youth to shut him off from the enjoyment of the pleasures of female society, of which he had for many years deprived himself.

The General not only called daily on Mrs. Clare, but, to the great surprise of all his acquaintances, he was often seen driving with herself and the young ladies in the Park and on the public ways. The influence of this intercourse upon the General was most salutary; the stern brows were often relaxed; the severe look which, by long use, had become all but stereotyped, began to give way to a more gentle and attractive one, and his acquaintances frequently remarked to him that he was reversing the order of nature, and growing younger instead of older with the advance of time. It is gravely to be doubted whether at this time he had any perception of the direction in which his steps were tending. It was enough for him that, having a certain amount of leisure time, he found it m re pleasurable to spend it in the society of Mrs. Clare and her daughters than in any other manner. In those old days, before disappointment had soured his mind, he was noted for his polite attention to ladies. Then he was known to be affianced to his cousin Belle and greatly attached to her. He made no secret of either fact; hence his attentions to other ladies excited no particular comment, and were never misconstrued by the individuals who were the recipients of them.

It seemed now that he had awakened to the appreciation of the charm of the society of woman. It is true he sought no new female acquaintance, and was unconscious of the comment his constant attendance upon the ladies of the Commodore's family excited. He knew that the hour or two passed in their society every day were the pleasantest hours in the twenty-four. He held Mrs. Clare in high esteem as a lady possessed of great good sense and intelligence, which had been embellished by education and observation of the ways and manners of the world. He knew she was a widow, and that she had remained in that condition for twenty years; and he did not regard her as being likely to marry. It had been whispered to him by William Wily who had obtained the information from Annette, that Rose had given her heart to Captain Bland, and, though he never heard it asserted, he did not doubt but there was a mutual attachment between Frank Carleton and Miss Stanley. If, therefore, at any time the thought crossed his mind that his attentions might be misinterpreted, he instantly dismissed it. By the ladies he was sure they would not be. To the remarks of the outside world he was quite indifferent.

The interest he felt in Geraldine was really his great attraction. From the first she had been a study to him. Now this daily intercourse was showing him new beauties in her mind and character, the unfolding of which to his observation gave him unalloyed pleasure, and excited new admiration every day.

Geraldine too began to look forward to these meetings with pleasant anticipation. Satisfied that her first estimate of the General, which was based on physiognomical observations, was unjust, she had sought to make amends, and had done so by extending to him a cordial friendship, such as she accorded to but very few. At the same time she found the study of the character of the General an exceedingly interesting one. Annette had told her of his generosity to Wily, which had opened the way for their marriage, and how happy she expected to be; and then she repeated all that Wily had said about the goodness of the General, and how, after the restoration of his properties, William had spoken to Mr. Equity, the General's attorney, about it; and Mr. Equity had told him that the General was always doing some act of kindness to somebody or other, and that he invariably forbade the people he benefited to make any remark about it.

Geraldine was not addicted to gossip with Annette, but when she began to speak of the virtues of General Sterne and the generous deeds he had performed, Geraldine would listen with a dreamy thoughtfulness and tender interest in the subject, which boded ill for the future peace of mind of Frank Carleton, if he entertained the views with which he was credited by the General. Even Mrs. Clare, who had latterly noticed how confidential the friendship between Frank and Geraldine had become, began to think she might have been mistaken. She had told her brother on the first evening of her arrival that she thought reciprocal love between Geraldine and Mr. Carleton was exceedingly improbable. And yet Mrs. Clare was puzzled. Mr. Carleton was as frequent a guest as General Sterne. Geraldine always received him with a calm, half-sisterly sort of pleasure.   There was no tremor or heightened color in those meetings; they were uniform in their character; but then Mrs. Clare reasoned, " Geraldine has always had, from a child, a calm, graceful dignity of her own; she is not like other girls." She could not bear the thought of losing either of her adopted daughters.   But she knew that in the nature of things it must be sooner or later.

If Geraldine decided to accept Mr. Carleton, he was in every respect eligible, and she could entrust her to him with confidence; though she still thought that, with all his excellences, he was not the kind of man that she had expected would win the affections of Geraldine.   With regard to Rose, she was troubled.   She had never seemed quite herself since that adventure in the park. She had lost much of her usual gaiety of manner. It seemed as if the old sunshine had gone out of her life. She was more sedate and thoughtful. Her eyes had in them a sad earnestness unlike the old sparkling look. Her step was less elastic, and the joyous, soft, ringing laughter of her mirth had given place to a quiet smile, which quickly subsided. Mrs. Clare was much distressed. The Commodore too had noticed the change, and spoken of it.

"What is the matter with Rose?" he asked. "She does not seem like herself. I am afraid she was more seriously injured by that unfortunate accident than we thought."

"I cannot tell," answered Mrs. Clare; "I have questioned the dear girl. She tells me she is quite well, but I fear such is not the case. I have asked her to let me send for Dr. Lancet, but she so earnestly requested me not to do so that I yielded to her entreaty."

"I think, sister," said the Commodore, "we must take the matter into our own hands. I will send for the doctor at once."

The Commodore left the room and dispatched his servant, Johnson, in search of the physician.

About an hour later Dr. Lancet entered, sat down beside Rose and conversed with her.

"Do you suffer any pain?" he inquired.

"No, sir," answered Rose, hesitatingly, and then added, "I felt stiff and sore after you were here before, but that is gone. I think I am quite well."

The doctor nodded his head and again "looked

wise." He next felt her pulse, and timed its beats by his gold chronometer. He next requested her to allow him to see her tongue, which he inspected as if he enjoyed looking into the rosebud mouth in which lay the member which an apostle calls "unruly," surrounded by two perfect rows of ivory molars and incisors. At length, thanking Rose, who was glad to end the performance, he sat still for some minutes, looking wiser than ever, whilst Mrs. Clare, Geraldine and the Commodore waited very anxiously until the oracle should be pleased to speak.

At length he said :—

"Miss Pye has not recovered from the shock she received ; her nerves are shaken. I will write a prescription. The medicine will combine sedative and tonic properties, and will, I think, completely restore her to health."

The prescription was written, and the physician's autograph appended.

" I should advise you, madam," he said, " to send it to Pestle & Mortar; they are very careful dispensers. I am always very particular about my prescriptions. You can rely on them."

The doctor did not see fit to add, " They credit me with a very handsome premium on every prescription I send them." His special commendation of the firm of Pestle & Mortar he knew to be an item of the humbug which paid him so well.

Several days passed, during which time Rose, to please Mrs. Clare, regularly took her medicine, but protested that it was unnecessary. She said she did not require it, in which she was quite right; she knew that the nostrums of the physicians could not "minister unto a mind diseased." Every day, morning and evening, she had searched the papers, and had seen the announcement of the arrival of Captain Bland at Portland, and also that he had organized a company of one hundred men and started for the front. And the Judge, who had heard the same by dispatch from Milton, had gone direct to the Baldwin to impart the information.

Rose already knew it, although she did not say so, and was very grateful to the Judge for calling to tell them.

No word had ever been spoken of the attachment of Milton by Judge Bland.

Milton had said to him, before he sailed :—

"Do not mention the subject, uncle. If I live to return, I will go to the Commodore and ask him for Rose. Dearly as he loves her, he loves still more the thought of making her happy. He will not refuse to give her to me."

The Judge had respected the wishes of "his boy," and so the matter rested.

Geraldine, who knew the cause of Rose's malady, greatly desired to impart it to Mrs. Clare, but Rose so earnestly requested her to keep her secret that she yielded to her wish.

"You know, Geraldine, dear," she said, "it would be so different if we were engaged. If he had asked me to be his wife, then I should be proud to tell mamma of it, and papa too. But I have nothing to tell them except that he said he would surely come back to me. You will keep my secret, darling?"

Rose wound her arms around Geraldine, and looked at her so beseechingly, as she made the request, that Geraldine instantly answered:— ·

"Yes, dearest, as long as you wish."

"And oh, Geraldine, I have a dreadful fear! He has gone to fight those savage Indians. I fear he will be killed, and I shall never see him again."

"Do not think so, Rose, darling," said Geraldine. "Rather believe that God will protect and preserve him, and I will help you pray for him."

"I do pray, dear, every hour of the day," answered Rose, "but my doubts and fears remain."

"Trust in God, and try to be happy, Rose, for Milton's sake. It would grieve him to know you were unhappy."

"I will try, dear," murmured Rose.

Half an hour later they were in the drawing-room together. Judge Bland and Mr. Carleton were there. Annette entered the room and laid the evening papers on the table. Rose observed that no one noticed them. She took them in her hand and went to her own room. Geraldine remarked and understood the movement. In her room Rose eagerly opened one of the papers and sought the telegraphic columns, where she read:—

"DEFEAT OF OUR TROOPS!

"FEARFUL MASSACRE!

"Yesterday Captain Bland, with his company, came upon a band of Indians, supposed to number two hundred. He at once attacked them, and had almost succeeded in dislodging them from their position, when a much larger body assailed his company in the rear. The carnage was frightful. Forty-nine of the company are reported dead or missing. When last seen, Captain Bland was fighting single-handed with three Indians, two of whom fell before his sword. Then he went down. So perishes a brave young officer."

Rose held the paper for a moment before her, looking at it in an agony of horror, and then sank senseless on the floor.

CHAPTER XXXVI.

HOPING AGAINST HOPE.

There was grief at the Palace as well as at the Baldwin. Judge Bland read that fatal dispatch in his room at or about the same time that Rose Pye read it in hers. His consternation and grief were terrible. Again and again did he upbraid himself for not hindering Milton from going to the front, or at least exercising all his influence to prevent it. He remembered Milton's forebodings. He did not now doubt but they were prophetic. A wail of grief broke from him as he remembered that he was his only hope and pride, and the solitary living relative who bore his name, whom he had fondly hoped would live to perpetuate that name and inherit his wealth when in the course of nature he himself should pass away. And now, in the hey-dey of his youth, in the very pride and glory of his young manhood, his life had been taken by a wild savage. He sat long in his chair, silently nursing his woe. Then remembering Rose, and what she had been to " his boy," he left his room and proceeded at once to the Baldwin.   He hoped the poor child would not have seen the paper.   For her sake, who was so loved by Milton, he must keep back his own heart's sorrow, whilst he gently paved the way for breaking the sad intelligence.   He would assume to have a hope, though hope had died out of his heart.   He would point out the uncertainty and unreliability of news-paper dispatches.   He would remind the Commo-dore's family, and all for Rose's comfort, of the numberless instances in which the telegrams of the day have been contradicted by those of the morrow. Yes; he would assume to have hope; though God knew   he   had   none.   His   kind,   sympathetic heart went out to Rose, and thinking on the grief which he knew was in store for her, he almost forgot his own.   But ever and again would the picture of " his boy " arise before him as he last saw him, in his manly beauty and high sense of honor and duty.   And then again, scalpless and mutilated by the Indian's knife, and left to feed the coyotes of the forest wilds.

Can we realize what Judge Bland felt during those early hours of his tribulation? No, we can-not—unless we have had such a grief.   But if we have loved and lost some dear one whom we prized as the apple of our eye, who was to us more than all the world beside, for whom we would have sac-rificed every other human tie, upon whom suddenly, and to us unexpectedly, the grim hand of death has been laid, and have seen the form we loved so untimely stricken, its beauty changed to the ghastliness of death, upon which we have gazed, and gazing have felt that the world no longer had a place for us, then can we realize what Judge Bland felt. But only in part, for we have had the sad consolation of laying with tender hands the loved one of whom we were reft beneath the silent sod. He knew not to what indignities, or to what foul uses all that was mortal of "his boy" had now been put. And even now, with this consciousness within him, he was bound on an errand of love and mercy to the child who had told him of her love for Milton with her eyes, and who had read in his own an answering look which said, "I know the secret." So each understood the other, and felt there was a tie, a bond between them of which they might not speak, for the Judge was bound by his promise to "his boy," and Rose's training, as well as her innate delicacy, forbade the mention, for Milton had only by implication asked her love.

When Geraldine observed that Rose did not return to the room, she went in search of her, and found her on the bedroom floor, just as she had fallen. One hand still grasped the paper, and its fore finger rested on the fatal dispatch.

Geraldine saw it all. By intuition she knew what was there. Gently unclosing the fingers that held it, she loosened the paper from Rose's grasp and read the dreadful lines. She hastily put the papers out of sight, and summoned Annette, with whose assistance she lifted Rose and laid her on the bed. She then sent Annette to ask Mrs. Clare to come to her. Mrs. Clare at once directed Annette to tell James Wily to find the doctor and bring him without delay.

An hour had passed; Rose was still unconscious, and James had not returned. Restoratives had been applied without avail. The grief of Mrs. Clare was terrible, but showed no sign. Hers was one of those natures which rise to great occasions. She moved about the room and assisted and gave her directions with as much calmness as if she were ice or stone.

I have known one other such woman. I saw her rise from the chair in which for years she had passed most of her time, the victim of a fatal sickness. I saw her stand and dress the arm of a laborer, which had been fearfully lacerated by machinery. There was no tremor in her hand, no weakness apparent in her then, and yet she was a tender-hearted woman, a loving mother, whose every act was the result of noble thought and high principle ; the man was nothing to her but an unfortunate sufferer. The enthusiasm of humanity upheld her until her work was done, then fainting from sheer exhaustion, she fell into the arms of her son, who bore her to her bed, from which she did not rise for days.

Mrs. Clare calmly pursued her efforts. At last Rose showed a quivering, shuddering motion, and opened her eyes and looked at Mrs. Clare. There was entreaty in the questioning look. Silently the watchers waited for her to speak.

" Mamma," she faintly murmured, "am I not

dead? I thought I was, and I was so glad."

"Do not say so, my darling," said Mrs. Clare; "it would break my heart, and your dear papa's also, if you were to die, we love you so. You must live and get well, and be happy for our sakes."

Rose did not answer; she closed her eyes and lay perfectly still.

The doctor entered. He was puzzled. For once, he allowed the look of wisdom to give place to one of incertitude. He examined his patient. He wished to ascertain if Rose might not possibly have sustained some injury that had previously escaped his notice. He could find none. If such injury existed, it was internal.

He returned to the drawing-room and asked Mrs. Clare and the Commodore if she had, at any time, been subject to fainting fits.

"No," answered Mrs. Clare, "beyond the ordinary diseases of childhood through which she passed, she has never known a day's sickness, and has always been believed to be unusually vigorous and healthy."

"Has she suffered any sudden grief or disappointment?" inquired the doctor.

"No, sir," replied the Commodore; "there is nothing she has asked or wished that has not been granted her."

Neither the Commodore or Mrs. Clare knew anything of her attachment to Milton or of the disaster which had befallen him.

"It is strange," said the doctor; and then, assuming the wise look which was meant to imply, "I know more than I choose to impart," he added: "and yet not so strange as may appear. Young ladies are taken in this way more frequently than any, save we of the profession, have any idea of. I will write a fresh prescription, and I think you will find Miss Pye much better in the morning."

The Commodore was not satisfied. He privately summoned another physician, but the result was no more satisfactory.

Meantime Judge Bland arrived. He found the Commodore and his family in great trouble. He was satisfied he knew the cause of Rose's sudden illness. He expressed his sympathy in the kindest terms. At such an hour he could not obtrude his own grief. He would call again in the morning, he said; he had resolved he would see Rose, and, if possible, alone. And then he would take the first steamer for Oregon, and learn all he could of the fate of his poor, unfortunate boy.

Mrs. Clare and Geraldine were much occupied with Rose; consequently, the Commodore was left alone a considerable portion of the evening. When at length Rose slept and Mrs. Clare found him in the drawing-room, he said to her:—

" I have been thinking, sister, that this city life may not suit Rose, who has been used to living in the country. Perhaps it would be better to try a change. Suppose we visit Yosemite, and then go on by easy stages to the East and take steamer for the Old Country. It is many years since I saw the home of our childhood. If you approve of my plan, I will accompany you, and will forward instructions to have the old place furbished up and put in order, and we will spend a few months there."

" I think, brother," answered Mrs. Clare, " it is the best course we can pursue. We will start as soon as Rose is well enough."

That evening, Frank Carleton, who had also read of Milton's death, called on Judge Bland. He found General Sterne and Mr. Equity with him. Both had called for the same purpose—to express their sorrow and sympathy. Mr. Equity was intensely grieved at the loss of the friend of his hour of need.

" We must not be too hasty in jumping at conclusions," said the General; " to-morrow may bring us better news."

" So have I said to myself a hundred times, my friend," sadly replied Judge Bland, " but I have no hope; had Milton lived, he would have hastened to telegraph to me. He would have well known the greatness of my anxiety. How is it," he continued, " that the hand of Death is so often laid on the noblest and the best, whilst the useless and the worthless are suffered to live on unharmed by the evils that overtake the just. An old writer, Toplady I think, represents God as walking in a garden of flowers and plucking the fairest and most beautiful and taking them to himself. But why is it so? Why does he not remove the blasted and withered blossoms and let the perfect ones bloom on ? "

" The acts of Infinite Truth are always right," replied the General; "the blasted, withered blossoms live, it is true, but their existence is a living death; and

" Worse than death ineded."

But let us not mistrust, Judge; we must not yet abandon hope."

"I can but believe," said Frank Carleton, hopefully, "that better news will come."

"I thank you for your sympathy, my friends; God grant our wishes may come true," said the Judge, as his visitor rose to leave him.

In the morning, Rose was much better. Part of the night she had slept; part of it she lay awake and thought. A great sorrow had come upon her. Should she selfishly succumb to it ? No. Joy, which had attended her from the cradle, had gone from her life. But she had duties to perform. The romance of her life had been acted. Its end was a terrible tragedy. Her tears flowed fast as she thought of it. Then she resolved. She owed much to her father, who had supplied all her wants. She owed as much to her aunt, who had been the dispenser of his bounty to her and had loved her as a daughter. For their sakes, she would try to hide her sorrow. She would think of Milton as of a spirit gone before, and somewhere in the spirit land, waiting for her. None, save Judge Bland and Geraldine, knew her secret. None other should ever know it. In the morning she left her bed, despite the protests of Geraldine and Mrs. Clare. To the latter she said : " It was only a little faintness, Mamma; I am quite well now." She tried to assume some of her old gaiety. The attempt was a brave one. The result a sorry failure. But she was evidently so much better that the Commodore and Mrs. Clare relieved and thankful, decided that in two days' time they would leave for Yosemite.

Mr. Carleton called in the early morning. He had asked and received permission to make one of the party.

General Sterne had heard with regret of their sudden determination, and experienced a feeling of sorrow which was real and earnest. His feelings, like his actions, were always earnest. When the announcement was made to him his eyes involuntarily sought Geraldine. Her gaze was intently fixed on him. The instant she saw that he was observing her she averted it, a blush rising and diffusing her face. "How beautiful she is," thought the General, " what a happy man is Frank Carleton."

Recovering herself, she quickly turned to him and said: "We shall regret leaving our San Francisco friends, General Sterne."

" Your friends will be the losers, Miss Stanley," answered the General, "you will leave us ' sunny memories.' "

"A compliment from you, General, should be prized by us," said Mrs. Clare. It was the first she had ever heard him utter.

Toward noon Rose was left for a short time alone in the drawing-room. She was musing on her sorrow and resolve, when Judge Bland was announced by Annette.

" I am glad to have found you alone, my daughter. You know my grief; you have your own. Things may be better than they seem. Let us not indulge in useless sorrow. We will still hope."

" May we hope ?" said Rose, a great throb at her heart rising as if it would choke her.

"Yes, daughter, we may, for God is good. We should never despair of his goodness. We have but a newspaper dispatch to guide us. It may be wrong. I go to seek him to-morrow. I wish to leave with you a token of my love for him ɛnl also for yourself." As Judge Bland uttered these words he drew the hand he held towards him and clasped on her wrist a magnificent bracelet, with a pendant heart, set with diamonds.

"Examine the pendant," he said.

Rose carefully examined it. "It is very chaste and beautiful," she said. "I do not care much for jewelry, but I shall always keep this in remembrance of your kindness. Thank you very much."

"It has a secret," said the Judge. Taking the pendant in his hand, he touched a cunningly concealed spring, and disclosed a miniature. It was a perfect portrait of Milton.

It was almost too much for Rose. Tears filled her eyes. She could not speak.

"If he lives," said the Judge, "he will come to you."

"Pray God he may," murmured Rose.

Mrs. Clare and Geraldine now entered, accompanied by the Commodore.

"And so you leave San Francisco, I hear, Mrs. Clare, for Yosemite," said Judge Bland.

"Yes, Mr. Bland," replied Mrs. Clare, "the day after to-morrow, and then we proceed on our homeward journey."

No one, save Geraldine, had mentioned Captain Bland in Rose's presence, they did not wish to shock her, being an invalid. To Geraldine Rose had poured out the sorrow of her heart the preceding night.

"And I," said the Judge, "go to Oregon to seek 'my boy.' God grant I may find him."

"Amen," fervently responded Mrs. Clare, and then asked: "Shall we ever see you again, Mr. Bland?"

"I trust so, madam," replied the Judge, "I propose to visit Europe in a month or two, and I shall find you. Till then this is my farewell."

With mutual good wishes the Judge left the room. His last and tenderest greeting was reserved for Rose.

CHAPTER XXXVII.

STOCK GAMBLING, FAREWELL.

Four days had passed. The Judge had been gone three and the Commodore's family two days, and Wily was wandering about in an unsettled state of mind. He had decided to sell one of his pieces of San Francisco real estate, in preference to mortgaging any part of his property, to provide the funds to stock his ranch, and make his contemplated visit to his father and mother. His brother, James, was gone, and what was worse, Annette was gone, also. He had endeavored to induce her to marry him right away. Annette had at first wavered, but after Rose's last attack, she had firmly determined to accompany the family back to Europe.

"William," she had said, "if you love me as much as you say, it is not long to wait. You are coming on after us. When you come I will not ask you to wait any longer."

William was first vexed, and then angry, and at last repentant. He told Annette he knew she was right and he was wrong, and he felt fully assured that the strong sense of duty which prompted her to remain with Mrs. Clare and the young ladies, against her own wishes and inclinations, augured favorably for their future happiness. So, whilst she went forward with the Commodore's family, he remained, hastening the operation of disposing of the piece of property he wished to sell, which he discovered, as some of us have found before him, is ordinarily a far more difficult thing than buying. The buyers of houses and lands are inclined to think their money much more valuable than the property offered to them. But no sooner have they parted with their money and acquired the property than, presto, change! the property is far more valuable than the money. If my reader has undervalued or despised real estate as an investment, let him buy some; he will be surprised to find how much it will appreciate (at least in his own estimation), the instant he is the owner.

General Sterne was not less at a loss than Wily. There was a void in his life which he could not fill. How had it come? It was not thirty days since the Commodore's family had arrived in San Francisco. It was many days after he first saw Mrs. Clare and her daughters that he made their acquaintance. From that time he had spent a portion of each day with them. Sometimes he had driven with, and on a number of occasions accompanied them to one or the other of the numerous theatres of San Francisco. He seemed to have an object in life whilst they were near him. Now he had none. But what was that object? This he asked himself again and again, and failed to find a satisfactory solution.

Some days earlier the General had wound up his stock transactions. He had netted some thirty thousand dollars beyond all he had ventured, and exclusive of the fifty-seven thousand five hundred dollars he had paid for the redemption of Wily's properties. The deal still went forward, and he saw that he might have made a great deal more had he held on. This caused him no regret. He had seen enough of the operations of the market to know that in ninety-nine cases out of a hundred the gain he might make would ultimately be a loss of an equal or greater amount to some unfortunate who could ill afford to lose it. He was convinced that, fortunate as he had been, he had only to go on and he would inevitably be ruined. He had noticed that the stock gamblers are like a flock of sheep, who invariably follow the bell-wether, and hurry pell mell in one direction, and that the leaders in the stock gambling scramble are but decoys, who are put up to lead and lure the masses to destruction. He had observed that the masses invariably rush to buy when prices are inflated, and that they do not care to touch them when they are low, and he had seen that this was the result of secret wire-pulling. Had the prices risen or fallen with the actual merit of each mine, he would have had nothing to say, but when he found that bogus developments, and not real ones, had been the means by which the public had been deluded and swindled by the controllers of the Comstock lode, his mind revolted from the whole business, and he would as soon have thought of sharing the spoils of a highwayman as deriving a personal benefit from a Comstock deal.

Wily had discovered and reported to him that Mr. Equity had lost over ten thousand dollars through the trickeries of Trackem & Cinchem. To him the General sent a cheque for ten thousand dollars. He knew nothing of the fact that the lost money was his own. With the cheque he sent a note, which ran as follows :—

DEAR MR. EQUITY:—

I have succeeded in wresting from Trackem & Cinchem the money you lost through their treachery, which you will oblige me by accepting, and preserving silence on the subject, even to myself. I make but one other request : Refrain from stock gambling.

Yours very truly

RANDOLPH STERNE.

With this money Mr. Equity redeemed all the notes given by him to Milton, held by Judge Bland. The remaining twenty thousand dollars the General scattered amongst various charities, as he had resolved.

It was on the third day after the Commodore's family had left the Baldwin Hotel that General Sterne, meeting Wily, asked him if he had any hankering after stock gambling.

"Not much, General," said Wily. "Do you know," he continued, "that Trackem & Cinchem have gone to grief? They have burst up. Trackem has already left the city, and I guess Cinchem won't be far behind him."

"I do not think it is a great loss to the city, but I am sorry," replied the General. He still had his doubts as to whether it was right for him to be the minister of punishment.

"Sorry, are you?" said Wily. "I am glad. They were a pretty pair of scoundrels, anyway; and that reminds me, I just met an acquaintance of mine, Mr. Playsphere; he was giving me his experience in stock gambling. He said about two years ago he invested considerable money in Julia, under the advice of a supposed friend. The stock rose to nineteen dollars. Playsphere sold out, and found himself possessed of forty-five thousand dollars. Then he was so unfortunate or so foolish as to tell his friend what he had done. 'His friend' replied, 'I am almost sure you have made a mistake. I will let you know in half an hour. 'His friend' left him, but soon returned, and said, 'I thought so; you are all wrong; the price of the stock will double in a week. Pile in all the money you have and double on that.' Playsphere acted on his advice, and in three days he was ruined. His friend professed great sorrow for him, and assured him he would make it all up to him, which he never did, or any part of it. When a little time ago the stock had declined to four dollars, Playsphere, who in the interim had worked at his profession and saved a little money, went to 'his friend' and asked him if Julia was not a good buy? 'By no means,' said 'his friend.' 'Don't touch it.' When some weeks later it was selling for fourteen and a half dollars a share, 'his friend' came to him and slapped him on the shoulder and said, 'Now Julia is a buy. Go in for all you can get.' 'Thank you,' said Playsphere, 'I am afraid your advice is not worth much. I don't want it.' I mentioned the publication of the proceedings of the 'Society in Search of Truth' to Playsphere, and he asked me to give these particulars to you for publication."

"All right, Wily, they shall be published."

When the General reached the Baldwin he found a note waiting for him. It was from Yosemite. He read :—

DEAR GENERAL STERNE:—

We are enjoying ourselves very much amidst the magnificent scenery of the most wonderful valley. We shall remain here a week. Mrs. Clare and Miss Stanley are well, and send their kind regards. I wish you were with us. Can you not come?

Yours, faithfully,

FRANK CARLETON.

Could he not go? Certainly he could, and he would. He started by the next train.

CHAPTER XXXVIII.

YOSEMITE AND AWAY.

That visit to Yosemite was full of delight to Geraldine. From Inspiration Point our travelers looked down into the immense chasm rent in the earth's crust by the hand of Omnipotence, and down upon the valley below, which is hemmed in by walls of solid granite, rising sheer upwards from the floor of the vale, in some cases, to a height of three thousand feet, perpendicular; and down upon the giant trees, which from the Point look no bigger than garden shrubs; and the peaceful river meandering along its sinuous course, appearing like a beam of light dropped by the god of day upon the floor of the valley; and the waterfalls leaping and crashing, precipitately casting themselves from the heights as if in reckless haste to join the stream below—striving with a vain endeavor to lose their own existence in the river, but ever flowing on, as they have flowed through centuries gone by, and still will flow through ages yet to come. As the party rested at the Point, and Geraldine looked on the scene mapped out beneath her, she realized emotions never before experienced by her. She had climbed up into the dome of St. Paul's Cathedral, in London, and still upwards above the golden cross to the golden ball which surmounts it, and surveyed from thence the monster city. She had visited the Cathedral of Notre Dame, in Paris, and the great Cathedral of Strasburg. She had viewed with astonishment and wonder at Rome the vast Cathedral of St. Peter

and the immense ruins of the Colloseum. She had
experienced a sense of reverential awe beneath the
shadow of Mont Blanc, and amidst the chasms
and ravines of the mountains of Switzerland, but
never had she felt the power of nature's God as
she felt it now. " What," she mused, " is man's
works compared to this great work of the Master
Builder of the universe ? Bring here the temples,
churches, monuments and pyramids which are the
glory and the boast of all the nations of the earth,
these everlasting walls which God has built have
room between them to entomb them all."

In the calm and evenly poised mind of Geraldine,
veneration held a high place. She had the power
of intellect without its pride. She had a consciousness of strength, but it was without Vanity. She
loved the beautiful, she worshipped the sublime.
Dead indeed must be the soul to its higher mission,
that can contemplate the stupendous grandeur of
Yosemite and fail to be impressed with the immen-
sity of the power of nature. It is a sad thing for
an individual—it is a sad thing for a people—to be
void of veneration. To worship is a necessity of
man. When veneration is lost, he still worships,
but it is no longer a worship that ennobles, it is one
that debases. If he does not worship God, or Nature, or science, or art, or home, then he worships
himself, or appetite or passion, or wealth. Nobility
has gone out from his life.

Geraldine's whole soul bowed down before the
majesty of beauty which revealed itself to her as
she gazed upon the scene before her. Nor was

Mrs. Clare less impressed, nor the Commodore, Mr. Carleton, or Rose. They sat long in silence. Words seemed too poor and insufficient to express their feelings. It is probable that each in those minutes, more fully than ever before, realized what an insignificant atom of the universe is one human being. When at last the Commodore waved his hand as a signal to move forward, not one word had been spoken by either of the party.

General Sterne hastened forward to join the Commodore and his family. He found them at the ——— Hotel, and became, whilst they remained, one of their party. He was received with unfeigned pleasure by them all. Geraldine's eyes lighted up with a delight she did not seek to disguise, and Rose, who had liked and admired him from the first, looked for a few moments almost her old self, but quickly relapsed into her later manner. She seemed to be changing places with Geraldine. The grave, calm dignity was hers, while Geraldine displayed an amount of vivacity and sprightliness, (the combined result of a desire to interest Rose, and of her own enjoyment,) which surprised Mrs. Clare.

The General, too, was rapidly changing. He was no longer the cold, indifferent man of a month ago. He entered into the engagements and enjoyments of each day with the zest and earnestness of an enthusiast. His old vein of satire was giving place to a more genial one, and instead of the old strictures on his kind, his utterances were now void of caustic, and not unfrequently full of mirth-inspiring

R

fun, sometimes provoking a smile even from Rose.

The Commodore noted the change in his friend, and esteemed him the more highly than ever.

The General was conscious of the difference in himself, and experienced a regret that he had allowed so great a portion of his eight and thirty years to pass in the shade of his own self-isolation, when he might have dwelt in sunshine all the time.

Mr. Carleton he could not understand. He seemed to have turned all his attention to Rose since her sickness, and never disputed the right of the General to be the escort of Geraldine in their rambles through the valley, an arrangement in which Geraldine always cheerfully concurred. The General did not doubt that each was so secure in the affections of the other, that neither had mistrust of him. "But how happy could I be," he thought, "if I could win the affections of Geraldine." But then would come the remembrance of Frank Carleton, to whom he had given the right of friendship. And so again and again he crushed back the traitorous thoughts.

Those were halcyon days, full of pleasure; they glided rapidly and imperceptibly away. And he could scarcely believe it was for the last time when the party took their final ramble amid the wonders of the valley. He was walking beside Geraldine, meditating on the fact. She said to him :—

" Is not this valley wonderful ? See yonder the South Dome, which rises upward a mile in height from the valley—see how the rays of the setting sun are gilding the vast globe, till it appears like the dome of a stupendous temple, built by giants, and sheathed with gold ; and then, observe that water-fall ; it is only one of the many that are continually pouring themselves from thousands of feet above us, to swell the river that waters the vale. Does it not make you think of God, who dwells above the hills and opens his hand to let flow never-ceasing streams of blessings for the dwellers in the vale be-low ? "

General Sterne's eyes rested on her as she spoke. The transfiguration he loved to see was now upon her. Her very soul was rendering homage to the matchless grandeur of the scene around her. To him it seemed as if it left its home within to illum-inate her face with a pure and holy beauty. She seemed wrapt and half-unconscious of his presence. The words she had uttered seemed to have been said as much to herself as to him, and did not re-quire an answer. He was strangely moved. At length he said :—

"To-morrow you will leave these scenes, Miss Stanley, and probably never see them again."

"Probably never again," answered Geraldine. " I shall leave them with regret, but I will bear them in my memory. The remembrance will linger while I live."

"And you do not think you will ever visit America again ? " inquired the General.

"It is possible I never may," she said, "but I shall carry with me pleasant reminiscences of my friends." Then, turning her dark eyes upon him, full of anxious inquiry, and with an almost tremulous concern in her voice, asked : " Will you visit Europe soon, General Sterne ? "

For a moment he hesitated, and then he answered : " I have no such intention at present, Miss Stanley."

Was he blind ?   He thought not.   He saw beside him the most peerless being he had ever beheld ; whose mind was gifted as her form was beautiful. Was he deaf ?   He thought not.   He heard a question which seemed to ask the continuation of his friendship, and he knew he dare not prolong it.   He began to fear himself.   Could he turn traitor to a friend ?   No ; perish hope, but let honor and Truth remain.

Geraldine did not speak again during their walk back to the hotel, and neither did the General. Each had a secret neither could disclose.   Geraldine's lips were sealed by the conventionality of the world in which she lived, and her own maidenly shame at the thought of loving where possibly she was not loved.   The General's were sealed by honor and duty.

The Commodore had secured his tickets for his family before leaving San Francisco, and sent forward such luggage as would not be required on the way to New York.   General Sterne and Mr. Carleton accompanied the party to Colfax, where they were to take the overland train.   The adieux were said at the station.

" If you come to Europe, General, while I am in England, I shall expect you to make your home, or at least, your headquarters, at my old place," said the Commodore, " you will be always welcome."

" Come if you can, General; " said Mrs. Clare, " we shall all be glad to see you."

Did General Sterne see traces of tears on Geraldine's cheek when, with averted eyes, she offered him her hand for a final farewell? He thought he did, and had no doubt it was because Frank Carleton was to accompany him back to San Francisco, and remain a week before going East to rejoin her.

And now they were gone.

On that return journey the General was almost as moody and cynical as in the olden time, whilst Frank Carleton was as cheerful and gay as usual, and did his very best to rally his friend.

Did my reader ever realize the conviction that he had, in some past time, been a fool, or a dolt, or a blind idiot? If such a conviction has never flashed upon him, he must be most consummately vain, or very young, probably far under twenty. Few fail to make the discovery by that age. It is doubtful if any reach thirty without experiencing the unpleasing consciousness. It is certain the General was, within a week, to find himself prepared to admit that he had been all three.

The General, after his return to San Francisco, was more than ever disinclined for society. He passed hours at his piano or organ, playing almost exclusively the most tender and pathetic music in his collection. The fact must be admitted, he was in a bad way. But he had firmly resolved to resurrect himself. He would take his time to do it, but it would be done. During those days his door was open to one man alone; that man was Frank Carleton. He believed that Frank stood between himself and happiness. He was too generous and too just to think less of him on that account, and for Geraldine's sake he was, and would at all times be, his friend.

The fifth day after their return Frank Carleton entered General Sterne's room and said to him: "Two days more and I shall leave you and proceed East. I shall spend a short time in one or two places by the way, and then go to England. In six weeks my bachelor days will be over. I wish you would go with me."

"That cannot be," answered General Sterne, "but I hope you will be happy. You should be—Miss Stanley is one of the most charming ladies I ever met."

It cost the General a great effort to praise her to her supposed lover.

"Yes, Geraldine is a splendid girl," said Frank Carleton, "she has been like a sister to me; in fact, she has been my only confidante ever since I left England."

"Sister? Confidante?" said the General, starting from his chair. "Is not Miss Stanley your fiancee?"

"Miss Stanley my fiancee? slowly repeated Frank Carleton in great amazement. "No, certainly not. I am engaged to my cousin, Violet Carleton. We shall be married when I get home."

" Fool, dolt, blind idiot that I have been," muttered the General to himself; and then taking Frank's hand, he said : " I have changed my mind, Mr. Carleton; I will go to England with you."

CHAPTER XXXIX.

HEMMED IN BY INDIANS.

Captain Bland was stricken down by a blow from behind, with the butt end of an empty rifle in the hands of the third Indian, as he was withdrawing his sword from its fatal work on his second foe. He fell to the ground, stunned and bleeding. As he went down to earth, the savage uttered a demoniac yell of delight. He grasped his scalping knife and was about to make an end of his work and strip the scalp of the unfortunate Milton, when a man cautiously emerged from the scrub at about fifty paces distant, unperceived by the Indian. He leveled his rifle; there was a crack, and a thud, and the savage fell dead beside the Captain. The man now drew back into the thicket, and waited and watched until the Indians, who were in full pursuit of the remnant of the outnumbered and flying company, were far away. When not one remained in sight, he crawled out of the scrub to the place where Captain Bland was lying. He examined him first, and found he was insensible, but did not think he was dead. He next turned to the Indians; two were evidently dead. Concerning the third, he had a doubt. He therefore drew a long bowie knife and plunged it into his heart.

As he did so, he said: "Take that, yer skunk; dead men tell no tales. Ye'd like to wakin up and seein' us, and settin' the other varmints on our trail. Now yer booked for the happy huntin' grounds; may the divil take ye on the way." Then, stealthily looking round, he saw Captain Bland's horse, from which he had fallen when struck by the Indian. The reins became entangled in the branches of a shrub, the leaves of which the horse was nibbling. He loosened the animal and led it beside the Captain. He next took off his coat and spread it over the saddle, and lifted Milton and laid him across it. Then, springing on the horse behind him, he moved forward into the scrub. In a short time he struck a trail, which he pursued for several hundred yards, and stopped in front of a log cabin. Leaping to the ground, he lifted Milton from the horse, entered the cabin, and laid him on the floor. He then turned the horse's head, and applying a stick to him, started him off on the trail by which he had come. He now opened a door, which served as a means of entrance to or exit from the back of the cabin. Taking Milton in his arms, he moved along a narrow pathway, roughly paved with stone, and walked into a pebbly bottomed stream, and proceeded up it for about eighty yards, when he stepped on to a ledge of rock and with difficulty threaded his way over and through a labyrinth of vast boulders. He finally stopped, and again laid down his burden, whilst he removed a slab of stone, disclosing the entrance to a natural cave. He drew Milton into it and laid him on a bed of dried grass and replaced the stone.

The cave had evidently been formed by some disruption of nature. It was simply a hollow between several huge masses of rock, upon which other rocks were heaped in wild confusion. Its length was about nine feet; its breadth a little over five. It was fairly illuminated by the beams of light which straggled through the crevices between the rocks which were piled above it.

Scattered about the floor were various articles of utility, and, standing in one corner, several weapons, chief of which were a heavy shotgun and a tomahawk. The cave had the appearance of having been suddenly occupied, which really was the case. The preceding evening, at nightfall, the man who owned the cabin had discovered that his locality was infested with strange Indians, of whose rising he had heard rumors. Not caring to hazard an attempt at passing through the lines, he had set to work, and, in the night, removed from his cabin to the cave by the creek such provisions and means of defence as he possessed, and anxiously waited for the day.

In the early morning he reconnoitered and found that he was hemmed in; he congratulated himself on having a good store of provisions, and hoped to escape discovery, as his passage up the creek left no trail. Shortly after noon he heard the sound of guns. Believing that an engagement was in progress, he covertly crept through the brush, and reached the scene at the moment when, but for his timely arrival, a period would have been put to the career of Milton.

Having closed the entrance to the cave, the man

turned his attention to Captain Bland, who had not yet recovered his consciousness. He examined his limbs all over, and could find no other injury than a scalp wound. He felt all round the injured part and satisfied himself that there was no fracture of the skull.

"That is all right," said he; "I'll bring him to, and there'll be two of us to foight the beggarly varmints."

He dipped a basinful of water from a bucket which stood on the floor, and bathed the wound which had bled profusely and stained Milton's face and clothes and matted his hair. As the man continued to bathe his head, Milton moved uneasily. He was evidently returning to consciousness, and memory was busy with other scenes far removed from those in which he had been engaged that day, for his first words, uttered with his eyes still closed, were, "Rose, Rose."

The man put down his basin, and looked at him.

"Faith, thin," said he, "is it a rose ye want? Sure, an' I think a dhrap o' whisky would be better for ye. Begorra, thin oi'd git ye a rose, but the divil a rose is there in miles an miles. Maybe a pertaty flower wud do for ye. If so, oi'd fetch ye wan."

At the sound of his voice Milton opened his eyes. He looked at the man, and then round the cave, and then at the man again.

"Tim Maloney," he said, "is that you?"

"Sure an' its mesilf, oi belave, Captain," answered Tim, "and it's well for yer honor I was near handby, tor that murtherin' Indian thafe wanted to stale the schelp of ye, when I livilled me roifle and sint a bullet through the heart of the baste."

"But how came you to be there?" inquired Milton.

"Faith an' oi was belaguered by the black divils; they camped all round me last night and didn't know oi was here. When oi heard the firin' oi jist crept through the scrub to see if oi couldn't escape, or put a shot into one or two of the varmints. Oi saw ye foightin' the three schoundhrels which surrhounded yer honor, and yer throop desertin' ye and runnin' as if the divil was behint 'em. Begorra, thin, ye musht be dhry, Captin; take a drap o' the crathur. It'll put new loife in ye."

Here Tim poured a good sized dram into a tin cup from a black bottle and handed it to Milton. He took it and drank part off. "Now some water, Tim," he said.

Tim handed him some water.

"Pity to sphile that same; ye'll lose the tashte." As he said this he drank the liquor remaining in the cup he had handed to Milton, and smacked his lips with evident relish. It was clear he did not wish to lose the "tashte."

Milton was much revived. He now rose from his couch to test his condition. He found himself much shaken. He had a bruised feeling; his head ached and felt light; on the whole, he came to the conclusion that he was but slightly injured, and would soon be able to resume his duties. He wondered what had become of the residue of his company, and mused with sorrowful regret on the disas-

ter which had overtaken it. His mind again
adverting to his present position, he turned to
Tim, who had slipped out and was re-entering the
cave with a handful of leaves of a wild herb which
he had gathered, with which he proposed to dress
Milton's wounded head.

" Tim," said he, " where are we now ? "

" Shure, thin, Captin," answered Tim, " yer within
half a moile of where ye were foightin' the three
murtherin haythens. But whisht ! The blackguards
will be comin' back soon, and we musht be still."

" Can we not get away from here ? " inquired Milton.

" Git away, is it ? " answered Tim ; " the divil an
inch can we sthir until the cut-throat thaves lave
the hill. They'll be round about us directly thick
as bees. Saints be praised, the wather is handy,
an' we've plinty av biscuits to ate."

Milton found that Tim was correct. In a short
time the Indians returned, and they were surrounded. On several occasions they heard their
voices near them, and knew that they must be at or
near Tim's cabin. Happily for Milton and Tim, their
presence was unknown and unsuspected. Each
evening and morning one of them crawled out to
reconnoitre, ascending rocks and climbing trees on
the hill above them, but always careful to avoid
planting a foot where its print would be left. During those days Milton had much time for thought.
He was greatly distressed at the knowledge that the
misfortune which had overtaken his company
would certainly be telegraphed to San Francisco,

together with the fact of his disappearance. He knew the grief it would occasion his uncle, and also Rose. At the thought of the latter he was ready to dare any danger, or to incur any risk. He proposed to Tim that they should, in the stillness of the night, steal through the Indian camp below them and make their escape, or die in the attempt.

"Bedad, thin," replied Tim, "yer honor talks about dyin' wi' great complacincy. Its mesilf has no fancy for that same. Shure an' if ye try it, yer schalp will be strung up in a bastely wigwam in no time."

Tim was right. There was nothing for it but to wait. There was only one possible mode of exit, and that was directly through the hostile camp. Should they attempt it and succeed, the world would characterize the action as a bold and brave one. Should they try it and fail, then as a foolhardy one. So prone is the world to measure the merit of an action by its success or failure.

On the fourth morning of their captivity Tim returned to the cave with the pleasing intelligence that there was no sign of an Indian anywhere. It was true—they had probably learned that a much stronger force was approaching them, and had decamped and disappeared as suddenly as they had come.

Milton and Tim immediately prepared to leave their retreat. When they quitted the cave Tim replaced the slab.

"Shure," said he, "that hole in the ground has been moighty sarviceable. Be jabers, its more like

a tomb than a house. Faith, an' it'll save me buyin'
a lot in the cimetary afther I've gone to Saint
Pether."

They immediately started on their march. The
settlements were everywhere deserted, and not a living thing was visible around them; the horses, cat-
tle and sheep which once surrounded and gave an
appearance of animation to the homesteads they
passed, had all been been driven away, or lay
putrefying on the ground where they had been wantonly destroyed by the Indians.

Milton soon discovered that he had overestimated
his strength and endurance; his head throbbed and
was giddy, and his limbs were weary and pained.
When towards noon they arrived at a deserted
cabin, he found he could proceed no further that
day. He partook of some biscuit and a little of the
whisky Tim had brought with him, and laid
down to rest, while Tim went out to scan the
country, with which he was well acquainted.
In about two hours he returned, riding on
Captain Bland's horse, which he had found
browsing in a sheltered glade, and had caught
with some difficulty. The reins were broken, and
the saddle considerably dilapidated by the efforts of
the animal to free himself from it. Tim had previously captured a rooster, which had, by some
means escaped the general destruction, and was soli-
tarily striding about the place formerly occupied by
his now devastated harem.

"By the piper that played before Moses!" said
Tim, as he entered the door, " yer honor shall have

somethin' to flavor yer biscuit for supper; ye shall have a roast of this fine Mormon gintleman."

Milton, though no gourmand, was almost as pleased to see the fowl as his horse; though the recovery of the former under existing circumstances was very gratifying. Tim collected some pieces of charred wood and made a fire—he wished to make as little smoke as possible—plucked and dressed his bird, and in less than an hour the Captain and himself, in a very primitive fashion, discussed it with great satisfaction.

Early the following morning they started on their march, Captain Bland bestriding his horse and Tim walking beside him, Milton several times requesting Tim to take the horse for a time. This Tim steadily refused. He wished to reach the Columbia river, and hoped to catch the steamer which he knew should pass down that evening.

On the afternoon of the same day Judge Bland arrived in Portland and of course could gather no more hopeful tidings,. The following morning he read in the Portland "Oregonian" :—

ESCAPE OF CAPTAIN BLAND!

Captain Bland arrived at Salem last night, accompanied by Tim Maloney. He is wounded, but not dangerously. He left by the steamer for Portland.

CHAPTER XL.

ON THE MOVE.

Early the following morning he forwarded the following dispatch :—

" GENERAL STERNE,
         Baldwin Hotel, S. F. :

  " ' My boy ' is safe. Kindly forward the news to Commodore Pye.

                              " REGINALD BLAND."

When this telegram arrived at the Baldwin, General Sterne was away at Yosemite.   When, some days later, he returned, the Commodore's family had gone eastward.   The General had no knowledge of their proposed stopping places, nor even the route they proposed to take after leaving Council Bluffs. He consulted Frank Carleton, but he was no wiser. The General had purposely refrained from asking the question.   Frank had not thought of the number of different routes, and had neglected to inquire. He only knew that they were to spend a day or two in Utah, and then go on.   The General finally dispatched the information to Utah, but, for reasons to be explained hereafter, it never reached the Commodore.

Judge Bland waited at Portland the arrival of the steamer which was to bring his boy to him. He was naturally very anxious to know what was the nature of the injury he had sustained, concerning which he had no information, save what was contained in that brief dispatch to the Portland "Oregonian."

When at length the boat drew alongside the wharf, he was delighted to see Milton standing on the deck, apparently not much the worse for his adventure.

"Thank God, 'my boy, that you escaped!" said he, as he grasped his hand; "were you badly wounded?"

"Only a trifle, uncle," answered Milton; "just a scratch on my head. Nature has endowed me with a thick skull, to which fact I may, in part, attribute my present safety, but I must introduce to you Mr. Tim Maloney, to whom I am indebted for saving my scalp, which would certainly have bid good-bye to its resting place had it not been for him. Tim, this is my uncle, Judge Bland, of whom you have heard me speak."

The Judge grasped the horny hand that was held out to him and said: "I am proud to know you, Mr. Maloney. The service you have rendered 'my boy' will never be forgotten by either of us."

"Shure, thin, Judge," answered Tim, "one good turn desarves another; the Captain saved my back from being skinned two years ago, an' I saved his schelp from the blackguard Injun last week. That's tit for tat, yer honor."

Milton and Tim accompanied the Judge to his hotel. Milton still suffered. Any strong exercise provoked vertigo, and he experienced much lassitude. His uncle was greatly concerned about him, and insisted on his consulting a physician.

The doctor said that absolute avoidance of violent exercise and exciting engagements was positively necessary to secure Milton's restoration to health.

The Judge, unknown to Milton, obtained a certificate to that effect from the physician, and dispatched it to Washington. The result was the receipt by Milton of a telegram which congratulated him on his escape and renewed his leave of absence.

Milton was more annoyed than gratified. He proposed to do his duty. So far he knew he had done it. Knowing nothing of the dispatch sent by his uncle, he was inclined to think of the one he had received as a dismissal from active service, rather than an act of kindness to himself. He laid the telegram before his uncle, and would have at once replied, requesting active employment, had not the Judge first forbidden the act, and afterward told him of the dispatch he had sent, enclosing the doctor's certificate.

"I am very sorry you did it uncle, but it cannot be helped."

In two days they were on their return voyage to San Francisco.

Captain Bland very handsomely requited Tim Maloney; the Judge supplementing his gift. Tim went with them to the wharf. His last words were: "May the saints purtect and save ye, Captin, and yer honor, too (to the Judge), and whin ye git to ther gates of heaven, may Saint Pether be waitin' for ye to bid ye welcome."

The third day after leaving Portland, the Judge and Captain Bland were again located at the Palace

Hotel. Milton used the earliest opportunity to visit the Baldwin. He inquired for General Sterne, but could obtain no other information than that he had left the hotel, and that his baggage had been sent to meet the overland train the preceding morning.

He then called on Mr. Equity, who was delighted to see him, and once more thanked him for the generous assistance he had rendered him in his day of difficulty.

"Do not mention it, Mr. Equity," said Milton; and then added, "I have called especially to see if you can give me any information regarding the movements of General Sterne."

"Very little," answered the attorney. "He called on me three days ago and gave me instructions regarding his business. He told me he was going East, and would probably cross the Atlantic before he returned."

"His sudden departure was not contemplated, then?" said Milton.

"I think not," replied Mr. Equity; "it was the first I had heard of it. I saw him off yesterday morning."

"Did he propose to go direct to New York?" inquired Milton.

"I believe not, sir," said the attorney; "a Mr. Carleton was with him, and I think I heard him mention that they proposed to visit various places on the road."

Milton had hoped to find General Sterne, and through him to gain some intelligence of the move-

meLts of the Commodore's family.   He knew of no
other source at which to apply, and he knew nothing of the letter which the General had written to
his uncle ; it had crossed them on their return
from Portland.

The Judge was greatly concerned when he found
that the General was gone, and wondered what
could be the urgent business that had induced
him to leave San Francisco on such short notice.
He also observed how great the distress of Milton
was at not being able to find any clue as to the
whereabouts of the Commodore and his party. For
a long time he pondered the subject.   Late in the
evening he astonished Milton by saying :—

"Suppose we take a trip to Europe, 'my boy.'   I
think it would do me no harm, and would be the
means of fully restoring your health."

There was a pleasant twinkle in the Judge's eye
as he concluded the sentence.

"Agreed, uncle," said Milton ; " I was thinking of
going myself, anyway."

" Very well," answered the Judge; " I will make
my arrangements with all possible dispatch. As
soon as they are completed, we will start."

In less than a week they were on the cars. They
made two or three short breaks in the overland
journey, and arrived in New York on the fourteenth
day after leaving San Francisco, and on the seven-
teenth steamed out of the harbor.

I have not described their passage overland,
though there are numberless points of wonderful
interest on the route. Neither shall I describe their

passage across the Atlantic. A sea-going experience of several score thousand miles has failed to reveal to me the charm with which some writers have striven to invest the situation. I have traveled on some ships on which officers and men sought every opportunity to add to the comfort and convenience of the passengers. I have been on others in which everything done for a passenger was performed grudgingly. I have traveled with passengers who did all they could to make the journey pleasant to each other, and again with companions amongst whom the preservation of harmony seemed to be an impossibility. I have seen seas on which no ripple moved for days together, and again, storm succeeding storm for weeks in succession. I have known a very few who really enjoyed the indolent, out-of-the-world life of a sea voyage. But I have never known a single individual who has proclaimed sea-sickness a pleasant sensation, or desired to have the contents of his soup plate emptied on his garments more than once at a meal. The majority of sea voyageurs from the beginning "long for the desired haven." When the novelty of sea-sickness has worn off, the traveler ordinarily realizes the consciousness of being in a prison, the walls of which are surrounded by the restless ocean, and longs for escape to a wider field of action. If he will be candid, he will express, if not the words, certainly the sentiment, Tim Maloney would inevitably have uttered: "Sure thin, the plisintist part av the say vyage is afther ye get ashore."

CHAPTER XLI.

DEERLANDS IN COMMOTION.

Great was the bustle and excitement at Deerlands that summer morning, when Commodore Pye's steward and his housekeeper each received a letter from him informing them of his intended return, accompanied by his sister, Mrs. Clare, his daughter and Miss Stanley, her two servants and his own, directing the steward " to have the house, stables and gardens in good order," and the housekeeper " to be sure that the arrangements for the comfortable installment of the ladies be made complete." Only three weeks were allotted them to have everything in perfect order.

The steward immediately mounted his horse and rode in quest of painters, upholsterers, chimney sweeps, and additional gardeners and house servants. The old housekeeper took off her spectacles, gave them an extra rub, and re-perused her letter, and then proceeded to overhaul the linen chests. She next inspected the china and plate, and finally prepared a memorandum of such things as would be required.

They were both very busy that morning. When dinner time arrived, the steward called with intent to dine with the housekeeper and discuss the necessary preparations. She said to him :—

" Only to think, Mr. Guarder, of the young master coming home to Deerlands after all these years. I never expected to see him again, and Miss Rose coming, too. Why, she must be a young lady grown. It is nineteen years the seventh of next month since Mrs. Pye died. Poor young thing, she looked so beautiful in her coffin I could not believe she was dead. Dear, dear, how the young master did take on! That was a sad time. When I think of it, it seems as if it was only yesterday."

"Yes, Mrs. Home," replied the steward, "the time has gone quickly by. Mr. Pye (though he is Commodore Pye now), must be greatly changed. He was not much more than a boy when he took the baby to France."

"And he calls himself an American now," continued Mrs. Home; "why he does that I cannot tell, with his fine old home here all the time. And then he tells me that James Wily is coming with Mrs. Clare, and Johnson is still with him, and that Will Wily, the little boy that ran away from home and was believed to be dead, has made a fortune out in California—I think he said twelve thousand pounds—only think of it, and he is coming home to see his old father and mother, and is going to be married. That must be a wonderful country, that America."

"Little Will, said Mr. Guarder, "ran away just before the young master went to France, so he must be nigh onto thirty, and James must be getting up in years. I shall be glad to see the master here again; it will be like old times to see life and stir in the place."

"And so shall I," said Mrs. Home. "Dear, dear! though, Mr. Guarder, it will make us feel very old to see all the young people round about again. Miss

Rose, I hear, is a beautiful young lady—just like her poor, dear mother. That reminds me, Mr. Guarder, we must see that the enclosure round the vault is in good order, and have some new roses and other flowers put in. They will be sure to go to see it."

Every day was a busy one with Mrs. Home now. She had to superintend the taking up and laying down of carpets; the removal of covers from furniture and pictures; the collection of household supplies for the company, and a thousand other things besides. The old lady was tired out every night, but she indefatigably persevered. She was determined everything should be in order, and in accordance with the wishes of the Commodore.

The news of the return of the family to the Hall had spread not only through the village of Deerlands, but also the surrounding country. Mr. Guarder was interrogated every day by members of the various families of the neighborhood. The older ones wished to know all about the young 'Squire, now an American Commodore, who had been so well known by them in his earlier days. The younger sought covertly to elicit information concerning the young ladies. The village bell-ringers deputed their Captain to see Mr. Guarder and request him to let them know, as early as he possibly could, the exact time at which the Commodore would arrive. They proposed, as he and his family entered the village, to make the old church tower resound with such joyful peals as had not been heard for many a day.

The expected hour arrived at last. The Commodore's carriage, newly painted and bearing the family crest on the panel of each door, was brought forth from its long seclusion, and a splendid pair of bays harnessed to it. They were the progeny of stock which the Commodore had highly prized in time past. A dog cart followed the carriage, to convey the servants from the railway station to the Hall. The distance was about three miles. To the Commodore and his sister the scenes through which they passed, on the way from the station to the Hall, were all familiar. The same cottages stood in the same garden patches; the same knarled old trees stood in the same old hedgerows of white thorn, blackberry and sweetbriar. It seemed to them that the same old rooks from the neighborhood of the same old nests, in the same old treetops, uttered the same old, querulous caw, caw, which might be regarded either as a welcome or a reproof.

But the people : here and there an old or middle aged man or woman doffed his hat or dropped her curtsey. They were the youth and middle aged of the Commodore's and Mrs. Clare's days in their English home; nearly all had passed from their memories, or were so changed by the ruthless hand of time that they scarcely knew them. The young men and maidens they passed gazed after them with a shy curiosity. The children looked at them with eyes wide open with wonder.

It was with a strange mingling of emotion that they found themselves strangers in their own land, where twenty years before every man and woman, and every apple-faced, dirty little urchin had known them as Miss Maude Pye and the young 'Squire.

Geraldine and Rose intensely enjoyed the drive to the old home, of which both had heard much from Mrs. Clare, but neither had seen, and they were gratified by the respectful salutations made by the elderly people they passed on the road to Mrs. Clare and the Commodore.

The park gates were visible from the church tower, upon which a watchman was posted. Deerlands church stood near the Hall.

As they entered the gates, which were thrown open on their approach by a chubby boy, a son of the keeper of the lodge, the signal was given by the watchman on the tower, and the bells sent forth a joyous chime. They wound along a serpentine avenue of giant elms, from which the Hall was occasionally visible. As they neared the Hall the music of the bells changed, and sent forth on the balmy summer air—

"Home, Sweet Home!"

It was too much for Mrs. Clare. Tears she did not seek to hide rolled down her cheeks, whilst the Commodore drew forth his handkerchief and appeared to be looking across the park, whilst he was secretly removing the moisture that damped his own cheeks, and which he had striven, but in vain, to suppress.

The Hall was a rambling, two-story building. The main or central portion was of the Elizabethian period; the two wings were of later date. That on the left had been added by the Commodore's great-grandfather. The right wing was built by his father before he brought home his wife to the old paternal mansion. It was one of those places always full of pleasant surprises, in which, as you wander through them, you are continually stumbling upon some pleasant room or some quiet snuggery when least expected.

The Commodore, when he left it, did not know how long he would absent himself. He had given his orders that the furniture, carpets and paintings should be covered and preserved, and from the time he quitted his home they had never been used or exposed, save for the purpose of cleaning, and now the rich curtains and hangings were all restored to their places, and the coverings removed from the furniture and paintings. The interior of the Hall presented much the same appearance as when he left it.

As the carriage drew up at the door, both Mr. Guarder and Mrs. Home stood on the steps waiting to receive them, whilst the servants formed in a double line on either side of the hall. The Commodore and Mrs. Clare shook hands with the steward and housekeeper, who exhibited great delight at their return.

" Dear, dear! Mr. George—I should say, 'Squire— I mean, Commodore," said Mrs. Home, " this does my old heart good, for I never expected to see you any more; and Miss Maude, too—I beg pardon, I mean Mrs. Clare—and Miss Rose, too! looking as beautiful as an angel; just like her poor, dear mamma; and this other beautiful young lady. Thank God! you are home again, at last, Mr.—I mean Commodore."

"Yes, Mrs. Home, we are here once more; and I am glad to see you looking so well; and you, also, Mr. Guarder," said the Commodore.

"Thank you, Commodore," said the steward.

And this time, following Mr. Guarder's lead, Mrs. Home, without stumbling, replied:—

"Thank you, Commodore."

CHAPTER XLII.

OLD AND NEW FRIENDS.

The following morning Rose and Geraldine roamed over the Hall with delighted interest. They examined every nook and corner, and Rose proclaimed it the dearest and pleasantest old home she had ever seen. In the left wing was the picture gallery, where hung life-sized portraits of her ancestors, both male and female, for many generations. One picture alone was veiled; an intuitive knowledge of the Commodore's wishes had restrained Mrs. Home from uncovering it. Rose drew aside the draperies and looked upon a portrait which, but for the fashion of the dress, might have been taken for her own. She knew it must be her mother. Long and earnestly she looked at the painting, Geraldine standing beside her with one arm around her.

"How beautiful!" Rose involuntarily exclaimed. "It must be a portrait of my dear mamma."

"Yes, darling," answered Geraldine. "Your papa is said to have been devoted to her. I do not wonder at his tender eare for you—you are a living copy ot her."

Rose reverently replaced the covering, and they left the gallery and returned to the drawing-room. They had a number of morning callers that day, and for many succeeding ones. From a circuit of many miles the leading families hastened to renew their old acquaintance with the Commodore and Mrs. Clare, or to establish friendly relations with a family which for generations had been honored in the county and out of it.

Invitations followed, and Rose and Geraldine soon found themselves reduced to the necessity of planning their time to avoid the conflict of engagements to ride, to drive, or to visit.

The third morning after their arrival at Deerlands Mrs. Clare received a letter from Mr. Carleton. It ran :—

CARLETON MANOR,
NEAR SALISBURY.

DEAR MADAM :

To-morow I propose doing myself the pleasure of calling on you; my aunt Carleton and my cousin Violet will accompany me. We shall come by the morning train which will reach Deerlands at 11:45, and will return by the 4:30.

Kindly present my respedts to Commodore Pye and the young ladies. Trusting this will find you all in perfect health and happiness, I remain, dear madam,

Yours very truly,

FRANK CARLETON.

Two hours after the receipt of the letter the Commodore's carriage returned from the station, bringing the expected guests.

When the introductions were effected, Mrs. Clare inquired how it came about that Mr. Carleton had missed them at New York.

Mr. Carleton expressed his regret at the circumstance. He explained that he had been delayed on the road longer than he had anticipated, and that, when he reached New York he had discovered to his great regret that his friends had sailed the preceding day.

Then followed a comparison of experiences on the journey, which was necessarily confined to the Commodore, Mrs. Clare, and Mr. Carleton. The three young ladies had withdrawn to a bay window at the far end of the room, and were carrying on an animated and evidently interesting conversation in a suppressed tone.

Presently Rose came to Mrs. Clare and Mrs. Carleton and asked them to join her party.

"And what are we to do, daughter?" inquired the Commodore, endeavoring to assume a look of dismay.

"I am sorry for you, papa," said Rose mischievously; "this is a ladies' private consultation, and you know, we have been in America, and believe in women's rights."

"Mutiny and desertion!" said the Commodore comically. "The ship's crew are rebellious. Carleton, we had better go—we are not wanted. Serious business on hand, evidently."

The Commodore, followed by Mr. Carleton, went to the smoking-room, where he offered Frank one of his favorite Cubans, and, lighting one himself, they strolled out to view the stables and the grounds.

They first went to the stables, where Mr. Carleton critically surveyed the stud.

"They were all bred," said the Commodore, "on the estate, from old stock which we have had in the family for generations, and have been continually improving. There is not one of the horses here that stood in the stables in my time—they are all gone. Guarder, my steward, has continued to breed the stock, and cull out and sell the older and inferior animals, and has always kept a number of the best on hand, expecting, he says, that some day I should come home suddenly and require them. I am anticipating an addition to my stables to-day. Unknown to my daughters, I sent one of my grooms across the Channel to fetch their favorite riding-horses—they should be here soon."

"I have heard Miss Stanley and Miss Pye speak of them," said Mr. Carleton. "Araby and Mesrour they call them."

"The same," answered the Commodore.

Leaving the stables, on their way to the gardens they passed the kennel, still so called, though no longer peopled by its once numerous canine inhabitants.

"Here," said the Commodore, "I had one of the finest packs of fox-hounds in England. Before I began my wanderings I presented them to the county."

As they were entering the garden the lunch-bell rang. The Commodore led the way back to the Hall and, they shortly afterwards joined the ladies at table.

"I omitted to ask you concerning our mutual friend, General Sterne," said Mrs. Clare. "Was he well when you left San Francisco?"

"He was quite well when I last saw him," answered Mr. Carleton.

The Commodore, Mrs. Clare, Geraldine and Rose all looking at Mr. Carleton, did not perceive the look, half inquiry, half amusement, with which Mrs. Carleton and Violet regarded him.

Four o'clock arrived, and the Commodore's carriage was in waiting. The friends having been vainly requested to stay till the morrow, parted with mutual expressions of pleasure at the meeting and regret at the necessity for such an early termination of the visit.

When they had driven off, the Commodore said to Rose:—

"And now, daughter, will you explain the proceedings of that mysterious conclave of ladies, or am I still to remain in darkness?"

"Oh, yes, papa, I will explain," answered Rose, smiling, and rising from her seat, she walked across to the Commodore's chair and placed her arms around his neck and stood looking down into his face.

"Now listen, papa," she said. "Violet and Mr. Carleton are to be married a fortnight from to-day, and we have accepted an invitation for you and ourselves to be present at the wedding. We are to go to Carleton Lodge, Mrs. Carleton's house, the preceding day, and Geraldine and I are to be first and second of the bridesmaids."

"This is beyond all precedent," said the Commodore. "The ship's company has entered into an engagement without consulting the commander. Suppose I veto the whole arrangement, what then?"

As the Commodore asked the question, his face was a study. He was trying to look stern, whilst contented amusement and satisfaction played about his mouth and eyes, and would not be repressed.

"That will not do, papa," she said. "You are under female government now. Ladies are admitted to the franchise. We claim our rights. You are a small minority of one, and law-abiding citizens always submit to the will of the majority."

"I am afraid that American visit was a mistake."

Rose and Geraldine both looked very serious as the Commodore made this remark. The thoughts of both had flown across the Atlantic.

The Commodore noticed the change, and continued :—

"Well, daughter, I suppose I must submit, lest worse evils should befall me?"

Rose bent down and kissed her father, saying: "Thank you, papa."

Not one of that group could foresee the results which would ensue from that accepted invitation. There would have been anxious minds and palpitating hearts, and wakeful thoughts and earnest questionings, could the vail which hid the mystic

T

future have been drawn from before their eyes, and the secrets of those days revealed. Infinite beneficence has willed that we should stumble on in ignorance alike of the good and the evil that are stored for us in the unfolding hours of coming time.

Whilst the family were entertaining their friends in the drawing-room, there was joy in the servants' hall. William Wily had come, and was being entertained by his brother, James, and by Johnson. Annette meantime flitting about in a fever of pleasurable excitement. No sooner were the Carletons gone than James informed the Commodore of his brother's arrival.

The Commodore immediately went to him and gave him a kind welcome. He learned that Wily had reached England the day before; had seen his father and mo᾽her, and come on to claim the fulfillment of the promise given by Annette, and that they were to be united in ten days, if the Commodore and Mrs. Clare interposed no objection.

"There will be none, Mr. Wily," said the Commodore. "My sister has spoken of you, and knows she may have to part with Annette any day; and, William," he added, "you can celebrate your wedding here, if you choose."

Ten days later the servants' hall was decorated, the Commodore had given leave to James Wily to cut whatever was required from the garden and shrubbery. The hall was resplendent with flowers of every hue.

The kind-hearted Commodore sent a carriage to bring the elder Wilys, who were too feeble to walk.

In the village church Annette and William Wily were made man and wife—the Commodore giving away the bride—Mrs. Clare and her daughters witnessing the ceremony. When it was concluded the marriage party returned to the Hall, where they were entertained at a midday breakfast, which Mrs. Home, following the instructions given by the Commodore, had made both bountiful and good.

After the breakfast was over, the tables were cleared from the room, and a violinist and harper invited the company to join in the festive dance, the Commodore redeeming his promise by leading off the first figure.

It was a happy though somewhat boisterous time. By the evening train Annette and William left for London, having received a parting blessing from father and mother, and reiterated good wishes from all present. It was their intention to spend a week in town seeing the sights, and then sail for their distant home in California.

The Commodore sent them to the station in his own carriage. When they were ready to leave, James Wily brought Annette a package, which she found to contain valuable souvenirs of the esteem and regard of Mrs. Clare, Rose and Geraldine for their late trusted and faithful dependent, with good wishes for her happiness and prosperity in her far away home.

CHAPTER XLIII.

THE VISIT TO CARLETON LODGE, AND WHAT CAME OF IT.

The flight of time is closely allied to the problem the philosophers of all ages have sought to solve, viz: the mystery of perpetual motion. They have not found the object of their search—they will never find it. It is the grand secret of the Omnipotent. We observe its presence on every side, but we cannot fathom it. Within the limited sphere of our observations, we mark its operations, but we cannot produce them. Perpetual motion is the master mystery of creation. We sometimes speak of the creations of man; it is only a figure of speech. Man cannot create—he can but imitate. Creative power is the prerogative of Deity alone. Everthing that lives contains the germs of other existences like its own. It is the stamp of God, who has willed that his work should have eternal movement. Creation and perpetual motion walk side by side. Look at that large oak tree; you tell me it will die. What of that? Has it not shed tens of thousands of acorns, each containing within itself the germ of another oak? The mystery of creation was in each of those little cones—the germs of the trunk, the spreading branches, the verdant leaves, and acorns yet to come, were there. And the tree—does it perish? Part of it goes to build a ship, part of it goes to build a house, part of it is burned. What then? The constituent parts remain. The weight and substance and proportion of the material of the Great Artificer are still the same. The very decay of the tree is not an end—it is part of eternal progression. When the philosopher can make an acorn which will grow he will discover the grand secret of perpetual motion. God's work never stands still. What greater mystery is there than Time? Man's labor is limited by time. It is his destroyer. It is God's factor. It annihilates man's work. It perfects God's. Who can measure it? We have a record of a few thousand years. What of it? We vainly try to fathom the illimitable ages that preceded them. Who shall estimate or measure the sum of ages yet to come?

We look forward to a time—we anticipate its approach—it comes at last. But even as we say: "It is here," lo! it begins to glide away, and ceases to be the living present—it is gone into the dead past.

A series of fully occupied days filled the interim between the call of the Carletons and the time appointed for the journey to Carleton Lodge. They glided almost imperceptibly away. Riding, driving, calls made and received, visits given and returned, filled up the time and it was gone. Rose and Geraldine scarcely knew how it went. Often during those days did they converse of Milton Bland. They had read of his escape in an Omaha paper. Of the telegram sent by General Sterne they knew nothing. It had not found the Commodore, and had been returned to the General. From the time that Rose knew that Milton was in safety, she continued to improve, and delighted her friends by the rapid return of her old gaiety. To Geraldine she often remarked : " I do not fear Milton—I know he is true. I feared those dreadful Indians. He has escaped. He will come to me." Her own unerring, truthful nature was free from mistrust—no doubt entered her mind. She rested on his promise, and never for one moment lost faith in him.

Far otherwise was it with Geraldine. Rose had observed in an indifferent manner the growing interest General Sterne and Geraldine exhibited for each other when at Yosemite. Bowed down by her own grief, her observations had drawn no remark from her. In the days of great sorrow the purest and most generous natures, as well as less lofty ones, are liable to self-absorbtion. Sorrow is a self-ish passion. The greater our love for the lost one the more intense is our grief. To the departed the end may be a happy release. To us it is a fearful sorrow, because our beloved will no more make glad our eyes, or receive and give back our warm embrace. It is for ourselves we mourn.

Hope had returned to Rose, and joy came with it ; her thoughts, no longer self-concentrated, went out to the friends around her. She thought Geraldine had a secret. She now felt for her the tenderest sympathy. She often spoke of General Sterne. Geraldine would listen with a pleased interest, until Rose would hint at a warmer feeling than friend-ship existing between the two, then Geraldine would shrink from the subject, and turn away as the sensitive plant of the East Indies shrinks and folds away its leaves when a hand is laid upon it. Not even her much-loved, adopted sister must know that she had given her heart where she had ceased to hope there was a return of love. There was in General Sterne's character much that was calculated to win the admiration of a mind like that of Geraldine. Its force and strength, its very stern features, were to her attractions, and elicited admiration that could never have been won by the mere surface graces of pleasing manner unsupported by strong mental characteristics. In her acquaintance with him she had passed through four distinct phases of feeling. She had first experienced a feeling of repulsion, which had yielded to one of interest; interest had changed to admiration, and admiration had grown up into love. She had thought—nay, more, she had felt certain, that her love was sought by him. She had given it; she could not recall it. But it was all a mistake. Should she allow other eyes to read her secret? No. She would think of the General as a kind friend, and would conquer and crush out of her heart her love for him. If after this there was a visible change in her, it was that her calm dignity was a little more grave, but so slight was the difference that none save Rose observed it.

Little did either of them dream how near was the happiness each believed so far removed. General Sterne was now in England; he was Frank Carleton's guest at Carleton Lodge; they had crossed the Atlantic together. An almost brotherly regard had grown up in the mind of each for the other, and the General had at last frankly told his friend the hope which was drawing him to England. Mr. Carleton had already divined it, and prepared the way for the acknowledgement. He told the General all about his own attachment to his cousin Violet, and that he had made a confidante of Miss Stanley on their journey to America, and then he could not speak, or the General hear, too much of the virtues and graces of Geraldine. "Whom I shall always regard," said Frank, " as a dear sister."

The day had come for the visit to Carleton Lodge, the Commodore and his family were kindly welcomed, and the evening passed by in discussing arrangements of the coming day. The wedding was to take place at Carleton church at eleven o'clock A. M. The following morning the Lodge was full of the bustle of preparation. At half-past ten the carriages were at the door. At a quarter to eleven, when Rose and Geraldine were about to enter the carriage which was to convey them to the church, Mrs. Carleton said : "Expect to see old friends, dears."

What did it mean ? There was no time to ask— Mrs. Carleton was gone to her own carriage.

The guests were all seated ; the procession moved forward.

At a few minutes past eleven they entered the church. A group was already congregated about the altar, waiting to receive the bride. They moved up the aisle. What was it made the eyes of Geraldine light up with a sudden glow ? What was it caused Rose's face and shoulders to be dyed with an instant flush ?

There, beside Frank Carleton, stood General Sterne, and with them were Milton and Judge Bland.

Did each see the earnest, questioning look bestowed upon her, as they almost mechanically occupied the places assigned to them ? Were their thoughts entirely with the clergyman as he commenced to read :—

" Dearly beloved, we are gathered together here in the sight of God, and in the face of this congregation, to join together this man and this woman in holy matrimony ; which is an honorable estate, instituted by Cod in the time of man's innocency ;"

Or were their thoughts with Frank and Violet, who, now free, would in a few minutes be bound by solemn promises given unto God and man to love each other and be faithful unto death?

If so, there were mingled with them reminiscences of scenes and incidents that had transpired six thousand miles away; in San Francisco; in the wilds of Oregon, and in the wondrous valley of Yosemite.

The service is ended; the names inscribed on the register. Frank triumphantly leads his bride to the carriage. The Commodore offers his arm to Mrs. Carleton, the Judge is the escort of Mrs. Clare; General Sterne singles out Geraldine, and Milton possesses himself of Rose; those two are heedless of the other guests ; they are restored to each other; their carriage has no other occupant ; the beautiful world seems to them to be newly adorned to-day; the cortege winds through the gaping and admiring crowd; they are out in the open country, between high hedgerows and tall, overhanging trees.

"Did you expect me to come to you?" asked Milton.

"I knew you would," answered Rose.

"Are you glad? Did you wish me to come?" he asked, gently taking her unresisting hand.

"So glad!" she said, glancing shyly for a moment into his eyes.

"And will you give yourself to me, Rose, to be my darling wife?" he asked.

She placed her other hand in his. It was her answer; whilst Milton pressed his lips to hers, tremulous with emotion and delight. What cared they if the blue-eyed forget-me-not, looking from the bank upon which stood the hedge-row, saw them? What cared they if the little birds flitting by should bear the tale of their love to the four corners of the world? Their hearts were full of a great content. Too soon the carriage drew up at the door of the Lodge. The guests assemble round the sumptuous breakfast table. The usual healths and toasts are drank. The bride retires to don her traveling attire. The carriage bears the newly united pair away, and the guests stroll forth upon the green lawn, and wander through the well-kept winding pathways of the shrubbery.

Geraldine and General Sterne are together and alone. They enter an arbor—one of the many scattered along the walks. The arbor is overgrown with climatis and honeysuckle. The balmy air is redolent of summer sweets. A lazy stillness has fallen on the birds of song. They are taking their siesta. A peaceful calm rests upon the face of the landscape. Geraldine and the General for a time yield to the universal spell, and sit in silent enjoyment.

At length he spoke :—

"Do you think," he inquired, "that our young friends, Frank and Violet, will make a happy pair, Miss Stanley?"

" I think so," she answered. " When we were in America he never tired of speaking to me of Violet. I seemed to know her the first time I met her. She speaks of Frank as if he were all the world to her. Yes, I think they will be very happy."

"Do you know," he said, " that until you left us I used to think that you were engaged to Mr. Carleton ?"

"I engaged to Frank!" said she, fixing a questioning, wondering gaze upon him for a moment, then turning it to the distant hills, whilst a thoughtful look came into her eyes. Her spirit was moving amidst the scenes of distant California, and her mind penetrating the mystery of those pleasant days. Here was the solution of which she had not dreamed. Recovering herself, she added :—

"He gave me his confidence as if I were his sister, and I learned to love him."

"You did love him then, Miss Stanley ?" As he asked the question a look of infinite pain crossed his features. " Have I come so many miles for this ? " he asked himself.

Geraldine saw the expression of pain, and answered :—

" Yes; I loved him as a brother; I never gave him any other love. I have no other love to give. I love another."

As she spoke she looked at him, and again saw that painful contraction of his features.

" Why can he not see ? " she murmured to herself. " Shall I tell you who that other is ? " she asked.

As she spoke she gently laid her hand on his. At her touch every pulse thrilled, every nerve quivered. He felt as if he should go mad.

Hastily withdrawing his hand, he answered, bitterly :—

" It is not my right to ask such a favor, Miss Stanley."

" And the world," she said, " will say I have no right to impart the information. I dare defy the world with Truth. The first, the only love of my life, was—and is—yours."

What did he hear ? Was he in his senses ? Was this not a chimera of his own brain ? Could it be true ? Turning to look at her, he read in the now blushing face and half tearful eyes, the record of the Truth.

Taking the late rejected hand in both his own, pressing it to his lips, he said :—

" God bless you, darling ! You have lifted before my eyes the cup of happiness, which in my folly I was pushing from me. I was too blind to see it.

But may you not repent, Geraldine. You know the record of my life. A wide span, eighteen years, divides our ages. It may be that as the years roll on the difference will seem greater than now."

"That difference I have always known," answered Geraldine, simply.

"And knowing it, you give me your love now and forever, without mistrust or doubt?"

"Yes, yes," she said, "forever. Without mistrust—or doubt."

———

CHAPTER XLIV.

SERIOUS QUESTIONS.

During the pleasant hours of that summer afternoon the Commodore's family learned that General Sterne arrived in England at the same time as Mr. Carleton; that affairs of great moment, with which he had been entrusted, had detained him in London until the day before the wedding. That whilst staying at the Charing Cross Hotel he had been pleasantly surprised by seeing Judge and Captain Bland at the same hostelry. They arrived the day before the General was to leave London for Carleton Manor. He had at once telegraphed to Mr. Carleton, who immediately forwarded a dispatch to the Judge, inviting him and Milton to come and witness the ceremony, and another to the General, requesting him to bring them down with-

out fail.   To neither did Frank Carleton communicate the information that the Commodore and his
family would be present at the wedding.   In fact,
he thought it would be most enjoyable, to witness
an all-round surprise.   But when the time of meet-
came, it was at the altar, and the novelty and gravity of his own position made him oblivious to the
proceedings of his friends.   Nevertheless, when the
guests were seated at the breakfast table, he fully
enjoyed the expressions of surprise and pleasure
uttered by them at the perfect reunion of the
Californian circle.

The Commodore at once asked all three to return
with him on the morrow, and spend a week or two
at Deerlands   The General and Milton both hesitated, and finally answered that they would give
their reply in the morning.   The two Blands and
the General were to stay that night at Carleton
Manor; the Commodore would remain at the Lodge.

Early the next morning General Sterne, Judge
Bland and Milton called at the Lodge.   Milton requested a private interview with the Commodore.
Mrs. Carleton directed a servant to show them the
way to the library.

When they had left the room, General Sterne desired the same favor of Mrs. Clare.

Mr. Carleton gave directions to show the General
and Mrs. Clare into the drawing-room.

When they, too, were gone, Mrs. Carleton turned
to Judge Bland, and said :—

" There is mysteriousness in the air this morning.

Do not you wish to have a private interview with some one, Mr. Bland ?"

" Life, madam," said the Judge, sententiously, " is full of Mystery," and then gallantly added : " I, madam, shall be content and happy in having an interview with yourself and the young ladies." But looking around he found that Rose and Geraldine had noiselessly stolen from their presence.

Mrs. Clare was not greatly surprised when General Sterne said to her : " I have requested the favor of this interview, madam, to ask your consent to the union of your ward, Miss Stanley, and myself."

" Is Miss Stanley aware that you intend to speak to me on this subject, General Sterne ? "

" I have come to you with her knowledge and consent," answered the General.

" Such being the case," said Mrs. Clare, " you have my approval. Geraldine's instincts rarely err, and her decisions I have never had cause to question. You have won a great prize—I do not allude to her fortune, but to Geraldine herself. There are few like her. Be tender and true to her."

" I thank you, madam," answered the General; " I will love and cherish her as long as I live."

Meantime Milton had asked the Commodore to give him Rose.

The Commodore listened to all Milton had to say, but made no reply. He arose from his seat and pulled the bell. To the servant who answered it he said : " Find Miss Pye, and ask her to come here."

With a palpitating heart Rose entered the library.

" Come to me, daughter," said the Commodore.

Rose walked across the room and stood beside him.

"This young gentleman (indicating Milton), has had the impudence to come begging to me, and of all my possessions he has seen fit to ask me for you. What shall be done to him, daughter? Shall we order him out of the house?"

Rose threw both arms around her father's neck and murmured: "No, papa," and then bowed her head on his shoulder to hide her blushes.

"Are you not angry with him?" he asked.

"No, papa."

"But what shall I do to him? What shall I say to him?"

"Say 'yes,' papa."

"Hey! What? But suppose I decline to say 'yes'?"

"But you won't, papa?"

The Commodore gently unloosed her arms, tenderly kissed her, then placing her hand in Milton's, he said: "Take her, Milton, and make her happy. May the Lord deal with you as you deal with her."

He opened one of the French windows leading out on to the lawn. "Now go," he said, and the lovers passed out into the sunlight and away to a shady seat.

Never was God's world so beautiful.

Again the Commodore rang the bell. This time he sent word to Judge Bland that he wished to see him.

The two gentlemen sat for some time discussing the prospects of the young people.

"I shall give Deerlands to Rose," said the Commodore, "and in event of her having a family, it must descend to her eldest son. It must not be sold. Its revenues amount to about twenty-five thousand dollars a year. It will be pleasant for them to visit it now and then."

The Judge informed him of the value and extent of Milton's own properties in America, and his intention to add to them by way of marriage gift to "his boy."

The General and Milton did not require pressing to accept the Commodore's invitation to stay at Deerlands now. That afternoon they all bid a kind farewell to Mrs. Carleton, whom they had enlightened with regard to the mystery of the morning. The good old lady was delighted to learn that her invitations had resulted in so much happiness to her guests. She kissed both Rose and Geraldine with motherly kindness as she bade them good-bye, wishing them every happiness. That evening the Commodore and his guests rested at Deerlands.

In six weeks the double wedding was to be celebrated. We will not linger over those intervening days. They were full of contented happiness. Mesrour and Araby were in almost daily requisition, and Rose and Geraldine, attended by Milton and the General, rode forth to visit the various points of interest for miles around. The neighboring families delighted to do honor to the Commodore and his guests. Onward rolled the never-tiring wheels of time. Picnics, water parties and social

U

gatherings filled up the happy hours.   But in
nothing did they more delight than their rambles
through the old, peaceful English lanès and mead-
ows, in the quiet calm of those summer evenings,
when the twilight lingered far into the night, and
the soft, mild air was laden with the odor of sweet
flowers, and a stillness rested on the face of nature
which was like " the peace of God."

CHAPTER XLV.

JOIN HANDS AND HEARTS.

What a short time is six weeks of happiness !
How long are six days of sorrow !   Six hours of
pain have seemed interminable.   Six minutes of
suspense have seemed a life-time.   Six seconds of
deadly peril have appeared to be an age.   Those
weeks of probation have rolled away.   The bridal
day has come.   Arrayed in white, airy, flowing
robes, Rose and Geraldine stand before the altar of
old Deerlands church.   It were hard to say which
was more beautiful, Geraldine, with her classic form
and features and graceful dignity, or Rose, with her
bright, fresh, simple sweetness.   It is probable the
General thought Geraldine; it is certain Milton
thought Rose most lovely.   The vails of rich Brus-
sels lace which enveloped them covered no ornament save the wreath of orange blossoms on
Geraldine, and but one other on Rose, the diamond

bracelet with the portrait of Milton, the gift of Judge Bland.

The interior of the church was decked with ever-greens and flowers. The aisle up which the bridal party was to pass was strewn with rosebuds. The building was full to overflowing. The day had been made a holiday at Deerlands, and all the labor-ing poor invited by the Commodore to partake of a feast which was to be laid for them after the wed-ding breakfast under the spreading branches of a clump of ancient elms in the park.

The mutual vows uttered, the golden circlet, symbolical of endless union and never to be broken fidelity, was placed upon the finger of each of the brides. The blessing was pronounced, and the wedding party moved to the vestry to inscribe their names on the church register, whilst the organ pealed forth the wedding march of Mendels-sohn. The formulas were now complete.

The spectators in the church waiting their return, observe the two newly married pairs with keenest scrutiny as they pass down the aisle. They make their remarks on both brides and grooms. All agree that none—no, not even the oldest inhabitant, had ever seen two such handsome pairs in Deer-lands church. As they enter the carriages the music of the organ ceases, and the bells break forth into peals as of delight, which continue far into the day.

Home again ! The carriages draw up in rapid suc-cession at the door of the Hall, deposit their living freight, and are driven to the stables.

The numerous guests assemble around the festive board. Servants glide noiselessly around the room, assisting the company to whatever they desire of the magnificent collation. The tables show marvels of culinary art. Fruits in season and out of season, the products of many climes, are there. The wines are all from the Commodore's own private bins, which have never been opened until now, since he left England eighteen years ago. The guests all feel and share the happiness of the hour. At length the Commodore rose and said :—

"Ladies and Gentlemen :

"Are your glasses full ? [The waiters hasten to replenish every glass with wine.]   I have the pleasure of proposing a toast.   It is the toast of the day. It is one in which I know you will all heartily join. I had a daughter ; this morning I have given her away. I believe I have not lost her, but have gained a son.   I had an adopted daughter ; she, too, this day will leave my roof to share another home. I have bestowed her with a perfect trust.   May their paths in life be strewn with joy.   May the love which to-day is consummated grow with the growing years.   May God, the bountiful, bless and prosper them.   May their homes be the abodes of happiness.   May all who know them see and mark the great content of General and Mrs. Sterne, and Mr. and Mrs. Bland."

The toast was enthusiastically drunk.   General Sterne and Milton both responded in grateful terms. Their words were few and earnest. Other toasts followed. At length Mr. Carleton, who had shortened his wedding tour to be present with his friends this day, arose and said :—

" Ladies and gentlemen, I desire to propose a toast. My recent visit to the United States has greatly impressed my mind with the grandeur of that great country. The vastnesss of its rsources, the indomitable energy of its people, and the wonderful development of its wealth. Although their institutions are in many respects different to our own, we have many things in common. I beg to propose ' The Great American Nation,' coupled with the name of Judge Bland."

When the toast was drunk and the enthusiasm had subsided, the Judge replied :—

"As an American I thank you, ladies and gentlemen, for the courtesy you have shown to us and to our country. We are proud of it. We believe there is no such other under one government in the world. One of your poets says :—

> ' Lives there a man with soul so dead,
> Who never to himself hath said—
> This is my own, my native land ? '

" I answer: If so, that man is not an American. Mr. Carleton has truly said that we have many things in common with England. Our language is your language. Our laws are built upon the basis of your laws. Very many of our oldest and best families proudly trace back their descent to an English ancestry. We are natural allies. May the revolving years never see the harmony of the two nations disturbed." [The Judge paused and was greeted with great applause.]

He then continued: "When we were in San Francisco we had a secret society. Its members numbered only four. Two of the number are the happy bridegrooms of to-day. Each has now a new monitor. Each has now an individual instructor in Truth. May neither ever merit from his partner the recital of unpleasant Truth. The records of the Society are now in course of preparation for the press. I propose success to the annals of ' The Society in Search of Truth.' "

*   *   *   *   *   *   *   *   *

General and Mrs. Sterne and Mr. and Mrs. Milton Bland are to spend the fall on the continent of Europe ; they are to winter in Italy, and return to America in the spring, where they will be joined by Judge Bland, Commodore Pye, and Mrs. Clare.

*   *   *   *   *   *   *   *   *

The carriages are at the door, the adieux are said. Our young friends have entered upon new lives. New hopes, new fears, new pleasures, new cares, new sorrows, and new joys await them. Geraldine has told us that nothing is beautiful that is not true. May their lives be adorned with the beauty of Truth.

FINIS.